DEADLY SONATA

By Paul Myers

DEADLY SONATA
DEADLY SCORE

DEADLY SONATA

PAUL MYERS

A CRIME CLUB BOOK
DOUBLEDAY
NEW YORK   LONDON   TORONTO   SYDNEY   AUCKLAND

A Crime Club Book
Published by Doubleday, a division of
Bantam Doubleday Dell Publishing Group, Inc.
666 Fifth Avenue, New York, New York 10103

Doubleday and the portrayal of a man
with a gun are trademarks of
Doubleday, a division of Bantam Doubleday Dell
Publishing Group, Inc.

Library of Congress Cataloging-in-Publication Data

Myers, Paul.
Deadly sonata/Paul Myers.—1st ed.
in the United States of America.
p.   cm.
"A Crime Club book."
I. Title.
PR6063.Y47D395   1990
823'.914—dc20   89-35087
CIP

ISBN 0-385-26364-3
Copyright © 1987 by Paul Myers

For Mary, Nicholas, and John

Geneva

1

A young man in a shabby raincoat approached Mark at the entrance to Victoria Hall. He bobbed his head apologetically. "Excuse me, monsieur, I am sorry to trouble you. I wondered whether you might have an extra ticket for the concert tonight." He hesitated, glancing round nervously. "I would be prepared to pay you whatever you ask."

"I'm sorry, but I only have my own ticket. Have you tried the box-office for returns?"

"Yes. I've been waiting for hours." He looked like a student, and his halting, slightly guttural French suggested that he was a foreigner. "It's terribly important that I hear Avram Gutman play." There was a hint of desperation in his voice.

"He's a great artist."

"It's not that. Gutman is a symbol! When he quit Russia, he was making an important statement. I must hear him!"

"I'm afraid I can't help you."

The young man looked crestfallen, and Mark felt a certain sympathy. Such passionate intensity evoked memories of his own student days, twenty-five years earlier, when everything seemed to be a matter of life and death. "Look, I happen to know some of the management here. Perhaps they'll let you stand at the back . . ."

"No. I already asked. I practically begged them." He scowled. "Bloody Swiss fire laws! Those bastards don't understand." His anger was tinged with self-pity.

"Well, keep trying. You may be lucky with a last-minute cancellation."

The young man nodded silently and headed in the direction of another group of arrivals.

Mark made his way into the recently redecorated foyer of the hall. Ever since the news of Gutman's defection to the West, Geneva had decided to make his visit a gala occasion. All the seats had been taken as soon as the box-office opened, and as a well-known local manager representing several distinguished artists, Mark had been supplied with his usual aisle seat, useful for hasty exits at intervals and finales. He had no professional reason to be there—Gutman was represented by one of the largest American managements which had a network of local agents— but he had always admired the great Russian violinist and, anyway, the city rarely played host to a musical event of such international interest.

Wandering through the foyer for a last-minute cigarette before the concert, he recognized most of Geneva's leading figures, many of whom had dressed formally for the occasion. The men probably complained about it, but it gave their wives and girl-friends the opportunity to display their latest extravagances. He was reminded of the Grosse Festspielhaus in Salzburg during the summer festival, where one was always guaranteed two shows each evening—the concert inside the hall and, almost more important, the fashion parade in the foyer outside.

Mark was surprised to see Yuri Schedrin standing by the entrance to the stalls, hastily finishing a glass of wine. The Gosconcert agent caught his eye and waved. He was a tall, heavily built man with a weather-beaten face and a casual, genial manner that was endearing. Why did spy films invariably depict Russians with bullet heads and brutish manners? As always, Schedrin was impeccably dressed. Mark assumed that a special clothing allowance must have been granted by the Moscow bureaucrats to supply him with his well-tailored business suit, which gave him the appearance of a prosperous genèvois burgher. He wondered how long it would be before Schedrin would have to return home for a spell of duty. He did not imagine the man looked forward to it with any great enthusiasm.

The Russian greeted Mark with a warm smile as they shook hands. Despite his size and bulk, he was still several inches shorter. "A pleasure to see you, Mr. Holland. This must be what they call a busman's holiday for you."

"I suppose so. I've always admired Gutman, and believe it or not, I

2

still go to concerts because I enjoy them!" He hesitated. "What brings you here?"

Schedrin grinned broadly, indicating that he understood the tacit question. "Oh, Avram Gutman and I are old friends. I often accompanied him on tours in the past. It's only natural that I would come to hear him."

"Despite his present . . . attitude?"

"Why not? His change of address hasn't altered the way he plays the violin, I hope! We're not quite as inflexible as you imagine, Mr. Holland. Nobody's watching me!"

"I'm glad to hear it." Mark wondered whether Schedrin had already downed several glasses of wine before the present one. His gestures were expansive.

As though reading Mark's mind, the Russian continued, "Avram is no longer one of our citizens. He does not concern us any more on that front." He emptied his glass with a swallow.

It would have been interesting to ask what might happen to Gutman if he returned to Russia, citizen or not, but Mark refrained. "He has been somewhat outspoken since he . . . changed citizenship."

The Russian nodded. "Of course. Like all converts to a cause, Avram has an excess of enthusiasm, not to mention a large and well-trained team of publicity men and scriptwriters! When Avram suddenly asked for political asylum a few months ago and made that dramatic announcement from the stage of the Alte Oper in Frankfurt, you have to admit the whole thing was very theatrically stage-managed."

"I suppose so."

Schedrin laughed. "Come, come, Mr. Holland, aren't you being a little naïve? The whole thing was pre-arranged between the Bonn authorities and the Israeli secret service. It wasn't by accident that the concert hall was surrounded by all those policemen as soon as Avram walked inside, was it?" Mark was silent, and the Russian grinned again. "Besides, if you want the sort of news and television coverage he received, you have to warn the media in advance. There was a television crew waiting for him at the airport, and an El Al jet standing on the runway. What an extraordinary coincidence!"

"It was well organized."

Schedrin still smiled. "It was beautifully done. I watched the Israeli Prime Minister embracing Avram at Lod Airport on my television set. I remember wondering where they found all those cheering crowds at such short notice!"

"You don't sound very troubled by it."

The Russian shrugged. "I am not in politics, Mr. Holland. Like you, I look after musicians, and that keeps me fully occupied." He placed his hand on Mark's shoulder, lowering his voice slightly. "Anyway, I must admit that I admire professionals who are good at their work."

"You seem to be taking it all very philosophically."

"That's because I have very little choice in the matter. What would you have me do—go into mourning? My country has broad shoulders. We will survive."

"And his speeches?"

Schedrin's face showed long-suffering patience. "Western propaganda —I'm sure you're familiar with that phrase. Of course Avram must lead a passionate crusade for Soviet Jews to be permitted to go "home" to Israel. It is expected of him, not only by the Israelis, but by the American public as well. He is their new champion." He winked. "I've even heard it rumoured that the President is a little upset by Avram's eloquence. It seems he feels he is being upstaged by him, and you should never do that to an actor!"

"Then you don't believe he means what he says?"

"Perhaps. You know, I've known Avram for nearly twenty years, and during all that time he never discussed religion or politics with me, even when we got drunk together—which we sometimes did!" He smiled at the recollection. "No, Avram has to pay the price for his new citizenship."

"Your country has been remarkably silent on the subject."

"Oh, we leave that to the Libyans and the PLO. Did you see their statements in the press?" Mark nodded. "It's all a matter of image, these days, Mr. Holland—what the Italians called *bella figura*. The Americans criticize us for being in Afghanistan, and we point out that their President announces he will not interfere in the domestic affairs of a sovereign state like South Africa and at the same time sends millions of dollars to help the Contras in Nicaragua. Our cold war has become an international war of words and appearances. You must admit they're less dangerous than bullets or missiles." He was surprisingly outspoken, and Mark wondered whether the wine was taking effect. "Aren't you glad we only have to deal with temperamental musicians?"

4

"Very."

Schedrin sighed. "I will miss Avram. We spent many happy hours together. But there are others." He placed a large and carefully manicured hand on Mark's sleeve. "You should come and see for yourself. We have some wonderful young musicians in Russia, waiting to be heard outside. Maybe you would like to represent a few of them? As a friend, I can offer you excellent terms."

Mark paused. An old and familiar shadow had fallen across the lightness of his mood. Russia had a long musical tradition, and without doubt, there were new artists waiting to be discovered by the Western world. Schedrin would not be able to change the terms, friendship notwithstanding, for the Russian government always demanded and received a fixed amount for its artists, irrespective of local taxes and other deductions; Western agents earned their fees from anything in excess of that amount. Schedrin could not cut through the bales of bureaucratic red tape to change that. There were other obstacles. Concerts and appearances were arranged anything from eighteen months to two years in advance; despite talk of cultural *détente*, there was no guarantee that it would continue, and when the political situation changed, the Iron Curtain had a habit of dropping suddenly and unexpectedly on all activities. As the local manager of an artist who failed to appear, he would be held responsible. On many previous occasions, opera intendants, orchestra managers, and independent entrepreneurs had demanded written guarantees before accepting Soviet artists. They had all suffered the discomfitures and embarrassments of last-minute cancellations.

But it was not those reasons that made Mark hesitate. Did Schedrin know anything of his past? Perhaps the offer was being made as a quiet reprisal for the Gutman situation. The Russian was smiling amicably enough, his bushy eyebrows raised quizzically, awaiting a reply. And even if Schedrin did not know, would there be others, still watching him after all these years, asking themselves whether Mark might be a "sleeper" deliberately placed in cold storage by the Department until some future date? It was unlikely that they were aware of the angry circumstances of his departure from that service, and his determination never to work for them again. Even so, the offer was tempting, the thought that at last he was free and clear of that other life. Or was that just wishful thinking?

He was spared the necessity of a reply by the arrival of Rudi, his perennially efficient Swiss assistant, looking more than a little embarrassed. Mark wished that he liked the younger man better, but there was something ruthlessly correct about him that he found unreasonably irritating. He should have been delighted to have an office so competently manned, but human frailty had its compensations. Rudi was, as always, carefully dressed in a modest pinstripe suit, slightly too tight at the waist. His white shirt was immaculate enough to be new, and the plain navy blue silk tie with its small knot was perfectly located within the V of the collar. His rimless glasses sparkled so cleanly that he must have spent several minutes polishing them with the chemically impregnated cloth that he kept in their carrying case.

The reason for Rudi's uneasiness was that Agnes, the pretty little receptionist from the office, was at his side, her hand tucked possessively through the crook of his stiffly bent left arm. Agnes, whose good looks were slightly marred by an excess of silver metalwork amid her strong Swiss teeth, had undergone a rapid transformation from the regulation blouse and tailored skirt that she wore at the office. Her auburn hair was fluffed out in a mass of curls and she was resplendent in a wine-coloured ball gown that revealed enough *décolletage* to cause more than an occasional admiring glance. It had obviously thrown Rudi. Mark nodded to her, and she blushed happily. She was a very attractive girl.

Rudi bowed stiffly, looking unhappy and clearly wishing Agnes would let go of his arm. "Good evening." For a moment, Mark feared he might add "sir."

"Hello, Rudi. Do you know Mr. Schedrin from Gosconcert?"

"Oh," Rudi almost clicked his heels, but did not offer his hand. "I believe we have met before." The Russian's presence seemed to embarrass him further.

"And this is Agnes—Miss Muret—from my office."

A change overtook Schedrin, and with a smile bordering dangerously on a leer, he bowed low over her hand, so that he appeared to be inspecting her cleavage at very close quarters. His voice was warm. "I am delighted."

Agnes blushed more deeply, clearly pleased, but any further conversation was interrupted by the final warning bell and a general movement into the auditorium. Mr. Schedrin retained possession of Agnes's hand and led her into the hall, while Rudi hesitated at Mark's side.

"I'm surprised to see him here. I would have thought it was more diplomatic to stay away." His voice was prim.

"He's an old friend of Gutman's. I rather admire his bravado in facing it out."

"Oh yes, of course." Rudi never disagreed, which was one of his more irritating features. He continued to hover for a moment. "I hope you do not object to my bringing Agnes—Miss Muret—to the concert." His voice was painfully correct.

"Of course not."

"It was just the Frau Emmi has been away with flu for the past few days, and Agnes has done extra typing for me." Explanations seemed totally unnecessary, but Rudi clearly felt he had committed a social *faux pas* by inviting a mere receptionist to accompany him. "She was very anxious to come to the concert this evening, and as I had a spare ticket . . ." His voice drifted off miserably.

Mark smiled, thinking, "You toffee-nosed little snob!" Aloud, he said, "It's nice to see her here, looking so lovely." Rudi bowed his head. "She's a very pretty girl."

"Really? I did not notice. I felt she was a little . . . overdressed for the occasion."

"Not really. It's a good excuse to dress up for a change. She certainly seems to have made a hit with Schedrin. You may have to rescue her."

"Of course." Rudi fled in the direction of Agnes and Mr. Schedrin, who was still holding her hand. He had bent his head close to her ear, ostensibly to make himself heard over the general buzz of conversation, and Mark could see that his cheek was brushing hers. Agnes looked happy.

The first half of the concert was pleasantly uninspired. Gutman's newly acquired New York manager had seized upon the opportunity of the current tour to insist that each concert should include a young American conductor whom he was anxious to promote. Mark had met the manager on several occasions: a grizzled, successful man whose Brooks Brothers suit and handmade shoes did little to disguise the brawling instincts of a street-fighter. He had swept through Europe on a series of one-day visits that suggested a presidential goodwill tour, bullying each orchestral management into accepting his protégé at outrageously high fees—otherwise they would not get Gutman—and shouting his way through each meeting partly because he knew he was overselling the young man's talent and partly because he spoke no foreign languages and assumed the locals would understand him better if he increased the decibel levels.

The concert opened with a smash-and-grab performance of Smetana's Overture to *The Bartered Bride*, during which the young conductor seemed to be in a race against the clock. His two-handed conducting style, whereby the left hand was linked by some invisible yoke to the right, leaving no room for expressive gestures, flustered the Swiss musicians. They only settled down half-way through the piece and ended more or less in unison. The audience applauded enthusiastically. Perhaps their reaction was in anticipation of Gutman's appearance. The conductor, flushed with triumph and energetic time-keeping, swept on and off the stage several times, moving with such rapid determination that sheets of music, caught in his slipstream, flew off several music-stands. Still, Mark had to concede that the young man conveyed a certain excitement. He remembered that his manager had used the word "charisma" frequently.

The Mozart *Jupiter* Symphony which followed was attacked with similar urgency and lack of expression. The orchestra had settled down more comfortably, encouraged by the applause for the overture, but for all their new-found accuracy, the performance lacked any sense of breadth or perspective. Each movement was disposed of with a heartless precision that lacked character, warmth, or any sort of charm. The conductor observed all the repeats, including—to Mark's disappointment—the second half of the finale. There is a moment towards the end, when the music resolves into the major key and the violins sweetly reintroduce the opening measures of the movement; for Mark, that had always been one of Mozart's most magical effects, a kind of serene resolution of all the conflicting themes that make up the kaleidoscopic development section. To repeat such a moment robbed it of its uniqueness, but the conductor insisted and drove the work home with the finality of a suburban housewife garaging a Volkswagen. The last chord resounded, and the audience exploded with cheers. Clapping politely, Mark wondered whether he was being overcritical or perhaps just reacting against the heavy sales campaign surrounding the conductor. Gala audiences were not always the most perceptive or alert, but at least the young man had generated real enthusiasm from Geneva's normally passive concert-goers.

Taking advantage of his "escape" chair, he slipped quickly through one of the outside exit doors, which led to a quiet side street. Victoria Hall tended to be too warm, and the cool air was a pleasant shock to the system. Standing in the doorway, he lit a cigarette. These days, he rarely went to concerts with anyone else. There had been a time when he had shared them with someone, taking pleasure in watching her enjoyment and savouring the closeness of her presence. But that was long ago. The tiniest details of her face or images of a particular gesture were beginning to fade, leaving only a slight stab of sorrow when something evoked her memory. It was a misty early November evening, with a light film of rain carried on the wind. Winter seemed to be approaching rapidly. After a few minutes the coldness became uncomfortable, and throwing the cigarette aside, he pushed open the door, to be greeted by a wave of warm air and animated conversation.

The young student was standing by a doorway, looking into the hall. He saw Mark and smiled.

"Did you find a ticket?"

"Yes, at the very last moment." For a moment, he was thoughtful. "I won't eat much for the rest of the month, but it's worth it!"

"I'm sure it is." If Schedrin was right about a war of words and appearances, the West had just won a major victory in the eyes of one young student.

He found Agnes and Schedrin standing close together in a corner of the bar, sharing a half-bottle of wine. Judging by his expression, the Russian found her fascinating, and Agnes seemed to blossom in reflected glory. As Mark approached, she was running a scarlet fingernail coquettishly against the Russian's cheek. He looked up towards Mark and waved happily.

"Come and have some wine, if you can find a glass."

Agnes handed him hers. "You can use mine if you like, Monsieur Holland." She giggled and eyed Schedrin reprovingly. "I think I have had enough already."

"Thank you. What's happened to Rudi?"

She shrugged. "Madame Renaud took him away from us. She wanted to tell him about a new pianist she has found."

Mark nodded. Madame Renaud was always discovering new musicians and taking them under her wing. For a moment, he almost felt sorry for Rudi.

Schedrin put a protective arm around Agnes's shoulder and winked. "We're not complaining. It gives me the opportunity to have this delightful young lady to myself. You should have told me about her before, Mr. Holland. I would have made a point of visiting your office sooner." Agnes blushed again and, after a sideways glance at Mark, placed her hand over the Russian's.

Schedrin held up his glass, saluting Mark. *"Zdarovyé!* I meant what I was saying before we were so delightfully interrupted earlier this evening." He gave Agnes a small squeeze. "We have a number of excellent young musicians who should interest you, if you can spare the time. I would be more than happy to arrange a visit for you and to extend my country's warmest hospitality."

"That's very kind." The moment of doubt returned, like the memory of an old wound.

"Not at all. It would be mutually beneficial." The Russian was expansive again. "There is a very special pianist I have in mind, as well as several conductors." He grinned. "Perhaps they are not quite as . . . dramatic . . . as this young American—"

"We can but hope not!"

"Ah." Schedrin's smile widened. "I was not sure whether it was my opinion or, perhaps, certain nationalistic reservations that coloured my judgement."

"No, I think we both reached the same critical conclusion."

"Good. Perhaps we have more in common than you think, Mr. Holland." Agnes looked puzzled, and he turned his attention to her. "You see, my dear young lady, our critical faculties are sometimes influenced by very unmusical considerations. We were discussing that before you joined us this evening." A warning bell sounded, and he quickly refilled both glasses, offering to share his own with Agnes, who took a small sip. "We will see how the young man manages the Brahms for Avram. I hope he will not be in quite such a hurry!"

Mark was surprised by Gutman's appearance. He had expected a larger, more impressive figure, but the violinist was small and compact, with narrow, rounded shoulders. Grey hair was thinning across his prominent forehead, and his face was deeply lined. He walked slowly, head down, and the athletic young American conductor loomed over him, leaning forward anxiously, as though urging him forward. The audience applauded noisily, and Gutman glanced towards them, nodding his head with an expression of slight bewilderment, as though taken by surprise. He had none of the imposing presence of an Isaac Stern or an Oistrakh, but stood, slightly sheepishly acknowledging the applause, then diverted attention from himself by shaking hands with the leader of the orchestra. There was a further delay while he checked the tuning of his violin, and after a brief nod to the conductor, who was anxious to begin, Gutman turned to face the front, his head bowed and his eyes closed, awaiting the long orchestral introduction.

The opening phrase of the concerto was almost a whisper, and Mark could sense the audience relax and settle back. Whatever youthful bravura the conductor had displayed in the first half of the concert must have spent itself, and the first movement began to unfold at a stately pace with an underlying intensity, giving the impression that he was embarking upon a long and noble voyage. The strings were rich and warm, the woodwinds were mellow and perfectly tuned, and the rolling phrases emerged with a grace and maturity that Mark had not anticipated. Either Gutman had given the American a few quick lessons in musicianship, or the young man was inspired by the violinist's presence. Whatever the reason, Mark was totally absorbed. Then Gutman began to play.

The sound was big, and the solo violin seemed to fill the hall. It was a dark-coloured tone with a rich "woody" quality that suited the music perfectly. With his eyes closed, his face expressionless in its utter concentration, Gutman played broadly and in an unhurried manner, and the conductor held the orchestra in perfect control, blending it with the soloist and never allowing it to become too heavy. Gutman's presence seemed to inspire every player, and at the start of the second movement the oboist played with a sweetness and delicacy of phrasing that Mark had seldom heard before. Traditionally, violinists were supposed to complain that the oboe "had the best tune" in the concerto, but it was clear from the gentle smile on Gutman's face that he suffered no such ego problems, and he joined forces with the orchestra in a subtle give-and-take collaboration reminiscent of the best chamber music. There was only the briefest of pauses at the end of the movement before he dug his bow mercilessly into the violin strings for the Hungarian fireworks of the last movement. The orchestra responded in kind, leaping from phrase to phrase, and the work danced to a dazzling climax. A perfectly

11

timed ritardando led to the final chords, and the concerto ended triumphantly.

For a magical moment, there was absolute silence as the sound of the last chord died away, and then the audience erupted, rising to its feet with a great ovation. Gutman stood back, seeming to retreat within himself as waves of applause echoed through the hall. With a quick jerk of his head, he nodded thanks to the conductor, who enveloped him with an enthusiastic hug, then turned to the first violinist and shook his hand. He looked exhausted. The orchestra stood, and the applause was redoubled.

Gutman and the conductor returned to the stage for call after call, and the audience stayed on its feet and cheered, unwilling to let them go. Mark found himself standing with the rest, his hands beginning to smart from clapping so hard. At length, Gutman returned alone, standing immobile, acknowledging both the audience and the orchestra. He paused for a moment, then raised his hand, asking for silence.

He spoke in French, his words slightly hesitant as he struggled with the unfamiliar language. "I thank you for your welcome and your kindness, but in this moment of celebration I ask you to remember with me those brothers and sisters who are still prisoners of a cruel regime. Tonight, I celebrate my freedom with you, but I ask you to think of all those who have not yet been allowed to leave the Soviet Union, to return to their true home in Israel." The audience received his words with a great sigh of sound, and he continued, "It is to all such persons that I would like to dedicate the Chaconne from the Partita in D Minor by Bach."

There was a ripple of excitement as people settled back into their seats and the concert hall quietened. Several early leavers tiptoed back into the auditorium, standing at the rear, and Gutman placed the violin beneath his chin again, closing his eyes, waiting for absolute silence. Suddenly, two gunshots echoed shockingly, stunning the audience. The harsh whiplash of sound seemed to reverberate unnaturally. Then all hell broke loose.

Several women screamed, a number of men jumped to their feet, shouting unintelligibly; those nearest the exit doors fled towards them, while others crouched low in their seats, hoping for shelter. Three shadowy figures dressed in worn bush jackets and trousers, their faces partially masked by the familiar headgear of the Palestine Liberation Organization, walked down the aisle towards the platform. The leading man was holding a revolver. He moved as if in a trance, his eyes unfocused, his unshaven face palely lit by the light from the stage. A few paces behind, two men followed, and as if obeying a pre-arranged signal, they began to shout. Their words were barked out in Arabic, meaningless to those present, but as the audience recovered its senses, their voices were lost in the noise and confusion.

From his aisle seat, Mark slowly rose to his feet, watching the terrorists approach. The first man was staring vacantly, scarcely conscious of the gun in his hand. The men following behind him did not appear to be armed. A man seated on the other side of the aisle said, "Oh my God!" and dragged the woman next to him to the floor, covering her with his body. The gunman did not notice them. As he drew level with Mark, he raised the revolver again, pointing it towards the stage.

Mark threw his full weight against the Arab's side. As they collided, his right hand snaked out to grip the wrist holding the gun, wrenching it upwards. The force with which he hit the man knocked him sideways across the aisle, and the vicious pressure on his wrist made him drop the revolver. They fell together, Mark using his weight to crush the body below him. He was conscious of the acrid smell of sweat and fear, but from the corner of his eye he could see the gun being scooped up by a young man two rows down. The Arab grunted with pain but offered no resistance.

The other two intruders paused momentarily, as though surprised by the interruption. Almost in unison, their attention turned to the new owner of the gun, and they stopped still, suddenly silent. Their hesitation betrayed them, and within seconds they were surrounded by angry, thrashing bodies. The man beneath Mark had not moved. He had covered his head with his arms and lay curled in a foetal position, as though anticipating a rain of blows.

Mark scrambled to his feet, watching the motionless body. He stood back, allowing a new group of men to reach down and lift the Arab, still curled in a tight bundle, and drag him towards a rear exit. Less than a minute had passed since the shot had been fired. The attack was over.

A hand pressed on his shoulder. It was Yuri Schedrin. "That was very brave, Mr. Holland." He hesitated fractionally. "You disarmed that madman like a professional."

13

Mark watched the Russian's face, but it was impassive. "He wasn't expecting me to try it."

Several uniformed policemen had appeared in the auditorium, taking charge of the prisoners. Their angry captors seemed disappointed to hand them over.

"Nevertheless, you risked your life. He was holding a gun."

Mark shrugged. "I think it was a put-up job, planned for show. They'd already achieved what they wanted."

"Why do you say that?"

"If they had intended anything more than a demonstration, they would all have been armed, and with machine-guns. They know what they're doing. One revolver between the three of them was little more than a gesture. I doubt whether he aimed it at anyone specific."

"Then why do it?"

"To make us aware of their presence, and show the Israelis they're not going to have it all their own way. They chose the right moment for the publicity." Ignoring his surroundings, Mark lit a cigarette, relieved to find his hands were no longer shaking. He inhaled slowly. The more he thought about it, the more he knew he was right. The PLO wanted to teach a lesson to Gutman and the Israelis, who had enjoyed too much favourable publicity. The three men would be locked up for causing a disturbance, but there were thousands more waiting for the opportunity to be martyrs to their cause. There was not even any need to harm Gutman; their presence was enough to illustrate his vulnerability. Concert halls were ideal targets for terrorist attacks, and the evening's demonstration presented a frightening prospect for the future.

The police departed with the last of the prisoners, and the audience, slightly subdued, left the hall. With the drama over, firm Swiss self-discipline took over, and despite a continuing buzz of excitement, order was restored. To his embarrassment, Mark was surrounded by a group of admirers eager to congratulate him. A stranger grasped his hand, pumping it up and down, saying, "Bravo, monsieur, bravo!" It was as though he, rather than Gutman, had been the soloist.

Rudi and Agnes pushed their way into the group. "Can I do anything to help?"

"No, thank you, Rudi. It wasn't as dramatic as it looked."

"But the man had a gun."

"I know, but it was more for show than anything. Anyway, he was as high as a kite. God knows what he'd been taking."

"We owe you a debt of thanks." He sounded pompous.

"I think you're getting carried away." Mark could feel himself relaxing. "The irritating part is that we didn't hear the Chaconne."

The crowd was moving away, and Schedrin put a heavy arm round Mark's shoulder. "My God, you Englishmen always have to affect such a lack of concern! You did a brave thing, my friend, and we salute you for it. Come, shall we go and see Avram? He will want to thank you."

Mark hesitated. "If you like. I'm not sure they'll allow us backstage after this."

"Don't worry." The Russian urged him towards a small side door leading to the dressing-rooms. "They know who we are." With his free hand, he held Agnes by the elbow, gently guiding her.

Rudi held back. "Does he expect to see you, Mr. Schedrin?"

The Gosconcert man looked surprised. "Of course he does! Avram and I have known each other for twenty years or so. He would be offended if I didn't go back to see him."

"But I thought—"

The Russian turned towards him, still smiling, but his eyes were cold. "I know what you thought. Don't worry, young man. Art and politics do not always mix very well. Avram is my friend, and that is all that counts."

A nervous usher was guarding the door that led backstage, but Schedrin brushed him aside, waving his party through with the authority of a tour guide. Fortunately the man recognized Mark and bobbed his head.

"Excuse me, m'sieur. I was told not to allow anyone through, but seeing that it is you—" They were long past him before he could finish the sentence.

Gutman and a lean, dark-complexioned man in an ill-fitting suit were standing in the dressing-room, talking quietly. Mark did not recognize the man, but suspected that he might be an Israeli bodyguard. It was possible that they had anticipated trouble during the tour. The man watched them approach, and Mark had the feeling that his hand was hovering near the edge of his open jacket. He had observed the same alert stillness on the faces of colleagues in the past. When the violinist saw Schedrin, he broke off his conversation and turned to the Gosconcert man with a welcoming smile. Schedrin grabbed him in a great bear-hug, kissing the diminutive violinist on each cheek and murmuring to him in Russian. He turned to the others with a look of triumph.

"You see, my friends: nothing changes between us!" He turned to Gutman again, speaking rapidly in Russian and pointing towards Mark. The violinist's eyes widened slightly; he nodded, and Schedrin moved back, opening his arms in a wide gesture. "My friend, Mr. Mark Holland, the second hero of the evening!" He grinned. "With your blond hair and your handsome face, my friend, you could be mistaken for one of my countrymen!"

Gutman stepped forward and shook Mark's hand. "Thank you for your bravery." He stood back gravely as Mark introduced the rest of the party, then nodded briefly to the man who had been waiting with him, as though to dismiss him. The man sauntered to the doorway, lighting a cigarette. He stood casually in the frame of the door, preventing any other visitors from entering.

Schedrin crossed the room to a small refrigerator. "I brought you a little something to celebrate with, Avram. I left it here before the concert." Opening the freezer section, he took out two bottles of vodka, partially encased in ice. Holding one in each hand, he lifted them shoulder high. "See, Avram: it is Moskva, your favourite brand." He grinned. "I'll bet your Israelis don't give you that!"

At Mark's side, Rudi stiffened slightly, but the violinist smiled. "No, Yuri. It seems we always have to sacrifice a few things in the name of freedom."

Schedrin laughed and reached into the refrigerator again for glasses. Handing them round, he broke open the first bottle and filled each glass to the brim. Then he turned to Gutman. "I drink to you, my dear old friend, and to happy times together." He drained his glass with a single swallow, then looked to the others to follow suit. Gutman mirrored his action, letting out a contented sigh, and Mark joined them. The icy vodka was smooth, with a pleasantly oily taste. It helped to settle his nerves, which still felt tense. Next to him, Rudi took a cautious sip, wrinkling his nose.

Schedrin beamed at Agnes. "Now you. Drink it all in one. I will catch you when you fall!"

She giggled and swallowed, her eyes widening as the strong liquor hit the back of her throat. Gutman nodded approvingly and smiled, while

Schedrin refilled the glasses. As he watched Agnes, it struck Mark that this could be her first encounter with the "glamorous" music world, which, for him, had long since become a place of cold corridors, stale dressing-rooms, and sweaty towels. She saw it through star-struck eyes. Because she worked in the office every day, he had taken for granted that she would be accustomed to the backstage tradition of extravagant congratulations and artificial celebration while the artists unwound from their performances. She was charmingly intrigued, taking it all in with a sort of childlike wonder. Her eyes shone, and there were two spots of colour on her cheeks. That could be the vodka. But he preferred her reaction to Rudi's. While the young man remained aloofly polite, trying not to look too disapproving, she showed genuine pleasure. No wonder Schedrin found her so attractive.

The Russian continued to play host, constantly refilling glasses, and it was apparent that Gutman was pleased to see him. They shared anecdotes from other occasions, and Schedrin, who was an accomplished mimic, impersonated various well-known conductors with deft and occasionally cruel accuracy. It was obviously his party piece, and he performed with the polish of a professional entertainer. But then, when people from the music world met, they often resorted to old stories because their association was based on music rather than any deep-rooted friendship between them. They were like men who, meeting after a long time, exchanged jokes because they had little else in common. It was a world of constantly changing acquaintances.

Partly from reaction and also because they were already drinking from the second bottle of vodka, Mark felt vaguely light-headed. If the alcohol was affecting Schedrin, he did not show it, but Agnes giggled frequently. Even Rudi's complexion was slightly pinker than usual, and he laughed openly when the Russian gave a particularly biting impersonation of Celibidache rehearsing.

At length, Gutman looked at his watch and sighed. He seemed unhappy to bring the party to an end. "Yuri, I must leave you soon."

"So early? In the old days, we used to wait for dawn to come up." He chuckled. "Do you remember that time in Helsinki?"

"Yes, but I have an early plane tomorrow morning. There is a rehearsal in Munich in the afternoon."

"You work too hard, Avram. At your age, you should be playing fewer concerts."

17

"Perhaps." The violinist looked tired. "But it is an important tour for me." He smiled wanly. "Anyway, I'm not so old as all that." His companion had rejoined the group, and Mark suspected that, at a certain moment, Gutman had caught the man's eye, bringing him back into the room to indicate the end of their meeting. Perhaps it was the other way round.

Schedrin again enfolded him in a warm embrace. "Goodbye, old friend. I'll see you again soon."

"I hope so." His voice was sincere.

When they reached the stage door, Schedrin said, "Shall we have dinner? It's still early."

Rudi was struggling into a heavy coat with a pretentious velvet collar. "I'm afraid I cannot. I have an early appointment tomorrow." He looked expectantly at Agnes, but she avoided his gaze.

"Then you will join me?"

Mark smiled. "Not tonight, thank you. I must go home."

The Russian grinned. "In that case, I will have to entertain Mademoiselle Muret alone, if she will permit me."

Agnes looked from Schedrin to Mark, uncertain. It was a shame to bring the evening to an end, and the vodka encouraged her.

Mark nodded. "I'm sure you'll enjoy yourself."

She accepted it as a benediction. "Thank you, Monsieur Holland. I will not be late in the morning."

"I wouldn't worry too much about it."

Rudi looked angry. "I must say good-night." He nodded curtly, ignoring Agnes, and set off at a quick pace. By the time he reached the corner, he was almost running.

As they stood in the street outside, Schedrin placed a hand on Mark's arm. "I have been thinking, Mr. Holland. Next month, our pianist Viktor Kaverin will give an important recital in Moscow, with a big press reception the following day. It is our official launching, and he is a very talented artist. We have invited a number of people to come and hear him. If I send you a ticket, will you come?"

Mark paused. The cold evening air helped to clear his head, but he was conscious that the vodka had given him a false sense of security. Perhaps it was nervous reaction setting in. It had been a long time since he had tried unarmed combat.

The Russian tightened his grip. "Listen, there is a daily Aeroflot flight from Geneva to Moscow. It only takes four hours. Come and see for yourself. I know you will not be disappointed, and it would give me pleasure to arrange a tour of the city. What about it?"

"All right. I'll be delighted." It was almost as though he were outside, listening to himself.

"Wonderful! You will receive an air ticket in a few days. As soon as you do, go and see the Intourist people, and tell them to arrange your visa and hotel accommodation. I will tell them to expect you." A new thought struck him. "I will also see what I can do about seats for the Bolshoi. They're difficult to obtain, but you're an honoured guest." Mark nodded slowly, and the Russian took Agnes's hand a tucked it into the folds of his overcoat. "Are you sure you will not join us?"

"Sure, thank you."

"Then we will see each other in Moscow." He looked very pleased with himself. *"Paka!"*

Mark walked briskly homeward in the cool night air, hoping that the exercise would help to clear his head and dispel the dull ache brought about by too much vodka. Crossing the wooden footbridge spanning the sluice gates feeding water from Lake Leman into the river Rhone, Mark stopped and leaned over the railing. The rain had ceased, but overhead clouds made the night seem unnaturally dark. Below, the rushing waters glowed whitely as they cascaded through the carefully controlled gates. What on earth had made him agree? Quentin Sharpe and his messenger boys from the Department in London would think he had gone temporarily insane. They would never allow it. And yet, they couldn't stop him. His life was his own, and they no longer controlled him. Maybe that was why he was doing it. Besides, he could always change his mind and cancel the trip. He would see how he felt in the morning. He smiled to himself in the darkness, and spoke aloud.

"You must be out of your bloody mind!"

Moscow

2

It was painfully cold. Stepping from the hotel lobby into a forecourt crowded with grimy, ice-rimmed cars busily discharging and taking on shapeless bundles of passengers, Mark breathed in and felt the freezing air attack his throat and lungs. Light particles of snow drifted in the wind, mingling with exhaust fumes and steamy breath, and the ashen sky threatened further falls. Beyond the concrete slope leading from the hotel lay a monochromatic wintry scene, a grey-white hillside dotted with anonymous building blocks and criss-crossed roads snarled with heavy traffic. Beyond, there seemed to be a lot of open space. Perhaps it was a park in the summer. Under snow and ice discoloured by the smoke and fumes, it was a wasteland.

The electric sign in the lobby alternately blinking time and temperature had not forewarned him. Despite all his years in Switzerland, Mark had not learned to think in Celsius readings. A cruel gust of wind cut across his face, which was beginning to smart, and some quick mental arithmetic told him that Moscow's temperature was about minus three degrees Fahrenheit—thirty-five degrees of frost, for Christ's sake!

He waited a few minutes longer, stamping his feet on the slush and regretting that vanity had stopped him from protecting his head with the thick fur *shapka* that everyone else seemed to wear, let alone a pair of heavy leather boots. Sartorial elegance was unnecessary in such intense conditions. After searching among the latest batch of cars for the cultural attaché from the British embassy, he gave up and returned to the inner shelter of the building.

Standing in the spacious lobby of the Kosmos Hotel, Mark ignored the rattle and noise of human traffic surrounding him. With its stone floors and towering cement walls rising several stories, the area looked more like the central hall of a railway station. Perhaps it was the queues that gave that impression. There were several lines of people at the long reception desk waiting to hand in or obtain keys for their rooms. Above them, on the mezzanine floor, the tail-end of a queue waiting to be seated for breakfast straggled all the way down a corridor and into one of the two foreign-currency lounge bars. In a corner of the ground floor, there were more lines. Impatient guests argued with two blank-faced receptionists because the taxis they had ordered in advance had not arrived. A harassed girl, unexpectedly pretty amid her sombre-faced companions, was trying to sort out the documents of travellers in the next line. Beyond her, an aggressive angular woman with thick glasses told the man at the front of his line that rooms must be vacated by midday and no later; the hotel did not make exceptions. Someone had told Mark that the average Russian spends about a thousand hours a year standing in line for something—food, clothing, transport; virtually any daily necessity. Why should tourists expect to be treated any differently?

He sighed, glancing at his watch. The man from the embassy had said he would arrive at about ten, but there was still no sign of him. Two coffee bars were tucked away on either side of the wide lobby—espresso machines surrounded by chairs and sofas, like small oases in a desert of stone and plaster—and he crossed the crowded foyer towards the nearest. He walked past a strange assortment of guests: a group of Finnish winter-sports enthusiasts in heavy sweaters with strange, multivowelled words embroidered on them; a worker's party from the Ukraine, uniformly dressed in parkas and peaked caps; Western businessmen looking strangely out of place in smart city overcoats; African visitors in ill-fitting bundles of heavy clothes. Moving slowly among them were two old women armed with wide brooms, which they pushed slowly across the surface in an effort to remove the worst of the snow and grit being trampled in by each new arrival. The lobby was a huge, airy space designed to accommodate the tenants of the hotel's thousand rooms, but there never seemed to be enough staff on hand to look after them. If it had been on the all-too-distant other side of the world, the Americans would have carpeted it, filled it with canned music and coffee shops, and called it an atrium.

Mark ordered a coffee. After inspecting the long line waiting for the regulation glass of grape juice, boiled egg, bread, and coffee, he had decided to give breakfast a miss. He handed the attendant a Swiss five-franc piece, raising his eyebrows in the international sign language to enquire whether it was sufficient. The man examined the coin and nodded silently before consulting a paper next to the till. All foreign currency was acceptable. He gave Mark change in Danish kroner.

Harry Cunningham, the attaché from the embassy, arrived just before half-past ten. He was a small, neat man with sandy hair, a pencil moustache and a practised smile.

"Hello. Sorry to keep you waiting, but the traffic's miserable at this time of the year. They keep piling the snow up at the side of the road, so there's only two lanes. Don't let me hurry you. Finish your coffee in peace." He had a habit of hovering, his hands locked firmly behind his back, in the best diplomatic style.

"I've finished anyway." The coffee was good.

Cunningham looked around the lobby disapprovingly. "I can't think why they shoved you all the way out here. This place is miles from the centre of town. They should have put you in the National or the Russiya."

"I know. Mr. Schedrin apologized about it yesterday at the airport. Apparently, all the hotels in town are full. There's some sort of congress going on."

"There's always a congress of one sort or another, but they can get you in if they want to."

"This was the only hotel Intourist could find. Schedrin had a hell of a fight with the ladies on the Intourist desk at the airport, but they wouldn't budge. They claimed their Geneva office never informed them I was coming."

"More than likely. Everything's inclined to get bogged down in bureaucracy." The attaché was cheerful. He had obviously encountered the situation before. "Actually, the quickest way in and out of town is the Metro. I'll show you how to use it if you like. Schedrin doesn't seem to have done his usual efficient job."

"I'm glad he was there to meet me. After dragging through immigration, I wouldn't have known to check in at the Intourist desk."

Cunningham nodded. "It's like most things here: quite easy, once you know the form. This is your first trip?"

Mark smiled. "Does it show?"

22

"Not really. Moscow takes a little adjusting to, after which you can settle in quite nicely. I love it here."

"I haven't had a chance to see it yet. Schedrin whisked me out of the airport, had another fight with the ladies at the check-in desk here, sent me up to my room to change, and raced into town in time for the recital."

"You didn't have much time, if you came in on the afternoon flight. It's a fairly long ride in from Sheremetyevo."

"Yes." Mark remembered little of it. There had been a long drive through dark, unlit countryside, followed by broad streets lined by tall, square-cut buildings. He had been reminded of the monotonous suburbs of Milan, with their endless, disconcertingly similar blocks of flats. It had been hard to believe he was really in Russia, and Schedrin had distracted him with a steady patter of conversation. He had asked several times about Agnes.

Cunningham led the way across the lobby. "What did you think of Viktor Kaverin?"

"He's excellent. As I said last night, I was very impressed. He wasn't what I'd anticipated."

"Oh?"

"Most people make a fuss of virtuosos with brilliant techniques and incredible displays. I suppose I'd expected something like that, but he turned out to be a superbly sensitive musician: very lyrical and poetic. For some reason, I'd got it into my head that he was going to be all fingers and fireworks."

"Yes, he is good, isn't he? I've heard him a couple of times, here and in Leningrad. The Russians are very proud of him. He's got the technique when he needs it, but he doesn't throw it at you. I think he's the best they've produced since Richter. I'm sorry I missed you after the recital. I was going to suggest a bite of supper, but you'd already gone."

"That was probably my fault. I was feeling rather tired, and Schedrin ran me home as soon as the concert ended. I found a restaurant here in the hotel and had a quick meal before turning in."

"I hope you didn't try downstairs, where they have the rock band. You can't hear yourself think in there."

"No, I persuaded them to let me in one of the upstairs places. The head waiter kept telling me they were closed, but I sat down anyway, and they finally served me."

Cunningham grinned. "You're learning fast!"

Mark decided not to mention that the food had been poorly cooked and overpriced. Newly arrived visitors who complained about everything were a bore. The long flight, coupled with a sensation of growing nervous tension, had made him tired enough to fall asleep as soon as his head had touched the pillow.

They emerged into the freezing air and hurried to a dirt-caked car with fogged windows. A small electric fan blew warm air against the back window to keep it relatively transparent, but the side windows were iced over on the inside. The cultural attaché spoke briefly to the driver in Russian, and the man nodded without turning his head. As the car moved off, he smiled.

"Bloody awful weather at the moment. I don't know how much you'll be able to see, but if you give your window a scrape, you might get the occasional view."

"I hope so. I've no idea what to expect." Mark gazed at a huge metal structure, many stories high, at whose base curved steel swept up in a graceful half-parabola. "What's that?"

"The monument to space achievement. It's supposed to be a rocket going up."

"It's rather handsome."

Cunningham shrugged. "If you like that sort of thing. They're big on space achievement here. There's a statue of Yuri Gagarin the size of a five-storey house." He looked towards the driver and grinned. "You can talk freely, by the way. My driver says he doesn't speak any English, but he probably does. So unless you're about to pass me a few state secrets, you can say more or less anything you like. My flat's bugged, too. They always know everything about me." He spoke quite calmly, as though still discussing the weather.

Mark was surprised by his frankness. "Isn't that a bit disconcerting?"

"Not really. They assume all foreign cultural attachés like me must be spies. I suppose it's because all theirs are. After a while, you don't think about it."

"I would have thought it made life somewhat claustrophobic."

Cunningham shook his head. "Not at all, especially if you've got nothing to hide. Mistrust of people in general and foreigners in particular runs very deep in the Russian consciousness. It's always been that way. They had just as many secret police at the time of the tsars, so it's nothing new to them."

"I see."

"Don't worry about it. Nobody's likely to follow you around or monitor what you do, particularly if you're here as a tourist or—better still—a potential customer. I think a lot of people are disappointed to learn that." He grinned. "We all see ourselves as putative James Bonds when we first arrive here."

"I suppose you're right."

"However, once you prove yourself to be a friend, they will trust you absolutely. There's a kind of national paranoia until they get to know you. After that, you couldn't ask for better friends."

The traffic consisted mostly of trucks and other commercial vehicles, seemingly old-fashioned in design and painted in dark colours. There was a noticeable absence of private cars. They joined a long queue of vehicles waiting at a traffic light, and even with the windows closed, Mark could sense the heavy, slightly sweet smell of petrol fumes that he associated with Eastern European cars—Czech and Hungarian—from the past. They were travelling down a broad avenue lined with solid, square-cut buildings, and Mark peered through a space in the ice-frosted glass.

"It's not a very inspiring view, I'm afraid. Soviet architecture isn't the most imaginative." Cunningham pointed past Marks' shoulder. "Every now and then, you'll come across a lovely little nineteenth-century building, all stucco and curlicues, carefully preserved, not to mention all those churches with the onions on top. Do you speak any Russian?"

"No. I found a Penguin guide with a few useful phrases. I'm still trying to transliterate the Cyrillic script."

"It's a popular tourist pastime. I've got a cat called Pectopah." Mark looked puzzled, which pleased the attaché. "If you substitute the letters, it becomes 'restoran,' or restaurant. Most new arrivals congratulate themselves when they spot that one, but there are plenty of others."

"I'll keep trying." He sat in silence, staring through the misty glass. The traffic wound round several corners, always hemmed in by heavy lorries and buses. After a while, they seemed to be in a more central area. The streets had become narrower, and Mark had the impression that there were more shops and office buildings. Amid the dark severity of the façades, few displayed anything in their windows. But then, Russia's shops were all state-owned, and there was no need to lure customers with colourful displays. Perhaps Gorbachev's determination to develop a commercial sense of competition would change that.

Quite suddenly, they passed a bright green building covered with ornate carved decorations and plaster work. "That's very attractive."

"Yes. I always forget what it is. They're inclined to have rather unlikely names, like Centre for the People's Marine Navigation or something of the sort. I really ought to brush up on them if I'm going to do a decent job as a guide, but I didn't want to bombard you with names on your first outing. We're coming into the centre of Moscow now. I thought we'd take the traditional tourist route through the Kremlin to Red Square. Keep an eye out to your right, we're about to pass the Bolshoi Theatre." Set slightly off the road in its own square, the stately classic building seemed a sharp contrast, with its pastel colours and white Corinthian columns.

They drove down Marx Prospeckt, past the enormous front of the Lenin Library whose grandiose neoclassical architecture reminded Mark of Italian buildings from Mussolini's era, then turned left to enter the Kremlin. The gate was closed.

Cunningham frowned. "Damn, they're not allowing traffic through today. There must be some big meeting going on inside." He smiled apologetically. "They're inclined to do that without warning. We'll have to go round the other way. It's a pity; the churches in there are worth seeing." He gave the driver further instructions, and they doubled back along the side of the Kremlin walls until they passed through a broad square, dominated by a tall building. Cunningham murmured again to the driver, who chuckled. "That's the KGB building, with a statue of Dzerzhinsky in front. I was telling the driver that it's one of Moscow's most famous buildings." He grinned. "A bit like Eros in Piccadilly, eh?"

Mark stared at the building. A pale sun was beginning to break through the clouds, and a ray of light shone on it. It was very different from what he had expected: rather a pleasant building. His thoughts were interrupted by Cunningham. "We're coming into Red Square from the other end, behind St. Basil's."

There was a large open space, and they parked next to several other cars. The air was bitterly cold as they trudged up the slight incline towards the church with its familiar onion-shaped domes.

The attaché looked concerned. "You should have brought a hat. Are

26

you sure you want to walk?" He was sporting an expensive-looking *shapka* whose light brown fur almost matched the colour of his hair.

"I'm fine for a few minutes. My God, it's cold!"

As they walked past St. Basil's, he was surprised to see that the decorations on the walls were all hand-painted. He had anticipated a mosaic, but the surface was coloured with the simplicity of peasant art, its naïve flowers and patterns a charming contrast to the severe buildings surrounding it. Before him was the immense open space of Red Square. He had seen it many times in newsreel pictures of May Day parades, but they had not captured its grandeur and size. The squat red building housing Lenin's tomb seemed dwarfed by the area surrounding it.

It felt very strange to be standing in this most famous of all Russian landmarks, symbolizing the awesome power of the Soviet Union. There had been a time when Mark could never have believed that he would one day find himself there, and yet he felt no sudden shock of realization nor any sense of danger. Perhaps he really had broken with the past forever.

"How does it strike you?"

"Extraordinary." It felt like a very English word to use.

"It is. 'Red' is synonymous with beautiful to the Russians, you know. I'm not sure I would call it that, but it's certainly impressive." Starting at Lenin's tomb and reaching almost to the far end of the square there was a long line of people dressed in peasant costumes waiting patiently in the freezing air. Following Mark's gaze, Cunningham said, "They fly people in all year round to see Lenin. By the look of them, that lot come from Kazakh."

"How long will they have to wait?"

"About two hours. In the summer, it can take anything up to four. There's devotion for you!"

"My God, they could freeze to death."

"No, they're probably used to it, and my guess is that they've got half a dozen layers of clothes under the folk stuff." He pointed to the opposite side of the square. "That's the famous GUM department store. We might find a hat in there if you want to try. You lose body heat through the top of your head faster than any other way."

"Don't worry. I'm only here for about forty-eight hours, so I'll manage." He turned almost unconsciously in the direction of the car, and Cunningham fell into step beside him.

27

"Well, it's something to tell your grandchildren about." The attaché deliberately slowed his pace, so that Mark felt obliged to do the same. He dropped his voice slightly. "As a matter of fact, we're rather curious to know what brings you here."

"How do you mean?"

Cunningham continued to smile cheerfully, but his eyes were blank. "My comments in the car just now were for the benefit of the driver. I'm afraid it was a rather clumsy effort on my part to be discreet, if you see what I mean."

"Not really."

"Well, let's just say that your name came up in conversation at the embassy from a rather unexpected quarter. We were anxious to know what would bring someone with your . . . qualifications . . . to Moscow at this time."

"Oh." They walked in silence for a few paces. "I wondered whether your records might turn up my name."

"They didn't. We received a message from London, if you must know. They wanted to know what you were doing here."

For a moment, Mark was angry. "I didn't know they still kept tabs on me."

"I doubt whether they do, but they take an interest in the passenger lists on Moscow flights. Presumably your name rang a bell somewhere."

"I see. Well, I hope their interest is academic. I left *England* a long time ago." He emphasized the word, because he knew that Cunningham would understand the implication.

"I suppose you could say that they're not so much interested as curious. Perhaps that's a better word. It's an odd sort of place for someone like you to visit, isn't it?"

"I suppose it is, but I think it's also why I'm here: to prove to them— and myself, if necessary—that I'm no longer involved with that life. When Schedrin invited me to come and hear Viktor Kaverin, it seemed like an interesting thing to do."

"Interesting?" There was a slight edge to the attaché's voice.

"All right. I took a calculated risk that it wasn't some sort of trap. I wanted to believe that he took me for what I am, an artist's manager in the music world, and nothing else."

"All the same, it was a risk."

"It seemed important to take it. I left London a long time ago. I

28

couldn't tell the Russians anything they don't know already. I wouldn't even be of any use to them in an exchange arrangement." He smiled bitterly. "London would tell them to keep me."

Cunningham nodded. "Fair enough. I'll pass it back to them, if you don't mind."

"You're welcome to."

"All the same, I hope you'll watch your step. If anything should go wrong, we couldn't do much to help you. You see, it occurred to us that it *we* recognize you from the old days, there's nothing to prevent our friends over here from doing the same."

"I realize that, but it was still important enough for me to take the chance."

Cunningham's voice was soft. "You must have had rather strong reasons for resigning."

"I did." Mark quickened his pace.

"When did you say you were leaving?"

He smiled. "As if you didn't know! Tomorrow."

"Well, perhaps we are being overcautious, but I thought it was just as well to mention it." He grinned suddenly, looking youthful. It struck Mark that he was probably not much more than thirty. Perhaps he saw a little of James Bond in himself. "I wouldn't go talking to any strange men, if I were you."

"I seldom do."

"Good." He hurried forward. "You must be freezing. I hope that blighter kept the car engine running. We've still got time for a quick run up to the Lenin Hills, by the university. You can see the whole of Moscow laid out from there. It's really quite a small town, you know— rather like Paris. You're not going to have time for anything else if you're leaving as soon as that. We'll have to hurry if we're going to be at Viktor's reception on time."

They returned at noon to the Mezhdunarodnaya Hotel, a modern building on a road overlooking the frozen Moskva River. The entrance was cement and stone, similar to that of the Kosmos, but once they had passed through the foyer to an inner section, Mark was surprised to find himself in a well-proportioned, airy lobby, not unlike a small reproduction of the Regency Hyatt House in San Francisco. The central hall rose many stories, and glass-enclosed lifts slid silently up and down the inner walls. Dominating the centre was a huge metal cockerel, reminiscent of

Rimsky-Korsakov's *Coq d'Or*, standing on a tall pedestal. As they entered on the stroke of noon, the giant metal bird stretched its neck upward and crowed, and panels opened on the column to reveal nursery-tale figures revolving. It was delightful and, in sharp contrast to Moscow's severity, almost frivolously childish. A large number of spectators, both on the floor of the lobby and along various staircases leading to other levels, had gathered to watch the display.

Standing at Mark's side, Cunningham said: "This is one of Moscow's newer showplaces. *Mezhdunarodnaya* simply means international, by the way, and this hotel is where all the foreign companies can rent space to show off their wares." He led the way up some stairs to a long corridor of shop windows. "Various countries use these shops to fly the flag. We have a place, and needless to say the Japanese are here in strength. No matter where you go in the world these days, you can count on them to be there first! The only problem is that very few Russians, apart from government officials, ever come and look at what's on display. There are several restaurants, and the food's good—much better than average."

Yuri Schedrin met them at the door of their restaurant. "My dear Mr. Holland. May I call you Mark?"

"I wish you would."

"Then you will call me Yuri. Welcome to our new hotel. Did you hear the cock?" He was so obviously pleased that, for a foolish moment, Mark wondered whether they had built the giant bird first and designed the hotel around it.

"Yes. It was lovely." They handed their outdoor clothes to a solicitous cloakroom attendant standing behind a polished wood counter that might have come from the Savoy Hotel.

"Very good. I hope Mr. Cunningham gave you a tour of the city. I must apologize that I could not do so myself, but my stay in Moscow is very short, and I must travel to Paris this evening." Mark noted that Schedrin was wearing a business suit whose cut was not as elegant as the one he had worn in Geneva. He wondered if this was deliberate. "Did you find time for the Lenin Hills and the university?"

"Yes. I enjoyed it all very much." Cunningham had been a good guide, supplying adequate information without overburdening the tour with details. He had pointed out the other four buildings almost exactly like the university, designed during the Stalinist era, without bothering to go into the details of what each one contained. And standing on the high ridge above the town, the wind making his eyes water, he had found the panoramic view across the city impressive. Moscow was a handsome town, but not very graceful, like a good-looking woman who would never be described as beautiful. From the pictures he had seen, Leningrad was truly beautiful.

Schedrin scarcely seemed to notice Mark's reply and hurried them through an elegant restaurant with white walls and dark furniture upholstered in a rich red. The décor was almost Spanish in style, although he suspected it represented another area of Russia. It felt like being back in the West again.

"You must let me introduce you to some of the other guests, although I'm sure Mr. Cunningham knows most of them already. Viktor has not arrived yet, but he should be here at any moment." He ushered them into a smaller dining-room with a single large table set for about thirty guests. The walls were decorated in pastel greens and blues.

Mark found himself placed between Cunningham and a chubby, balding man who, by the cut of his clothes, was either German or American. It was surprising how, in a foreign land, one began to identify nationality by the style of clothing. Opposite, one of his Russian hosts— a small, nervous man who smiled and nodded his head frequently, possibly because his English was not strong—poured a shot glass full of vodka and raised it in a silent, genial toast.

The man at his side held out a pink hand. "Joe Ross, *New York Times*." He nodded past Mark to Cunningham. "Are you with the British?"

"Not exactly, although I am English. I run an artists' agency in Geneva."

Ross nodded. "That's why I saw you at the concert last night. You get to notice any new faces. What do you think of him?" He nodded in the direction of Viktor Kaverin, who had just entered the room with Schedrin.

"Outstanding. He's a fine pianist."

Ross grunted. "They're certainly putting on a show for him. As things ease up, I guess they plan to launch him in the West."

"He deserves to be heard there."

"If you say so. I don't have much of an ear for music, but he sounded good to me."

"Then you're not an arts reviewer?"

The American smiled. "It doesn't work like that here. We cover anything that happens, from party congresses to piano recitals—anything that rates a story."

"How long have you been here?"

"Too long. I've done eighteen months, so I reckon another six before they ship me home."

Mark smiled. "You make it sound like a prison sentence."

"You could say that. It'll make a great chapter in my memoirs."

"Do you speak Russian?"

For a moment, the American looked contemptuous. "I wouldn't get very far if I didn't. I learned it from my grandfather."

"Really?"

Ross drank his vodka Russian-style, with a quick upturn of the glass. "Don't let the name fool you. My family came from these parts. Their name was Rosenbloom, but they changed it to Ross when they got to Ellis Island. The old man would have been pleased to see me come back here, God rest him. Even after fifty years in New York he still had a yearning for Mother Russia."

"But you don't?"

"Nah, I like my comforts." He surveyed the table, which was covered with a wide assortment of hors-d'oeuvres. "I'm glad they picked a good restaurant."

The food was excellent. Black and red caviar, cold meats, fish, and half a dozen salads were accompanied by lavish refills of ice-cold vodka, to be followed by filet mignon and fresh vegetables (a rarity in December, Ross assured him) with a good Russian Burgundy. The meal was rounded out with the delicious ice-cream that everyone had recommended to Mark before he left Geneva.

At the end of the dinner there were speeches. A microphone was placed at the head of the table, and Schedrin introduced a sombre-faced junior minister of arts who read a prepared speech in Russian, pausing at the end of each sentence for an earnest young woman to give English and French translations. The volume of the loudspeakers was turned much too high, and the minister's words came from the wall at the opposite end of the room, so the effect was slightly unreal. He described Viktor Kaverin's career in a monotone, itemizing his educational background and concerts to date like a railway timetable. It made Mark

32

wonder whether he had heard Kaverin play. The pianist sat throughout the speech with his head bowed, a dreamy smile on his face. Perhaps the only comment that Mark found interesting was that Kaverin had not finished his studies at the Moscow Conservatory until 1978. By his calculation, the pianist was already well into his thirties.

While the interpreter was translating into French, Mark turned to Cunningham. "He's not exactly straight out of school."

The attaché shook his head. "He's a late starter, with an unusual background. He always played the piano, of course, but he started out as an athlete. He tried for the Olympic gymnastic team but didn't quite make it. After that, he had two years of military service and only settled into serious music when he was in his middle twenties."

On Mark's other side, Ross was making notes on a small pad. The American shook his head. "It's interesting, but hardly likely to hit the headlines."

The minister droned on for a few more minutes, adding official platitudes, then sat down to polite applause. Schedrin thanked him and placed the microphone in front of Kaverin. The pianist stood up, smiling cheerfully as they applauded. He was dressed casually in a black rollneck sweater and slacks, with a grey nylon zip-front windjacket. His face was rather pale beneath dark hair that was long by Russian standards, and Mark noticed that he had very long eyelashes, like a girl's. The night before, he had been dressed formally in white tie and tails, but Mark could now see that he had an athlete's broad, muscular shoulders and narrow waist.

Kaverin spoke in English. His accent was marked, but he was fluent. For a moment, the interpreter looked uncertain, but he waved her aside, and she sat close to the minister, whispering a rapid translation in his ear.

"First, I would like to thank Minister Kharpov for his generosity in coming to this reception and for his kind words. I would also like to thank Mr. Schedrin and his colleagues from Gosconcert for their generosity in arranging such a reception on my behalf." He bowed to each, then turned back to the room with a smile. "Perhaps you are surprised that I speak to you in English, but it is a language that I have studied for many years and one that I hope to put into regular practice in future years."

Ross raised his eyebrows and murmured, "That's an odd thing to say."

As though replying to him, Kaverin continued, "I make this statement because I know that the agency is eager for me to play in Western Europe and, if circumstances permit, beyond." To Mark, it seemed a commonplace remark, but he noticed that the American had leaned forward, showing greater interest. "You see, my friends, as a member of the Soviet Union's younger generation of musicians, it is my greatest wish to show the world that we in Russia share with them a great love of music, as well as a strong desire for peaceful friendship and understanding. What better way could we choose than by performing the great music of the masters, whether it is Bach or Beethoven of Germany, Ravel and Debussy of France, or our own Tchaikovsky and Rachmaninov? Until now, I have been given the wonderful opportunity to play in concert halls all over my own country, and I am very excited to learn of the new plans that will take me farther afield, beyond these boundaries." He paused for a moment, glancing in the direction of the minister, who listened impassively as the young woman whispered in his ear. Mark had the impression that the pianist was tense, but he smiled and continued, "In fact, one of the greatest ambitions of my life is to play a recital for the President of the United States."

This was greeted with scattered, self-conscious applause. Under his breath, Ross said, "He'd never stay awake long enough!"

Mark watched the minister's face for any reaction as the translation progressed. Except for a brief nod of his head, his expression did not change.

Kaverin surveyed his audience. "In the next few months, I will be appearing for the first time in several West European cities. I hope my performances are worthy of my training and preparation, and I look forward to meeting people from other lands and extending the hand of friendship and fellowship wherever I go." He sat down, and the applause was suitably prolonged.

The minister left a few minutes later, and as the guests drank coffee and liqueurs, their Russian hosts vacated their chairs to allow Kaverin, shepherded by Schedrin, to move down the table, shaking hands and chatting briefly with each group. When he reached Mark, Schedrin made the introductions, and the young man's face lit up.

"Ah, you are the one I am taking to the Bolshoi tonight."

34

Schedrin placed a hand on the pianist's shoulder. "I promised that you would go, Mark, but I cannot take you myself. Viktor has the tickets. I hope that is satisfactory?"

"Of course." Mark shook Kaverin's hand. "I enjoyed your recital very much. I look forward to hearing you again."

Ross said, "Did you mean that about wanting to play for the President?"

The pianist nodded gravely. "I could not be more sincere. I have thought about it for many years." He shrugged slightly. "Who knows? One day, such a dream could come true."

The American smiled. "Who knows?"

Kaverin turned back to Mark. "Shall we meet in the foyer of the theatre ten minutes before it begins?"

"Certainly. I have to confess, I don't know what's on tonight."

The pianist seemed surprised. "It's the ballet. They are dancing *Swan Lake.*"

Schedrin smiled. "Viktor may have another little surprise for you, but I won't spoil it for him."

Viktor shook Mark's hand again. "Until this evening, then. Stand inside the building, Mr. Holland. It will be too cold to wait by the pillars. I will find you."

He moved on to the next group, and Mark turned to the American journalist. "Did you get a story?"

Ross patted his notebook and grinned. "I think I just have. The Russian pianist who wants to play for our President. It's the sort of headline the wire services might pick up." People were beginning to drift towards the exit, and he stood. "I'll call this one in. Is that kid really as good as they say?"

"Yes, he's first-class; one of the best for years."

"Great. It makes the story all the more interesting." He shook hands with Mark and Cunningham, and made his way to the exit.

Watching him, Cunningham shook his head. "He looks as pleased as Punch. I can never understand our American friends. That remark about playing for the President was all he appeared to want."

"Why not? He's a reporter, not a critic. I'll keep an eye out for the item."

"In Switzerland?" The attaché looked sceptical.

"The *International Herald Tribune.* It picks up pieces from all the major American newspapers. When you think about it, it's a good story." Mark looked at his watch. "I'd better get back to the hotel."

"Of course. Do you want to have a go at the Metro? It's quite an experience."

"Why not?"

"Good for you! I'll take you to the right station, and all you have to do is go six stops. Your one is called Vdnya, but you'll have to remember to look for a sign that reads B, Delta, H, X. Actually, you can't miss it, because it's the only one with four letters on the line."

They said goodbye to Schedrin, who asked to be remembered to Agnes and promised to call on Mark on his next visit to Geneva. It was nearly four o'clock, and Mark suspected that the attaché wanted to go home early. He directed their driver to the nearest Metro station. Inside, Cunningham dropped a five-kopek piece in the turnstile and grinned. "That's about five pence. It's cheaper than London, and much more efficient—no strikes!" He pointed. "When you reach the bottom of that moving staircase, take the platform on your right. Any train will get you there. Remember, it's six stops."

"Thanks." The entrance to the station was busy, and Mark could feel himself being urged forward by the crowd.

"Will you call me in the morning? We could have an early lunch before you trek out to the airport. You have to allow a minimum of about two hours for the check-in."

He rode down the long escalator, which seemed to reach deep below the ground. The tunnel down which he was travelling was wide and airy, its white walls illuminated by 1930s-style lamps facing upward. It was like a greatly enlarged version of the London underground, but there were no posters or advertisements. When he reached the platform level, Mark found himself in a broad, high-ceilinged avenue lit by handsome old-fashioned chandeliers. Walls, floor, and ceiling were spotlessly clean, and he had the impression that he was entering the extended lobby of a rather grand hotel. The crowd moved forward, and he walked steadily, as though keeping pace with an army of pedestrians. A large, ancient-looking train rattled into the station, and after some polite jostling, Mark found a place by the door.

The people surrounding him were silent, their faces impassive, as though wrapped in private thought. Mark had been told before that the public faces of Russians were expressionless as a matter of habit, suggesting an unnatural severity. He glanced around and smiled to himself. They looked like deportees. Occasionally he detected a curious, sidelong glance in his direction, but most of the people studiously ignored him. Sneaking a direct look at the faces that were nearest, he was unable to discern anything particularly Russian about them. Their winter clothes were heavy—perhaps a little shabbier than in the West—and their features suggested a wide variety of ethnic backgrounds, but they were not noticeably different. He might have seen the same people on the underground in Glasgow.

The train stopped at the next station, and a muffled loudspeaker in the carriage made an unintelligible announcement. It was hard to read the name of the station, because it was picked out in mosaic on the opposite wall, but Mark was able to compare the script with the map on the inside of the carriage. He wondered whether Russians or Japanese visiting London for the first time found it all equally puzzling.

After six stops, he stepped off the train, childishly relieved to recognize the four-letter name, and joined the crowd walking to a tall escalator that reached seemingly endlessly upward. It climbed slowly and for a long time. Mark estimated that it was more than a hundred yards from top to bottom. Coming through the exit, he was struck by a blast of icy air and the sight of the Kosmos Hotel a short walk away. It was already growing dark, and following other pedestrians, he picked his way cautiously across frozen snow and ice in a sort of no-man's-land between the street and hotel. With almost a shock, it occurred to him that he had never once wondered whether he was being followed or his movements monitored. It looked as though Cunningham was right after all. James Bond was for amateurs.

3

The heavy-faced lady at the desk glared at him. "You have to book taxis twenty-four hours in advance."

Mark took a deep breath. "I know, but as I've already explained, I didn't know that yesterday, when I arrived. Anyway, I wasn't here twenty-four hours ago." The woman shrugged eloquently. "Look, I'm supposed to be at the Bolshoi Theatre in half an hour. I am a guest of your government."

It had little effect. The woman turned down the sides of her mouth. "What can I do? Taxis must be ordered in advance." Like most bureaucrats, she had no solutions for anomalous situations. "You could take the Metro."

"I could, but I don't know the way, and I don't speak any Russian."

The man standing behind him in the queue tapped Mark on the shoulder. "Did you say you're trying to get to the Bolshoi?" By the sound of his accent, he was a Yorkshireman.

"Yes."

"You can ride in with me, then. That's if my bloody taxi's here." He scowled at the woman, who consulted her notepad.

"What is your name?"

"Lumsden. I booked yesterday."

"Then your taxi will come." She wrote numbers on a piece of paper and handed it to him. "It will be there in a minute or two."

"That's what you said last time, and I had to wait a bloody half-hour!" The woman ignored him, and was already glaring at the man behind.

As they walked to the door, Mark said, "Thank you. I don't know how you're supposed to know about the system here."

"It's the same with every bloody thing in this God-forsaken hole! I've been in and out of Moscow for the past five years, and it doesn't get any better." He was a stocky, red-faced man in his late forties, wearing a battered sheepskin coat with a woollen ski hat pulled low over his forehead. "This your first time?" Mark nodded. "You have to learn two main rules: first, be patient until it's your go; then, be bloody rude, or you won't get anywhere. What brings you here, then?"

"Classical music."

"Oh yes? I'm in water purifying myself."

"I hope I'm not taking you out of your way."

"No, I'm catching up with some of the lads at the Intourist Hotel on Gorki Street. It's just past the Bolshoi. I'd hoped they'd put me in there too, but it was booked up. There's some sort of a congress going on."

"There always is, I'm told."

"Aye." He consulted the paper he was holding. "This is the number plate of our taxi—4467. See if you can spot it." He gave a grunt of disgust. "Bloody taxi service is a disgrace, and the airport drive's a rip-off."

"How do you mean?" They were standing outside, facing the forecourt. The air was oppressively cold, but the cutting wind had dropped and the threatened snow had held off.

The man watched the steady flow of taxis coming and going. "When you pay your hotel bill, you'll find they've charged you twenty-five rubles for transport to and from Sheremetyevo. Right?"

"Right."

The man scowled. "Except they double you up with three or four others, or cram you into a bloody minibus with half a dozen people, and still charge the same. Average it out at four people a trip, and that's a hundred rubles—near enough a hundred quid."

"I see what you mean."

"That's not all." He was angrily triumphant. "If you take your own bloody taxi to or from the airport, it's only about nine or ten rubles on the meter, so they're ripping you off, anyway!"

Mark smiled. "That sounds like capitalism!"

At that moment, their taxi arrived. Lumsden bore down on the driver, brandishing his paper, but the man shook his head, indicating that he must check in at the transport desk. This irritated Mark's fellow passenger further. "Come on, Ivan, I've got your bloody number!" The driver ignored him and disappeared into the hotel. The Yorkshireman got into the cab and sat down heavily. "We'd better stake our claim before they give the bloody cab away to someone else. What a dump!"

"How is the Intourist Hotel?"

"Not much better, if you're talking about the rooms, but it's in the centre, which is a damned sight more convenient. The girls are just as bad."

"Girls?"

The man eyes him with an air of exasperation. "Pick-ups, call girls, whores. Don't tell me you haven't noticed them. They work all the bars, day and night."

"I haven't been in any of the bars. I only arrived late last night."

"Oh. Well, every hotel catering to foreigners is full of 'em." The driver returned, and Mark's companion stared at him. "Bolshoi Theatre, *da?*" The driver nodded. "Then, the Intourist Hotel for me, OK?" The driver nodded again and edged the car out of the busy forecourt. He turned back to Mark. "As I was saying, the bars are full of bloody girls. Hypocrites!"

"The girls?"

"No, the government! It's typical of your Russian hypocrisy, isn't it?"

"How do you mean?"

The man seemed angrier than ever. As he spoke, he counted off each point with a stubby finger. "In the first place, there's no such thing as prostitution in Russia, right?"

"I suppose not."

"But in the second place, they want the foreign currency—as much as they can lay their hands on—right?" He did not wait for Mark to reply. "Now, the girls only offer their services for foreign money, so the government turns a blind eye to what they're doing, and they spend the money in the foreign-currency shops and bars."

"I see."

The man looked pleased with himself. Mark had the feeling that he had repeated the story many times and was glad to find an uninitiated listener. "That's only the first part of the story. Now, because there's officially no such thing as prostitution, officially there's no such thing as VD either, nor anything in the way of clinics and proper treatment. So, if you should happen to fancy a bit of fun for the evening—not that I do, mind you!—the chances are even that you'll end up with a nasty little souvenir of your visit." His face darkened, and Mark had the suspicion that he was speaking from experience. "Why should they care? The only customers are from outside Russia, so it's no skin off their noses if they go home with a dose of good Russian clap! And all the time they're acting so bloody prim and proper—bloody hypocrites!"

"I'm surprised the authorities let them get away with it."

The man was silent for a moment. Around them, the lorries and commercial vehicles had finished for the day, and the roads were relatively empty, making the journey into town much quicker. There were few pedestrians braving the freezing temperatures. The overhead street lights were bright, but the buildings were dark and anonymous.

"If you ask me, the authorities are running it. I wouldn't put it past them."

"Oh?" Mark remembered that at one time the Czechs had run a government-operated pick-up bar in Prague.

"One of the girls tried it on with me yesterday evening. Spoke fair English too. They speak half a dozen languages between them, and you can watch them dividing up according to who's there—Germans, English, Swedes. You name the language; they've got the girls. Anyway, my one came over and started to talk to me." He gave a gruff laugh. "She wanted seventy quid. Bloody cheek! I thought I'd try bargaining with her—just to pass the time, you know—and she was off like a shot. If you ask me, they've got set rates, like everything else here. I've never met a girl on the game who wasn't prepared to do a little haggling over the price, but this one didn't want to know the time of day. So, either business is booming, which is unlikely at those prices, or she's a government employee, like everyone else. Probably has to report on what she picks up!"

Mark smiled. "It's just as well you don't go in for that sort of thing."

"Quite right." The man was self-righteous. "I wouldn't touch them —a lot of bloody scrubbers! Anyway, I'm a decent family man. I've got better things to do with my money!"

Mark arrived at the theatre a few minutes early and passed the time watching the audience enter the foyer. They were little different from their counterparts anywhere else in the world. Perhaps they were not very fashionable, but their heavy winter clothes hardly allowed for that. There was a fair sprinkling of pretty girls sporting headbands or silk scarves thrown around their necks with carefully contrived abandon.

From the good bone structure of the faces, the drawn-back hair, the slightly hollowed cheeks, they looked like dancers. He had seen similar young women everywhere else whenever the ballet was performed. It was interesting that different forms of entertainment seemed to attract different types. In London in the 1960s, the Boulez evenings of contemporary music always brought in the "hairies" with their intense expressions, corduroy trousers, and open-toed sandals; and the only time he had visited a Philip Glass opera, the place had appeared to be full of punks, whose outré make-up and violent hair colours had been more interesting than most of the music.

Viktor Kaverin was late and found Mark pacing by the main entrance door wondering whether he had misunderstood their arrangement. The pianist was dressed in a smart full-length leather overcoat. His *shapka* looked as if it might be sable.

"I am sorry to be delayed. I hope I haven't kept you waiting too long." He took Mark's arm, leading him down a corridor to a small side door. "Come this way, please. We are to go to the special guest room."

They arrived at a small cleanly painted entrance, which seemed to be somewhere between front- and backstage. Mark could see a door leading to an office with a desk. After hanging their coats up, Viktor led the way up a staircase to an elegant waiting-room, thickly carpeted, which was decorated in dark red velvet and gold. Ornate gilded armchairs and sofas stood against walls covered with a rich red silk. It was very grand.

Viktor lowered his voice. "This is our VIP room. It goes straight to the box, through there. Shall we go in?" He led the way, and Mark found himself in a box situated next to the stage, directly above the orchestra pit.

The hall was beautiful. The dark red and gold and white that greeted his eyes was perhaps the most unexpected sight he had encountered on the trip. For some reason, he had supposed that the Bolshoi would be plain and utilitarian, like the rest of Moscow, but he was faced with luxurious nineteenth-century magnificence and splendour, rich in fabric and design. There was an ornate "royal" box dominating the centre of the rear wall of the auditorium, and it struck him absurdly that if Tsar Nicholas and Alexandra had suddenly stepped into it at that moment, he would not have been surprised. Elegant chandeliers provided lighting, and the tall building rose to many levels. It was more splendid than

Covent Garden, and the Vienna State Opera by comparison looked like an Odeon cinema.

The audience did not match the surroundings. Some of the men wore business suits, and there were women in dark cocktail dresses, but there were also many in open-neck shirts and comfortable sweaters. It seemed to Mark that there were more men in uniforms than one might see elsewhere. At his feet, the orchestra was tuning up in the very large pit. It appeared from the sound that he was sitting directly above the French horns and the percussion.

Viktor motioned him into a wooden armchair at the front of the box. It was very close to the stage, but he found he could see well enough. "I have a small surprise for you tonight."

"Really?"

The pianist smiled. "My sister. She is a member of the company. I will point her out to you." As he spoke, the box was filling up with other guests: an elegant young couple who spoke quietly together in Italian, two burly men looking uncomfortable in tight-fitting brown business suits, and an elderly woman in a black silk evening coat that had seen better years. From her delicate features and porcelain skin, Mark assumed that she was a retired ballerina. It would have been interesting to examine his fellow guests more closely, but at that moment the lights dimmed and a young conductor picked his way through the players to mount the podium.

It was a good performance, but not great. The orchestra played well, although it was hard for him to judge at the start because from his position over the orchestra pit the sound was dominated by brass and timpani. However, when the dark red velvet curtain rose, Mark was able to see the size and depth of the huge stage and became absorbed in the dancing. At a certain moment, Kaverin tapped him on the shoulder and whispered.

"My sister is the third swan from the left."

Mark nodded and smiled to himself. It was an unusual family introduction! She was very pretty, with the large eyes and sensitively moulded face of a dancer. Her movements were graceful, and her body seemed slightly more sensuously curved than some of her anorexic companions. Perhaps there was even a slight family resemblance to Kaverin, but he could have imagined it. Under all the make-up, it was really impossible to tell.

43

The first act passed quickly. The ensemble work was not as perfectly disciplined as he had expected it to be, but the soloists were excellent. Even within the restrictions of classical ballet movement, Mark was aware of a controlled masculine athleticism that was sometimes lacking in many European companies, and his attention did not wander throughout the performance. It was only when he stood that he realized how uncomfortable his wooden chair was. If he was honest, he had to admit that the aesthetics of the great classical ballets like *Swan Lake, Giselle,* and *La Sylphide* had never appealed to him as much as later works. They were too stylized—almost too perfect—and he preferred later ballets with better stories and more easily identifiable emotions. It was a shame the Bolshoi had not chosen Prokofiev's *Romeo and Juliet.*

There were queues in all the foyers for cold drinks, and Viktor led him upstairs to a long, elegant gallery with crystal chandeliers.

"I am glad that we can have this opportunity to talk this evening. Will you join us for a little celebration afterwards? It will be just a few close friends."

"Thank you." What had Cunningham said about talking to strange men?

The pianist seemed a little embarrassed. "You see, now that you have heard me, I was hoping to ask a small favour of you."

"I'll be delighted to help if I can."

Viktor hesitated. "The first engagement I have been offered is a concert in Bergen, a little over a month from now, but there is a small problem."

"What is that?"

Reassured, the Russian spoke faster. "The guest conductor of the Bergen Symphony is Maestro Konstantin Steigel, and there is the opportunity for me to perform a concerto with him before I give a solo recital. The problem is that the maestro has never heard me play and has expressed some doubt about my appearing with him. Mr. Schedrin received a letter from the manager of the orchestra. He was a little embarrassed by the situation. I have been told that you are Maestro Steigel's manager, and we were hoping that . . ." He left the sentence unfinished.

It began to dawn on Mark why Schedrin had been so eager to bring him to Moscow. He smiled. "I don't think that will be a problem. I'll be

44

delighted to call Steigel with the warmest recommendation that he engage you. What have you proposed to play?"

The Russian's face lit up. "Thank you. I am so grateful! We suggested the Beethoven G Major, but I would be pleased to change to something else if you think it would be more suitable."

"The Beethoven is an excellent choice. I'm sure Konstantin will approve."

It seemed to Mark that Kaverin overreacted in his delight. "You have no idea how much this means to me. I have admired Konstantin Steigel all my life. I have even bought many of his records, which are hard to find in Russia. They are amazing!"

Mark nodded. Steigel disliked recording; he considered it an irritating and unmusical occupation for a conductor of his generation, which had grown up in an era of live concerts. The intrusions of technology distracted him, and he always claimed that he undertook recordings because the royalty income would provide a valuable pension when he retired. Mark suspected that he secretly hoped the despised recording sessions would add a touch of immortality to his readings of the great masters.

Viktor's eyes shone. "I could not ask for a better way to make my debut in the West. I know that Bergen is not as important as London or Paris, but I am sure those will follow. Is there any chance that you will come to hear me?"

"I suppose I could. What is the date of the concert?" He remembered Steigel grumbling about having to plough his way through Norwegian snow "for the questionable pleasure of bringing Beethoven to the descendants of trolls."

"The concerto will be on the twenty-seventh."

"I'll try to be there. It will be a pleasure to hear Konstantin again, and he and his wife, Heidi, are always good company. I'm sure you'll like them."

The pianist grinned charmingly. "I'm much more concerned that he will like me!"

The second half of *Swan Lake* seemed to drag a little, and Mark became increasingly conscious of the discomfort of his wooden chair. He passed some of the time trying to identify Kaverin's sister on each entrance of the *corps de ballet.* Unless her make-up was very skilfully applied, it seemed to him that she was an unusually pretty girl, standing out from the others. When the final curtain calls had been taken, Viktor hurried him down to the vestibule where they had left their coats.

"If you will wait here, I will go to fetch Irina. It is much warmer than in the street!"

He returned quite soon, accompanied by the dancer. She was as beautiful as Mark had suspected, with delicately pale skin and fine features. Like her brother, she had large brown eyes, tapering to the corners with a hint of oriental heritage, unusually long eyelashes, and a sensuous mouth that was almost inappropriate to her classically ascetic ballerina's features.

Her grip was firm as she shook hands. "Vicktor tells me you will help him when he goes to Bergen next month. That is very kind of you." She spoke gravely.

"Not at all. Talent such as his deserves to be heard. I'm glad I can help."

Looking more closely, Mark realized she was not quite as young as he had assumed. There were delicate lines at the corners of her mouth and eyes which she had not bothered to disguise. She wore only a trace of lipstick, and the vague shadows beneath her eyebrows might have been the remains of her theatrical make-up. Like many beautiful women, she did not need to enhance her appearance.

Irina paused by the exit door. "Viktor is bringing the car. It is better to wait here until he arrives." Her English accent was better than Viktor's, but she spoke carefully, like a student experimenting with the words.

The pianist was driving a small Lada—the Russian transmutation of the Fiat—and had turned all the fans to full power so that the icy windscreen would clear. As Mark joined him in front, he patted the steering wheel proudly. "My baby!"

"Is it new?" Presumably, like most consumer goods in Russia, it had only been available after a long wait. Babies probably took less time to produce.

"It is not new, but I have only just bought it. There is a sort of unofficial market square where you can find many things on a Sunday morning. All the dealers are Georgians. They are the great traders, but you have to be careful—they are worse than gypsies! If you could stay a little longer in Moscow, I would show you the places that are not listed in the official guidebooks. They are less historical, but much more interesting! It is lucky you are at the Kosmos Hotel. Our apartment is very near."

He drove rapidly through quiet streets whose surfaces were turning white under a new fall of light frozen snow. The city seemed to be empty. From time to time, Mark thought he identified a building or recognized a particular corner of the road, but the architecture had a monotonous similarity. Looking out, he said, "I'm still too new to know where we are."

"The town is not very big, and we all use the same roads in and out of it. That is why it is so busy during the day. We are driving on Prospekt Mira. That means Peace Avenue."

From the back, Irina added, "It is a word we use often, especially when we entertain visitors." Mark thought he detected a trace of irony in her voice, but remained silent.

The apartment building was a modern five-storey block hidden from the main road by a small wood of fir trees. It looked like one of the many blocks of post-war flats that had sprung up in London's suburbs.

In the lift, Viktor said, "We have invited a few of our friends, mostly musicians or dancers. They are the only people we ever seem to meet, and we have chosen the ones who speak English," he bowed slightly, "in your honour."

"That's thoughtful of you. I'm afraid my Russian's non-existent."

Most of the guests had already arrived, and Mark found himself introduced to five or six couples, all in their late twenties or early thirties. They had not been at the Bolshoi, and by the way they greeted Viktor and Irina, he assumed that most of them had spent the early part of the evening at the flat. Introductions were somewhat formal, creating an uneasy hiatus, but within a few minutes, everyone seemed to relax again. The women congregated at one end of the room where a table had been laid with a cold buffet, while the men stayed closed to a makeshift bar. Beer and vodka were the chief drinks, and Mark found himself nursing a tumbler filled with spirits. Despite Viktor's promise, the conversation was in Russian, but various people engaged him in the usual polite enquiries: Was this his first visit to Moscow, and was he enjoying it? What had he seen? If the atmosphere surrounding his arrival had been vaguely tense, that soon passed.

A group of men were arguing amicably with Viktor. Seeing Mark, the pianist held up his hand. "Come, I promised Mr. Holland—Mark—that we would speak English for him."

A young man with bushy red hair and the sproutings of a beard laughed. "You make it difficult for us. If I'm supposed to describe the way Oleg played yesterday, I do not know the right swear-words. All I can tell you is that he pedalled the piano like a bicycle, and missed half the notes in the left hand." He glanced at Mark. "His Chopin was a piece of shit!"

Mark smiled. It was reassuring to know that Russian musicians were no different from their counterparts anywhere else. The apartment was modern and comfortable. The sofa and chairs were simple and contemporary, with polished wood frames covered by rectangular pillows and cushions in simple basic colours. He was reminded of the old G-Plan furniture of the 1950s. There were several framed posters of concerts and music festivals on the walls, and he could identify the word "Kaverin" in Cyrillic letters. The living-room was quite large, and he had left his overcoat in one of the two bedrooms. Presumably, there were a kitchen and a bathroom somewhere, leading off the central corridor. Probably the only surprising feature was that it was so similar to an apartment anywhere else in the world. But then, what had he expected: a crumbling tenement, filled with old women in *babushkas?* A stately old room that had seen better days, with heavy furniture in dark wood, icons on the walls, and a steaming samovar in the corner? It occurred to him that his visions of Russia had been coloured either by spy films or Chekhov plays and the novels of Tolstoy and Dostoevsky. Perhaps the Russians assumed that, as an Englishman, he lived in a baronial hall surrounded by dogs and servants. He was finishing a second vodka when Irina invited everyone to help themselves to food.

Viktor joined him on the sofa, balancing a plate on his knees. "Do you have enough? Ballet always makes me hungry!" He surveyed his own generous serving. "I will have to run an extra distance tomorrow if I finish all this!"

"Do you jog in this weather?"

"Yes." He grinned. "You see, I am preparing to become Westernised. It is cold for the first few minutes, but I need to keep fit."

"Someone told me you were once a gymnast."

The pianist nodded. "I took it very seriously when I was a teenager.

Unfortunately, I was not good enough to be selected for the Olympic team, but the training helped me. One needs great muscular control to play the piano, especially in the quiet sections. I find it very helpful to me now. Here, let me bring you another drink. There is some wine."

As the party progressed, Mark found himself accepted by Viktor's friends. Questions asked timidly and often in halting English soon settled into relaxed discussions. The young man with red hair bombarded him, asking about one musician after another, and whether he had ever heard von Karajan conduct. Music and musicians were universal subjects, and it occurred to Mark that his interrogators discreetly avoided any subjects vaguely related to politics. Either they were showing natural caution, or perhaps he was ultra-sensitive. An hour or two passed, the bottles on the sideboard were steadily depleted, and laughter and conversation became more animated. With some of the lights lowered, several couples danced, moving slowly to the music.

Quite suddenly, Mark was aware that he had drunk too much. His forehead was damp, and he felt unsteady on his feet. Despite a general sensation of lightness and well-being, he realized that he was slurring his words. Walking carefully, he found his way to a small kitchen and after searching in the refrigerator for ice cubes he drank a tumbler of cold water. It refreshed him, washing away the oily taste of vodka. He sat on a chair, resting his elbows on a kitchen table, the cool glass pressed against his temple.

"Are you feeling ill?" Irina was watching him from the doorway, a look of concern on her face.

"No." He smiled. "Clearing my head. I'm not used to your vodka."

She sat at the table next to him. "It is not unusual in Russia. The government is always reprimanding us for drinking too much."

"I've read about it."

"Really? Is that what they print in your newspapers?"

"Not all the time, but it has been mentioned. It depends which newspapers you read." He could still feel the effect of the alcohol, making him garrulous. "Anyway, most of the British newspapers are comics."

She looked puzzled. "They print jokes?"

He laughed gently. She was charming. "No, I mean they're designed for entertainment rather than news: pictures of topless girls, sensational stories about sex and crime, gossip about film stars, competitions promising huge money prizes. If you want the news, it's better to watch television."

"Oh." She was thoughtful. "Perhaps I will see it for myself. Our company is to go on a tour in the spring, and we will dance at your Covent Garden. It will be my first visit."

"That's very exciting." It seemed to Mark that she was an extraordinarily attractive woman. He was touched by her childlike seriousness. "I'm sure you'll enjoy yourself, but you'll find it very different from here; very . . . democratic." He grinned. "Perhaps I shouldn't say something like that."

Irina shrugged. "We do not really think about such things. We are dancers, and that is all all that matters to us. We see enough about the West to understand that life is very different there, but it is not important. Few of our friends are interested in politics."

"I thought you had little choice in the matter. Most of us are told that the Russian people are preoccupied with political ideals." As an afterthought, he added, "And chess, of course. Doesn't everyone in Russia play chess?" It seemed to him that he had made a clever remark, but he could not think why.

Irina laughed, and he noticed that her teeth were very white and even. It struck him that she had not smiled very much that evening. It made her more beautiful than before. "I don't know how to play chess. It always looks very boring."

"That sounds like treason." There was a glass of vodka on the table, and despite himself, he sipped from it, knowing that it would affect him further. He felt a sense of adventure.

For a moment, Irina was serious. "You should not stereotype us, Mark. We are all different individuals, with minds of our own. I was born on the day that Stalin died, and that marked a very great change for my country."

"Because you were born?"

It made her smile again, which pleased him. "Of course not. What I mean is that by the time I was grown up, I was living in a very different country from the one your writers like to describe. I have read what they say, and I find it hard to believe they are writing about people like me."

"You're probably right. Our films and books have a very one-sided view."

She sighed. "We must seem very poor to you. Sometimes I see magazines from France and America. They are full of such luxuries. It's hard to imagine a life like that."

Mark drank again, emptying the tumbler. "That's a very glossy picture, but for some people it's real enough. They take it for granted." He was holding her hand, but she did not appear to notice.

"I would very much like to see America."

"You too?" He remembered Viktor's speech at the reception.

"Yes. Are they really all so rich?"

"No. A lot of them are poor—poorer than anything you know here."

"The black people?"

"And the white. Don't believe everything you read. There is a wide gap between the rich and the poor."

"Really?" She was like a fascinated child again. "I cannot imagine such a situation. Have you been there yourself?"

"Often. I used to love it, but I don't feel the same way any more." His words seemed to be slurring again.

"Why?"

"It's hard to explain." He tried to concentrate on the images in his mind. "There used to be such optimism—such confidence! You could live out all your fantasies there, no matter how childish or immature they were. With a few dollars in your pocket and a heart filled with ambition, you owned the place." She looked puzzled, but he continued, carried away with a false sense of articulateness. "If a young man saw himself driving down a sunny coast road in a big convertible with the top down and a pretty girl at his side," he gave her hand a reassuring squeeze, "he could do it, even if the car belonged to Hertz and had to go back in the morning! There were no restrictions to the possibilities, or so it seemed: jobs, money, friendship—sky's the limit! But that was before the crime and the recession and the paranoia set in, before the fear and the mistrust and the need for self-preservation, before the realization that politicians—all of them—were just seedy, dishonest little men, serving themselves. God, you should have seen what it was like when Kennedy was around! He gave one a sense of change and hope and optimism." He knew that he was rambling senselessly, enjoying the words for their own sake, and that she could not understand him, but the vodka persuaded him that his speech was stirring. It was like being in a play. "People were so charmingly naïve. They had such faith in the rightness of what they were doing, even when they were wrong. It was

51

such an . . . innocent time. Perhaps not. Maybe I'm just talking about my own naïveté, my own innocence." He gestured with his free hand, knocking the tumbler over.

"I don't understand what you're saying."

For a moment, Mark focused his thoughts, aware that he was drunk. "I'm sorry. I'm just sounding off stupidly. Please forgive me. I'm making a fool of myself."

Irina looked concerned. "Shall I make you some coffee?"

"I think you had better, before I pass out on you!" He shook his head, but it did not help. Then he smiled at her. "You know, you're very beautiful. I watched you all evening, during the ballet."

"Thank you." Her voice was soft. "I will make the coffee."

"And I apologize again." He leaned forward and kissed her on the mouth. Her lips felt cool, but she did not move away from him. It might have been his imagination, but he thought her hand held his more tightly for a moment.

Irina stood, leaving her hand in his. "Coffee!"

"Yes. Have I offended you?"

"Because you kissed me? No. I accept it as a very nice compliment. Thank you." Like a solemn child. "But I think you should drink some coffee before you feel worse."

"You're very thoughtful."

She busied herself, pouring water into a kettle. "You forget that I am a dancer. We learn to live with our emotions on display. Perhaps that makes us different from other people." Turning towards Mark, her face was serious. "I suppose I was curious to see how you would behave. I have never met an Englishman before. I had always been told that they were very cold and formal."

"The Englishman with his usual bloody cold?"

"What do you mean?"

"It's an old joke, translating from the French; something to do with *sang-froid habituel.*" He shook his head, hoping to clear it. "It's not important. Anyway, I'm probably not typical, although everyone says that."

"In that case, I am glad. I think maybe you are a nice man." Mark tried to stand, but she placed a hand on his shoulder to restrain him. "I do not think you are accustomed to our vodka. Stay where you are until the coffee is ready."

"I leave again tomorrow. I'm sorry about that. I would like to see you again."

She shrugged, watching the kettle. "Perhaps you will come back to Moscow."

"I might. Will you go with Viktor to Bergen?"

She hesitated fractionally. "No, I have to work. We will be preparing for the tour."

"Maybe I can find you somewhere along the way." The idea was appealing. "I could show you round whichever city you were visiting, if you would let me."

She smiled. "That would be wonderful. I would enjoy it very much, but you must remember that I will be working. Ballet dancers have a very strict routine."

"But you would find time for me?"

The kettle began to boil. "There is always time if we need it. Your coffee will be ready in a moment."

Viktor drove him back to the hotel late in the night. The streets were white and empty. Coffee had helped to sober him, leaving behind the throbbing sensation of a sick headache and an overwhelming tiredness. At the door of the apartment, Irina had first shaken his hand formally, then quickly leaned forward to brush her cheek against his, murmuring, "I hope you will keep your promise. It will be good to meet again."

"I'll check the itinerary of your tour when I get back." He wondered whether Moscow had shops that delivered flowers. It would be an appropriate gesture. "I look forward to next time." Viktor said nothing.

The hotel was deserted. A solitary uniformed guard stood by the door, to check the credentials of visitors. Even the old woman with brooms had deserted the lobby for the night.

Viktor shook his hand. "Thank you again, Mark. I cannot tell you how much I appreciate your help."

"I'll call Konstantin tomorrow or the next day, depending when I get in."

"And I will see you again in Bergen?"

"I hope so."

He walked slowly along the shabby circular corridor with its strong aroma of scented polish and disinfectant. Wallpaper had been torn off the cement and plaster surrounding the door to his room, making it easy to identify from a distance. He wondered who had done it: the York-shireman, venting his frustration with bureaucracy, or Russian revellers capping their celebration of a night on the town? In the morning, he would call Cunningham and cry off the lunch invitation. It would be easier to sleep late and travel directly to the airport. Besides, he was not sure that the attaché would approve of his evening out. It had hardly been in the best tradition of British diplomacy. Oh well, the hell with that!

Bergen

4

"He is a very talented young man." Konstantin Steigel sank into an armchair in his dressing-room, letting his long, spare body relax. "But I cannot think why he had to involve himself in all those ridiculous news-paper statements. A musician should dedicate himself to his music and leave the sordid business of politics to politicians."

"To do him justice, I don't think he set out to make headlines. He offered the statement as a gesture of international goodwill at a Moscow reception, and the man from the *New York Times* picked it up. The wire services got hold of it, and before anyone knew, it was all over the press."

Steigel grunted. "If he wants to make important statements, he should do so with his piano. Heidi, where's my shirt?"

"Here, Tino. I'm just bringing it."

The conductor slumped deeper in his chair, frowning abstractedly. He was wearing his old black roll-neck rehearsal shirt, now discoloured and damp, with a towel wrapped round his shoulders. As ever, his glasses were perched on the end of his bulbous nose, and he removed them carefully before drying his face. He tired easily these days, Mark thought, and the energetic morning rehearsal seemed to have left him exhausted and irritable. In a corner of the room, his wife, Heidi, almost the same age but indefatigably active, produced a dry shirt from a battered leather hold-all. Scarcely a line furrowed her red, apple-cheeked face, which seemed youthfully incongruous against her pure white hair. She had been his companion, supporter, assistant, protector, and handmaiden for nearly fifty years and usually managed to anticipate his commands before he barked them. Mark wondered what the old conductor would do if anything ever happened to her.

"Anyway, I'm glad you like Kaverin, maestro. I was very impressed by his recital in Moscow."

"*Ja*, there are not so many talented pianists coming out of Russia these days. It is a matter of teaching, I think. There is nobody to hand down the great traditions." He dropped the towel on the floor, and Heidi collected it. "On the other hand, there are not so many talented pianists coming out of anywhere. They all play like well-programmed machines, producing a kind of synthesis of all the correct interpretative attitudes—a little bit of Schnabel here, a spot of Rubinstein there, but nothing of themselves. This one has originality." Sunlight was streaming through the window of the Grieghalle, its brightness amplified by reflection off the snow outside. The narrow tonsure of silver hair remaining on the conductor's head sparkled in its rays. Steigel closed his eyes against the glare. "Heidi, there is too much light."

"Yes, Tino, I will look after it." She moved to the window. "Don't sit around in that wet shirt. You know what it does to you."

With a long-suffering sigh, the conductor struggled to his full height and made his way to an inner room, supervised by Heidi, emerging a few minutes later in a checked woollen shirt. There was a large plate of open Norwegian sandwiches—rare roast beef and king-sized prawns—thoughtfully left by the management, and he paused to help himself to one, signalling to Mark to do the same, before settling again in his chair. Heidi poured black coffee from a vacuum flask she had remembered to fill before leaving the hotel.

"How do you find the orchestra?"

"Not bad—better than I had expected. I had feared that a constant diet of Grieg would make them unbearable." He chuckled. "Imagine a country with only one national composer, and even he was Scottish a couple of generations earlier. Did you know the family name was really Greig? No, on the whole, they play quite well."

"I think their repertoire is more varied than that. It's supposed to be the oldest orchestra in Europe. The hall sounds beautiful. It was designed by acousticians."

"Then I am amazed you can hear anything at all." Steigel seemed to be recovering his strength, if not his normal good humour. He was a mild, scholarly man by nature, and Mark had the feeling that he frequently contrived his histrionics in order to live up to his reputation as a conductor of the old school.

"Apparently, they designed the whole thing, long before the architects got hold of it. It's a very handsome building."

"I suppose so. All that glass and metal seems out of place against the fine old wooden buildings." Like most musicians of his generation, Steigel had a heartfelt mistrust of modern buildings or acoustical expertise. Most of the world's great concert halls had been designed and built long before the science of sound had been a consideration.

Heidi seated herself on a hard-backed chair by the window. "You have to forgive his ill humour, my dear. He's still grizzling over a telex this morning from that dreadful man in New York."

"Which one?"

"Laufer." Greg Laufer, vice-president of artists and repertoire, was the senior executive of Magnum Records.

"What does he want? I told him you'd asked me to look after all requests."

Steigel held up the palms of his hands in a gesture of frustration. "My dear Mark, it's no use telling an American executive—especially a dangerously ambitious one like that—anything at all. In the first place, he was probably not listening, being too busy composing polysyllabic words for his next pronouncement. Why do they always speak in a kind of convoluted civil service vernacular? I suppose it's because they think long words make them sound more important. And in the second place, I am sure his arrogance and sense of self-importance would never allow him to discuss anything with a mere messenger, if you will forgive me. I expect he has a useful handbook on how to be a success, which advises him always to go to the top."

"You're probably right. What was the telex about?"

"Repertoire. He regretted to tell me that my proposal to record the

Brahms symphonies was unacceptable. It appears that Brahms is not "moving" the way Mr. Laufer would prefer. He therefore counterproposed something of equal importance: the *1812 Overture* and *Wellington's Victory.*" Steigel shook his head in mock despair.

"Oh Lord!"

The conductor finished his sandwich and sat with his fingertips touching. He looked like an ageing schoolmaster. "I wrote him a short letter before leaving the hotel—I saw no point in wasting money on telexes—in which I said I was prepared to consider the overture, which is not such a bad piece, even if it has been done to death, but *Wellington's Victory* is out of the question." His smile was sad. "Even a genius like Beethoven had an occasional off-day. Anyway, I am not a young man, Mark, and without doubt the time will shortly come when I will, if I'm lucky, come face to face with my Maker."

Heidi said, "Tino, you shouldn't talk like that!" but he ignored her.

"When I do, I hope I can look Him in the face and tell Him that I have served music with honesty, probity, and taste. I realize these are qualities with which Mr. Laufer is unfamiliar, but my day of reckoning is unfortunately a good deal closer than his."

Mark smiled. "Did you write that?"

"No. What's the point of discussing taste with a man who has none? I simply suggested that we add the usual Tchaikovsky lollipops to the overture, preferably the Serenade for Strings. Since that uses a reduced orchestra and saves him money, I hope he will agree. It is hardly a substitute for Brahms, but it will have to do." He sighed. "I do wish you could find me another record company, Mark. It is so difficult to communicate with people who do not speak the same language."

"I'll see what I can do. Their distribution is very good."

"That is not enough of a recommendation. I hate to descend to the level of such people. There is much to be said for snobbery."

"Really?"

"I don't mean social snobbery, the sort of head-waiter philosophy that sums up each person, deciding whether to patronize or grovel. That's appalling! Do you know, I once met an American on an aeroplane who confided to me that whenever he enters a person's house, he makes a mental estimate of the total cash value of the owner's furniture and decorations. *Gott,* what a mentality!" He rose from his chair, striding across the room and gazing at the snow-clad street outside. "No, my dear, I mean intellectual snobbery, which discriminates between the excellent and the shoddy, and which is not influenced simply by commercial success. Otherwise, we have no way of distinguishing between music and the popsy-wopsy canned trash that the radio plays all day, and we would have to assume that great literature now consists of those dreadful sagas of sex and success that fashionably liberated ladies with typewriters exalt in. I hope that I will always remain an intellectual snob."

From her corner, Heidi said, "Sit down, Tino; you have had a busy morning." She looked at Mark. "We should go back to the hotel for a rest."

Mark rose. "Yes, of course."

Steigel waved a hand, brushing her comment aside. "In a while. I'm not a child! I want to stop at the museum by the park on the way to the hotel. They have the finest collection of Edvard Munch in the world."

"I know, Tino," her voice was placid, "but I thought we could go there tomorrow morning. Our plane does not leave until four."

"Oh, very well." He looked depressed. "I thought we might stay an extra day or two. Bergen is charming, and the people are very hospitable. The manager of the hall offered to take us out to Troldhaugen, to see Grieg's house. I understand it is very beautiful. Besides, I would prefer to go to Kaverin's recital tomorrow night. I want to hear more of that young man."

Heidi looked slightly flustered. "Very well, Tino, I will arrange it, but you should have told me sooner. It means changing our reservations."

"So change them! We have nothing else to do this week."

"Why don't you let me look after that? I'll talk to the concierge at the Norge."

Heidi looked grateful. "Would you, Mark? That would be very helpful."

"No trouble at all. They have an airline desk in the hotel. Let me know when you would like to leave, and I'll make the arrangements."

Konstantin was already at the door, struggling into a fur-lined overcoat. "We should leave now if I am to rest before the concert." He seemed in a better mood. "I must say, I find the people here very pleasant and most eager to please, but they look so young!"

Mark smiled. "Yes, when I was walking across the park to the hall, I passed what I thought was a young girl of about fourteen. Just as I went by, a five-year-old child ran over to her, calling her 'Mama'! I'm also amazed by their English. I asked the young manager how long he'd been living here, because I thought he was an Englishman, and it turned out he'd never been outside Norway."

Steigel nodded. "Presumably they have to learn other languages because nobody is going to learn theirs. It's like being Hungarian. Are you walking with us?"

"No, I said I'd pick up Kaverin from his dressing-room and take him on a little sightseeing tour. He's very impressed with everything. It's his first time outside Russia."

"Let's hope he doesn't make any more statements to the press about it. Please tell him how satisfied I am. I believe the Beethoven will be a fine performance tonight, especially if I can persuade the violins to play the opening quietly enough. We won't have dinner after the concert. It's too late for me, but perhaps he would like to take an early lunch tomorrow."

"I'll ask him."

"Good. Heidi!" He watched impatiently as she gathered her own coat and the leather hold-all.

"I'm coming, Tino."

Viktor was in his dressing-room with Schedrin. Both men were already wearing their overcoats.

"I hope I haven't kept you?"

"No." Viktor indicated an empty plate. "Yuri and I ate lunch while we were waiting. The manager and his staff are very generous, and the sandwiches were magnificent."

Schedrin nodded. "I am impressed with everything I see in Norway; and what a marvellous theatre! Did you know it has the biggest stage in Europe? The rear wall weighs twenty tonnes, but it slides back and forward with electric controls to give you enough space for anything from a solo recital to a basketball game. Fantastic! What does the maestro say?"

Mark smiled. "I think Konstantin's basketball days are over, but he asked me to tell you that he was delighted with the rehearsal. He's decided to stay on in Bergen an extra day so that he can hear your recital, and he wondered whether you'll have lunch with him tomorrow. I think you'll find he'll be too tired to eat after the concert tonight."

Kaverin and Schedrin exchanged glances, and the Gosconcert man opened his arms wide. "You see, Mark? I told you Viktor is special. Now, perhaps you will consider representing him for us."

"I'll see what I can do. I would certainly like to, but I need a little time to think about it. As a matter of fact, I have one proposal to pass on to you. There is a series of Sunday afternoon recitals at the Salle Paderewski in Lausanne. They called me just before I left Geneva yesterday to say they have had a cancellation, and they asked me to recommend a substitute."

"When is the concert?"

Mark looked in his diary. "March 23."

"And you will represent Viktor?"

"No. I don't think the recital would pay enough, but I could pass them straight to you, which would leave you free to negotiate directly."

Schedrin looked at the pianist. "This would fit your plans very well, Viktor. This first year will be experimental most of the time, and you will not use up your quota." Turning to Mark, he explained, "Our artists are not normally permitted to spend more than a hundred and twenty days a year outside the Soviet Union, but it is doubtful whether Viktor will even spend half that time—unless you can develop something very special for him!"

"I wish I could. Shall I ask them to contact you?" He handed Schedrin a business card from the Swiss entrepreneur.

"Thank you. I will telephone them straight away."

They stepped out of the hall into brilliant sunlight and clear blue skies. It reminded Mark of winter in New York. The heat of the sun was beginning to melt some of the snow, and sparkling drops of water fell from the overhanging façades of the older houses. Kaverin put on a pair of outsize sunglasses, and Schedrin said something to him in Russian which made the young man laugh.

"Yuri says this is my first trip outside Russia, and I am already trying to look like an American film star!" He surveyed the ornamental park through which they were walking. "This town is so beautiful! Everything is warm and soft and friendly—and luxurious! It is like a fairy tale."

Mark nodded. "It's very attractive. The houses and streets are so neatly planned and carefully tended that the whole place reminds me of a model train layout. I keep expecting a giant hand to come out of the sky to lift one of the buildings and set it down in a different place!"

Schedrin laughed. "You are almost as much of a dreamer as Viktor, but you're right. There is a simple charm that is most appealing."

"Are you going back to the hotel to rest?"

Viktor shook his head. "No, I am much too . . ."—he searched for a word—". . . animated to relax. Maybe, when we have walked for a while, I will lie down. I did not run this morning."

For a moment, Mark thought Schedrin looked flustered. "I did not think it was a good idea for Victor, as a stranger in a new country." He laughed. "I was certainly not prepared to accompany him on such a vigorous enterprise!"

"I spent a few minutes before breakfast walking near the hotel. Who is this Ole Bull I see everywhere?" He pronounced the name as though it was a contraction of "old."

"I think he's called Ole." Mark made it sound like "early." "He was one of Bergen's most distinguished international musicians: a self-taught violinist who was said to have been inspired by hearing Paganini play. He travelled all over the world, especially in America, mostly playing his own pieces, but he never bothered to write them down." He smiled. "I think he and Grieg represent about ninety per cent of Norway's musical history!"

Schedrin smiled. "That's wonderful!" At a corner of the park, he shook hands. "I will leave you here. There is a shop I want to visit on Sverres Gate, but first I have work to do. I will also try to call Switzerland. Thank you again, Mark. You know, whether you want to or not, you are becoming Viktor's sponsor."

"I'm pleased to help. I should explain that it's not a very important recital series—"

"It doesn't matter." The Gosconcert agent put a hand on Mark's shoulder. "It is important that Viktor should be heard as much as possible. The word will soon spread."

"I'll make sure the manager of the Lausanne Chamber Orchestra comes to the recital. He's an old friend. We might also invite a few people from La Suisse Romande in Geneva. They're less than an hour away."

"Wonderful!"

"I'll see what I can do."

"Then we will see each other again tonight at the concert. If the maestro will not join us for dinner, I will book a table for three at the Villa Armorini restaurant. I am told it is good, and it is just across the street from the hall. Everyone goes there." For a moment, it seemed to Mark that Schedrin became serious. "I will leave Viktor in your care while I am gone." He was about to reply that Viktor was old enough to look after himself, but the Russian had already departed, walking swiftly in the direction of the Norge Hotel on Ole Bulls Plass.

Mark strolled with Viktor along the broad main shopping street, heading towards the harbour. The pianist scarcely spoke as they walked, pausing frequently to stare at windows filled with attractive ceramics, food shops with a wide array of goods, men's clothing stores.

After a while, he looked up. "You must excuse me if I seemed distracted, but I am converting the prices into rubles. Everything is so expensive! How can the people afford to buy?"

"They earn good salaries. Norway has a very high standard of living."

He shook his head in wonder. "There is so much and such plenty. I could not imagine luxuries like these before I saw them for myself." Viktor lowered his voice slightly. "To be honest, Mark, I thought some of it was just Western propaganda."

"It's real enough, but Bergen is a very small town. I suppose that's what makes it so pleasant. You have a shock coming when you see Paris or London."

"It's unbelievable, like waking up in the middle of a beautiful dream to find it has all come true!"

"How is Irina, by the way?"

Viktor was looking in the window of a patisserie, piled high with assorted biscuits and *petits fours*. "She is very well and asked to be remembered to you. They are working very hard at the moment, preparing for their tour."

"Yes, I know. I looked up their itinerary in Switzerland." He wondered whether he should keep his promise. The thought of seeing her again appealed to him.

"They will dance in London next month, at the time I will play in Lausanne—if Schedrin allows me to."

"I'm sure he will."

"I hope so." For a moment, Viktor's face clouded. "I am not permitted to make such decisions for myself. It is sometimes a little frustrating."

"Well, at the beginning of a career, it's always like that."

"Perhaps." His face was blank.

"As your audience develops, you'll find yourself going wherever you choose."

"No."

"Why do you say that?"

For a moment, Viktor paused to face him. "Mark, I think perhaps you are being a little too discreet. I am a Soviet artist. I am only allowed to go where the authorities permit. I cannot travel at will."

"I realize that, but Schedrin told me the agency has very high hopes for you. From what he said, I have the impression that Gosconcert plan to put everything they have behind you. Besides, once Russian artists are successful, it seems to me they travel as freely as anyone else. Look at Richter."

Viktor shrugged. "He's Richter."

"They give me the impression that you may prove to be his successor," Mark smiled. "As a matter of fact, I think they're right."

"That's very kind." Viktor walked on a few paces, then paused to look at antique Persian carpets in the next window. "Unfortunately, the authorities are not very pleased with me at the moment. I made a foolish statement which created too much publicity."

"About playing for the President?" The pianist nodded sombrely. "I would have thought that was regarded as an international gesture of goodwill."

"It was meant to be, but when it received so much publicity I was officially reprimanded." He sounded bitter. "It was not considered appropriate for a musician of my age and experience to make political statements, especially as I had not told anybody I was going to say something like that. I was warned that my travel permit could be withdrawn without notice and threatened that it would be if I made any similar comments in the future."

"I see."

Kaverin relaxed slightly. "This trip is to be a sort of test. That is why I am so happy that I will make my début with Konstantin Steigel. He is a great conductor! My only fear is that they may still withdraw permission in the future."

"But why?"

He shrugged. "As a punishment, to teach me a lesson. I spoke too soon, and said too much."

"I think you're exaggerating. Schedrin sounded eager enough to accept the Lausanne recital. He just went to telephone them."

Kaverin laughed. "No, Mark, I think he went to telephone Moscow first, to ask their permission. After that, according to what they say, he will call Lausanne. Yuri is only an errand-boy!"

"And if the answer is yes?"

"Then I will have passed the test—this time." Mark detected a familiar Slavic gloom in his voice.

"I'm sure you won't have anything further to worry about."

"For the moment." Viktor looked uncertain. "Please, will you help me to avoid any interviews? There have been some phone calls already, but I have refused them. I think it would be better if I did not speak to the press while I am here."

"If you wish. I suspect they'll want to ask you again about that recital. It was reported world-wide."

"I know. That is why I must not speak to them. In this way, I can make sure I cannot be criticized."

"That's very sensible."

Viktor stared at Mark for a moment. "It should not be necessary, should it? I should not have to behave like a guilty man because I said what was in my heart."

Mark spoke softly. "They misinterpreted you, Viktor. I'm sure they'll understand."

The pianist took in the street with his gaze. He seemed close to tears. "Everything is just beginning for me. They should not have such rules!"

They continued in silence across the town to the old Fish Market, and Mark paused to admire the row of ancient wooden houses on the Strandkaien, their timber fronts freshly painted in browns, ochres, and dark greens. The windows of a dairy displayed an enormous selection of local cheeses, most of which were unfamiliar. The quays were deserted for the afternoon. They continued to the far side of the natural harbour created by the narrow spit of land on which most of Bergen stood, resting between two rocky promontories of the mainland. The mountains rose steeply around them.

Viktor pointed. "What's that?"

"A funicular railway up the mountainside. It takes you into a national park at the top. Bergen is built on seven hills, like Rome, but these ones are more spectacular."

"Can we ride in it?"

"If you like. I was going to walk you as far as the Rosenkrantz Tower on the far side of the harbour, but the trip up the mountain is just as good. There's a restaurant at the top, where we can have a cup of coffee. The view is beautiful, especially on a clear day like this. Are you sure you don't want to go back to the hotel?"

"Certain. I can rest later." He quickened his pace up the slope towards the terminus at the base of the mountain. "I would like to be out in the open countryside, where the air does not smell of towns—even a beautiful town like this!"

Mark bought two tickets which welcomed them bilingually to the Fløibanen funicular and wished them a pleasant journey. The reverse side of each ticket was decorated with charming folk art depicting the ascent of the little train. The Norwegians, it seemed, had a sense of design and colour even when it came to public transport.

Three children, aged somewhere between eleven and thirteen, were waiting for the train. Dressed in ski suits, with red woollen caps that emphasized their blond hair and fair skin, they looked as though they had just stepped out of a winter sports brochure. Viktor caught the eye of one little girl and winked. She giggled and whispered to her nearest companion.

The wedge-shaped carriage hugged the hillside, climbing steeply and disappearing occasionally into tunnels or passing through deep glades of fir trees. They could feel the temperature falling as it made the steady ascent a thousand feet above the town. Kaverin stood, both hands grasping the rear rail, and watched the roofs recede below them. His face was expressionless, so that Mark could not read his thoughts.

At the summit, the gate clanged open, and the children bustled forward, carrying their skis. Mark and Viktor followed them up a path leading to thickly wooded hillsides. The trail cut narrowly between tall trees. They stood in silence, watching as the children fitted their skis. Moments later, the three small figures tipped over the edge of the nearest slope and almost noiselessly sped away towards the pine woods. Despite their age, they skied like professionals.

Mark led the way back towards the restaurant, wondering whether it would be open at this time of the year. Below them, Bergen sparkled in the afternoon sunlight, surrounded by the dark blue of the sea and the varying shades of white, green, and brown of the mountains.

Viktor said nothing, staring into space and breathing deeply. The sunlight outlined his handsome features, and a light wind pulled at a loose lock of hair on his forehead.

"You're very thoughtful."

The pianist stared at the glowing panorama as though disturbed from a reverie. "I was thinking that it would be good to be like those children —to ski down the hillside, free and unhindered, and disappear for ever." He smiled to himself, but his voice was sad. "I think I would like that."

Lausanne

5

Sitting with Schedrin in the quiet but solid luxury of the Palace Hotel, Mark wondered how such grand old establishments managed to stay in business. The hotel seemed, as always, to be empty, which was hardly surprising at those prices, but this apparently had no influence on the staff or the standards. It was as though the place remained superbly aloof, unaware of changing times or fluctuations in the cost of living. It would remain, majestically comfortable and quietly efficient, until the last guest had departed. But how did they keep going? Perhaps they brought in clandestine coach parties of wealthy Germans and Americans late at night, making sure that they had departed again well before the morning traffic of isolated residents appeared for their breakfast. It was unthinkable to have braying Midwestern accents or bullying Frankfurters disturbing the subdued elegance of the foyer, with its heavy sofas and armchairs, while uniformed concierges and desk clerks whispered from behind their desks. Even the ebullient Gosconcert man reduced his voice to the sort of murmur one reserved for the smoking room of an English club. He was dressed in a smart Harris tweed jacket with tan slacks, which gave him a vaguely retired military look. It occurred to Mark that he had previously always seen the Russian in a business suit.

Schedrin placed a hand on his arm. "We are making progress, Mark, but it is proving more and more difficult. The British offer tiny fees and only ask for pot-boiling programmes, and the Germans hold out for big names to attract maximum audiences. As for the French . . ." He shrugged his shoulders in a fair imitation of Gallic indifference. "We have had a good response from Holland. I am flying to see the manager of the Concertgebouw this week."

"How about the Americans?"

Schedrin looked unhappy. "We have to wait. They have not yet lifted the ban on most Soviet artists. It is very difficult." He looked at his watch. "I don't know what has happened to Viktor. Perhaps I should call his room."

"We're still quite early, and the hall is just down the road. I told them Viktor would come in some time after ten to try out the piano and practise for a while." He smiled. "Even the industrious Swiss like to take things quietly on Sunday mornings! I have a small surprise for you, by the way. Agnes asked if she could come to the recital, so I drove her over from Geneva with me this morning."

The Russian's face lit up. "Miss Muret?"

Mark nodded. "She wanted to hear Viktor play. I think she has aspirations towards becoming a manager one of these days. As a matter of fact, I also have the suspicion she was looking forward to seeing you again too. You seem to have made something of a hit with her."

"I am delighted and very flattered. Where is she?"

"I dropped her off at the corner of the rue du Bourg. She wanted to find some flowers to welcome Viktor." He looked up. "Here she is now."

Agnes entered the foyer looking flustered. She was carrying a bunch of daffodils and narcissi. Mark watched, slightly amused, as the Gosconcert man rose and walked across the room to meet her. It had been a long time since he had played Cupid, especially for such an unlikely pair.

At that moment, Viktor arrived at the steps leading down from the hotel elevators. He waved a hand at Mark and greeted him with the traditional hug that musicians reserve for each other.

He spoke rapidly. "I am so pleased to see you again, Mark! For a long time, I did not know whether I would be coming to Switzerland or not. They only told me ten days ago. Irina sends you her greetings. The company will be in London all this week. She asks whether you might see her there. I have a telephone number if you would like to call her." He seemed unusually animated, and Mark had the feeling that he was very tense.

"I'll see what I can organize. I haven't been to London for several months, so she's giving me a good excuse for a visit. Let me introduce you to Agnes Muret from my office. She has come to Lausanne specially to hear you."

Viktor bowed gracefully, and Agnes—slightly self-conscious in front of Schedrin—presented her bouquet. He accepted it with a dazzling smile. "You must excuse me for being late, but my hotel room is so beautiful that I did not want to leave it. I could not imagine having enough clothes to fill all those huge cabinets . . . and the bathroom!" He rolled his eyes in mock astonishment. "I have never seen anything like it! There was even an electric hair drier attached to the wall. I have washed my hair twice—last night and again this morning!"

Yuri Schedrin laughed. "My God, Viktor! This is only your second trip, and you are already behaving like a capitalist!"

Viktor smiled, slightly embarrassed. "I am sorry. I must seem very childish to you."

"Not at all." Mark led the way to the front door. "It's nice to see the hotel's facilities are appreciated. I'm afraid you won't be so impressed tonight. After the concert, we'll drive back to Geneva, where I've chosen a small hotel close to the airport, to save you having to hurry in the morning."

"I am happy. I will still have time to wash my hair again before the concert. They even supply the shampoo!"

Standing in front of the hotel, Schedrin hesitated. "You know, I have never had the opportunity to visit Lausanne before. I understand it is a very fine old town, with a handsome cathedral and a château." He turned to Agnes. "I hoped I could persuade Miss Muret to show me round this morning while Viktor is at the hall." Agnes looked hopefully at Mark.

"That sounds like a good idea. I'll look after Viktor for you. There's not much point in our all going there."

Viktor nodded eagerly. "We can all meet again later. I do not expect to practise for very long." He laughed suddenly, and Mark was again conscious of his uneasiness. "It seems to me that I have done nothing but sit at my piano for weeks."

Schedrin tucked Agnes's hand in the crook of his arm. "That is settled, then. At what time shall we meet here?"

"Three o'clock." Viktor answered first and grinned. "I'm hoping Mark will show me some of the district in his car. I want to see as much of everywhere as I can."

"Very well."

As they walked down the hill towards the Salle Paderewski, sunlight filtered through a pale overhead haze, breaking up the morning mists. It felt pleasantly warm.

"I can understand why you chose to live in Switzerland. Everything is so calm and well ordered. Look how carefully they have clipped their trees for the winter!"

Mark smiled. "Yes, it's efficient and uneventful."

"You do not sound very convinced. It must be strange to be able to choose where you will live."

"It's not quite as easy as that. I received a certain amount of . . . help when I first came here." For a moment, Mark frowned, remembering the long hours of acrimonious negotiation with the Department for his freedom.

"Yes." Kaverin was thoughtful. "One always needs help."

At the piano, Viktor closed his eyes for a moment before playing. Mark noted again that he sat very straight-backed, his head erect, in a manner reminiscent of Artur Rubinstein. So many of the younger pianists slouched over their instruments, their noses almost touching the keyboard. Perhaps Viktor's teacher had been one of Steigel's approved older generation. He played restlessly, experimenting with the pedals and trying the action of the keyboard with rapid runs and trills. He began the Mozart F Major Sonata that was to open his recital, but broke off after a few bars, apparently unable to settle himself.

"How is the piano?"

"Very good. I like it." He seemed distracted. "This hall is good, but quite small. Is it the only one in Lausanne?"

"No, there's a bigger one—Beaulieu—but it's rather dry and not very flattering. Shall I leave you alone for a while?"

"No." He locked the fingers of his hands together, stretching his arms, then began again with the opening of Chopin's B-Flat Minor *Funeral March* Sonata, playing with savage passion. It was startling, almost brutal, and very different from the way he normally played. Despite an excellent technique, with great resources of strength, Kaverin was a sensitive, lyrical musician. He seemed now to be playing with controlled fury.

After a moment, he stopped again. "I would like to make this sonata my special work, one with which I will always be identified." He smiled, relaxing slightly. "I have the recording by Vladimir Horowitz; the one he made in the sixties. It was a great inspiration to me. Shall we go?"

"If you like. I thought you would want to practise for a while."

"No. I would rather get out of here. I need to talk to you about several important matters. Can we take a drive?"

Mark made his way through empty Sunday streets and, passing through the suburb of Pully, drove along the shore road to Vevey and Montreux. Morning mist still hung over Lake Leman, but the sun was beginning to burn it away. The road hugged the sides of hills which began to rise steeply. Kaverin was silent and preoccupied, staring vacantly through the windscreen at the ribbon of tarmac.

"This is one of the chief wine-growing districts." Mark glanced up towards the carefully terraced hillside neatly lined with bare vines. "Some of the local brands are very good, but you don't hear much about them outside Switzerland. We can try a bottle of Saint Saphorin at lunchtime."

"Yes, that would be good." Kaverin glanced nervously through the rear window of the car almost as though he expected to be followed. "Where are we going?"

"I thought we could drive as far as Montreux."

"I have heard of it."

They approached a small village of houses clustered against the hillside. A narrow road, climbing steeply, provided parking space outside. "Would you like to stop and have a look? The village is very old and picturesque. It's home for many of the local growers. I seem to remember a shop with ancient wine presses and vintners' equipment on display."

"No, I would prefer to keep driving, if we may. I would like to find somewhere we can talk undisturbed."

"Why not here, in the car?"

Kaverin smiled briefly. "Perhaps, in a while. I am trying to assemble what I have to say."

They continued in silence, passing through a sleepy Vevey. It was too early in the year for tourists, and the residents were either in bed or in church. On the promenade by the lake, a few couples were enjoying the first rays of sunshine.

Viktor seemed to relax. "It is so peaceful here, like another world. Can we drive into the mountains? I like to be high up."

As they entered Montreux, Mark indicated a building perched on a mountaintop overlooking the town. "I'll head up to Caux. The view is beautiful, but it may still be very cloudy."

"I would like that." Viktor looked at a large mirrored glass-plated building with an imposing view across the lake. "Is that an expensive apartment building?"

Mark smiled. "No. Believe it or not, it's a chocolate factory!"

He turned left, steering the car through narrowing roads, which curved and twisted, slowly climbing into the hills. "There's another funicular here, but I doubt whether it's operating at this time of day." As the car ascended, they passed through misty glades of trees and patches of meadow still brown with winter. The temperature was dropping, and on several shadowed corners that the sun had not penetrated, there were still stretches of unfrozen snow. The road was slippery and Mark reduced speed, steering the car through a series of hairpin bends and steep slopes. Every now and then, they ran parallel with the track of mountain railway. Beads of water formed on the windscreen. "I don't know how much of a view we'll find at the top. We seem to be driving through low clouds."

At the summit of the hill, they broke through the mist into sudden, bright sunshine. Snow on the ground added to the brilliance of the light.

Viktor smiled. "This is perfect." He looked at the long, low wooden building that they had seen from below. "What is this place?"

"It belongs to the Moral Rearmament people. It's a sort of international centre for world peace. The Swiss are specialists at that sort of thing." Mark smiled. "But not on Sundays. It looks as though it's closed tight." He drove to the end of the deserted parking lot behind the building and stopped the car by the rim of the plateau. They walked to the edge of the mountain on which the building was perched. Below them, the valley was still shrouded in swirling fog, but they could see across it to the distant mountains and hills which rose around them. It was as though they were mysteriously cut off from the world below. A cool breeze counteracted the heat of the sun. Viktor was silent.

Mark watched him carefully. The muscles on his jaw were moving restlessly. "Is this a suitable place to talk?"

Viktor nodded. He spoke suddenly. "Mark, I need your help."

"I know, but I explained to Yuri—"

"No, you don't understand." He took a deep breath. "I want to leave Russia. I don't want to go back tomorrow. I cannot go back!"

"What's happened?"

Viktor hunched his shoulders angrily against the breeze. "There is nothing specific, but if I do not leave now, I may not have the opportunity again for a long time—perhaps never."

"I don't follow you."

"They have told me that this is to be my last concert outside Russia for the moment."

"Why?"

"I explained when we were in Bergen. My behaviour at the press reception in Moscow has been officially condemned." His voice was bitter. "Because I was outspoken, I am to be punished. I must return to playing concerts only within the Soviet Union."

"I see. Why did they allow you to come to Lausanne?"

"Because you proposed it. You do not understand the way my people think, Mark. When Yuri called Moscow to tell them that you had recommended this recital, they did not like to refuse because you could be a valuable friend in the future—if not to me, then to other Soviet artists. It is difficult for them to find partners in the West."

"That doesn't make sense. If they cancel your future trips, I'd hardly be eager to represent anyone else."

"That is not how they calculate. They will say I am not free, or Yuri will tell you that I do not want to travel. They can tell you anything they want!"

"But Yuri's supposed to be going to Amsterdam on your behalf. He told me about it earlier."

Viktor shook his head. "You are too innocent, Mark. Yuri will say that he had no success and that, for one reason or another, he has lost faith in me. You do not realize how these people twist the truth! He will bring you other musicians—maybe good ones—and tell you that I am no longer interested in travelling. He will say that I was disappointed with the lack of response to my concerts."

"I see." Mark was silent.

"That is why you must help. You are my friend, Mark—the only friend I can turn to. What do I have to do?"

Mark shook his head slowly. "I don't honestly know."

"If I give myself to the Swiss authorities, will they let me stay?"

"I doubt it. You're not exactly seeking political asylum, on the face of it. On the other hand, you're not well enough known as an artist to have any influence on their decision. Have you really thought this through?"

"Of course!" He was angry. "I know what is in store for me. I have thought about nothing else for weeks. I am not a fool!"

"But you're only assuming that they're not going to let you out again. In a few months, when things settle down, and if I can develop new engagements, they could just as easily relax the conditions and—"

"No! You do not understand how they think, Mark. Believe me, I know what I am telling you." He was close to tears. "Now that I have seen for myself, now that I realize what lies and propaganda they have fed me all my life, I cannot go back!" His hand gripped Mark's arm fiercely. "You must help us."

"Us? Are you including Irina?"

"Yes, of course. I wouldn't leave without her. It is the perfect opportunity, don't you see?"

"No."

Viktor made a conscious effort to calm himself. "It is unusual for two members of the same family to be allowed to travel outside the Soviet Union at the same time. Husbands and wives sometimes travel together, but only if the authorities are very sure of them. Under normal circumstances, they insist that one of them stays behind. Because you offered the recital at the last moment, they did not expect me to be absent from Moscow at the same time that Irina is dancing with the Bolshoi. Perhaps they thought it would be safe because she is in London and I am in

Lausanne. It is almost a miracle of coincidence! That is why we must take this opportunity."

"Have you discussed it with her?"

"Of course I have! We have talked about nothing else for days!"

"And she agrees?"

"Yes, yes!" He was becoming excited again. "From the day I returned to Moscow, I told her what I had seen. I told her it was all true—everything we had heard about and the things we had read in books and magazines. I was so angry! At first, she would not believe me, but we looked again in books and magazines, and I showed her the postcards that I had brought back with me. It is amazing how differently you can interpret even a picture when you know what you are looking at."

"What did she say?"

"At first, she was astonished and a little frightened, but the more I told her, the more angry she became too. Please, Mark, what must we do?"

Mark hesitated before replying. "Let me think about it for a moment." It seemed to him that the air was very cold, and he turned up the collar of his overcoat.

Viktor reached into his pocket. "I have money." He produced a wad of crumpled banknotes. "Here! I have more than two thousand dollars. Take them, please, if they will help."

"Where did you get them from?"

"My car. I sold it last week at the market. It was not very much, but it was all the man could give me. If I had asked for rubles, he would have paid me twice as much. Please take it." He held the money out.

In the distance, at the far end of the building, another car entered the parking space. It was too far away to see the occupants. Momentarily distracted, Mark returned to Viktor. "You'd better hang on to that money for the moment. Keep it well out of sight."

"I have." He smiled suddenly, looking very youthful. "I was terrified when I walked through the customs at Sheremetyevo. I do not think I would make a good smuggler!"

Mark stared across the valley. Despite the sunlight, the mist seemed to cling to the treetops, forming an opaque barrier.

"What can we do?" Viktor was breathing heavily, like a man who had been running.

"I'm not sure. I need to think."

74

"We have so little time. I am supposed to fly back to Moscow tomorrow morning. That is why I did not practise at the hall. Mark, you must help me. You cannot let me go back!"

"What about Irina?"

He spoke quickly. "We made a plan, before she left. I told her that I would call her from the hotel when I knew that you would help us."

"What sort of plan?"

"It is very vague, because we don't know what to do. When I call, she will ask the British authorities to let her stay while I ask the Swiss. Later, we will join each other. I hoped you would go and see her in London. When you were in Moscow, you promised that you would try to meet her during the tour, do you remember?" He watched Marks' face. "This will work?"

"No, I don't think it will."

"But why?"

"Because you can't just ask to stay, no matter where you're from. Nor can Irina. You have to prove that your life's in danger or that you're escaping for political reasons or that you can be of value to the country where you apply or God knows what else. You can't just tell them it's because you like it better than your own country!"

"But people—what is the word?—defect. Why can't we defect?"

Mark sighed. "It's not as simple as that. They usually ask for political asylum, or they offer to trade information that might be useful to the government. There has to be a reason, Viktor. I don't think it would be enough to tell them it's because you don't think you're going to be allowed to give concert tours in the West!"

"But I cannot go back. It is too late! Do you know anyone who can help us?"

"Not here, no. You forget that I'm only a resident alien myself. The Swiss won't want to know my problems."

"How about England? Is there anybody there? There must be someone who can help us!"

Mark was silent for a long time. From the corner of his eye, he noticed that two men had got out of the other parked car and were now walking slowly towards him. There was nothing particularly remarkable about them, except that they walked side by side, their faces in his direction, without talking.

"Please, Mark!" Viktor's voice was urgent.

He spoke slowly. "There is someone in London I could talk to." Viktor seemed to catch his breath. "I don't know whether he would help, but he might be able to tell us what to do."

"Can you call him?"

"I suppose so. We're not exactly the best of friends, but he might help, under the circumstances."

"I do not understand. If he is not your friend, why would he help you?"

Mark chose his words carefully. "He's a specialist in all sorts of . . . immigration problems. He was a sort of working colleague at one time, but we never liked each other very much. I suppose I could call him in his professional capacity."

"Yes!" Kaverin started towards the car. "We will call him from my hotel. Do you know where to reach him on a Sunday?"

"Yes." Mark's face was set. "I remember the number."

"Then we must hurry. There is so little time!" Viktor started to walk toward the car, when he noticed the two men. They were still fifty yards away. The pianist halted, becoming motionless.

Mark joined him. "What's the matter?"

Viktor had not moved. "The men walking towards us. Do you recognize them?"

"No, I don't think so. Do you?"

Viktor's voice was tense. "I am not sure. I think perhaps I have seen them before." He was trembling slightly.

"Where?"

"In Bergen." He hesitated. "And in the Geneva airport when we arrived yesterday."

"Are you sure?"

"No, but I think it is the same two men." He moved forward again, walking casually to Mark's car. "If we leave now, they will be a long way from their car, won't they?"

"Yes."

"Then we should go quickly."

Mark unlocked the door of his car. "Who are they?"

"I don't know. They are probably assigned to watch me."

Mark backed slowly out of the parking lines and drove steadily towards the men, who had now stopped, watching uncertainly. The taller of the two said something to his companion, but they did not move. A moment later, as they drew level, Mark accelerated suddenly and his car leapt forward, racing towards the main road. Glancing in his rear-view mirror, he saw that the two men were now running towards their car, fifty yards away.

He entered the first curve too fast, braking at the last possible moment. "I don't know about you, but I don't like being spied on."

"It is a way of life in my country. That is why I must leave. What will you do?"

Mark smiled, skidding the car through the next bend. It slid dangerously towards the steep bank of the hillside, but he adjusted it with a quick spin of the steering wheel. "We'll give them something to worry about, if only to put them in their place. Hang on."

He continued downhill with a burst of speed as the car entered a straight section that passed through a meadow. Looking up, high above him at the top of the hill, he had a momentary glimpse of the other car as it entered the first bend; then he locked the wheel to skid through a ninety-degree turn that took the vehicle into a wooded tunnel of trees. They were travelling along a narrow path cut into the forest, and two turns later, he found a small dirt track leading deeper into the trees. He coasted to a stop, turning off the engine and parking the car amid a shady clump of pines. Between the trunks, he could see the road winding farther down the hill.

"Why have you stopped?"

As though in reply, the other car roared past them down the hill, its tyres screaming on the tarred surface. They watched in silence as it skidded and swerved down the road. Within moments, it had disappeared.

Mark turned to Viktor with a smile. "That should keep them occupied for a while. If they want to see you again, they know where to find you. Let's hope it gives them a few anxious moments at the Salle Paderewski, waiting to see whether you'll show up!"

Kaverin nodded thoughtfully. "Do you think your friend in London will help?"

"I don't know. He was never much of a friend, but he might pass us on to somebody who will."

"There's so little time!"

"There's enough, if he'll help. Is Yuri travelling back with you tomorrow?"

"No. He is staying on. He is staying on. He is going to Brussels and Amsterdam."

"Good."

"Why do you say that?"

"I have an idea. I wonder where our companions have got themselves to."

As they re-entered Montreux, Mark searched the streets for the other car, but it was not visible. The town was coming to life, and sunlight was glittering on the still waters of the lake.

In the hotel room, Mark asked, "Won't Schedrin question your phone calls?"

"No. He knows that I have been speaking to Irina. Yuri is a civil servant at heart. It's not his money."

Mark dialled London. It was a number he was unlikely to forget. He was conscious of Viktor's steady gaze. After a brief pause, a voice answered. "May I speak to Quentin Sharpe, please?" He wondered whether his own voice betrayed his emotions.

The voice was impersonal. "He's not in today. Who is calling?"

"Mark Holland. I'm sure he'll remember me."

"Is it urgent?"

"Yes."

"I'll see if he can be reached. Please hold."

There was a long silence, broken only by the occasional crackle of static. Viktor paced nervously and was about to speak, but Mark motioned him to silence. At length, there was a distant click. Mark recognized Sharpe immediately.

"I'm surprised. I hadn't really expected to hear from you again." He sounded vaguely amused.

"I hadn't expected to call."

Quentin's voice lowered slightly. "It's rather difficult for me to talk at the moment. Do you have a problem?"

"Not personal. I'm calling on behalf of a friend." Mark glanced at Viktor. "He's the Russian pianist Viktor Kaverin. Have you heard of him?"

"I don't think so."

"I met him a few months ago when I was in Moscow."

"Ah yes, I heard you'd been there on a visit. Rather an unusual choice, under the circumstances. I hope the trip was enlightening." His tone was bantering again, and Mark could feel his temper rising.

"It was very interesting, thank you, but not quite as I had expected. Perhaps I had been given a rather distorted view of it." Quentin was silent, offering no comment. "I thought you might remember Viktor's name. There was a certain amount of publicity surrounding a speech he made at a press reception. He said he'd like to play a recital for the President of the United States."

"Oh, that one. I thought the name sounded familiar." Mark wondered whether Quentin had recognized the name immediately. It would be typical of him to play a cat-and-mouse game. "What about him?"

"We're together in Switzerland at the moment. He's giving a recital in Lausanne this afternoon."

"That's nice."

Mark paused for a moment. "We've been talking about future plans. Viktor would like to change his base of operations."

There was a very slight hesitation before Sharpe replied. "Permanently?"

"Yes. He was hoping you might be able to offer some suggestions."

"I see." He spoke slowly. "No, I don't think I can offer anything. He's a pianist, you say?"

"Yes."

"Well, he could always come in for a chat the next time he plays in London."

"It's not as simple as that. In fact, it's unlikely that he'll be coming to London. He's supposed to return to Moscow tomorrow, after which his plans are very vague."

"Does he have any interests outside music?"

"None that I know of. His sister's in London at the moment. She's a dancer in the Bolshoi Ballet, and they're appearing at Covent Garden all week."

"Ah. He had some sort of a package trip in mind."

"Something like that."

"Sorry. I can't help."

"Look, he's pretty desperate at this point."

"Oh, quite." Quentin raised his voice slightly. "You must forgive me if I have to run. I don't like to impose any further on my host. I will be home in a couple of hours, if you'd like to call back."

Mark looked up, to see Viktor standing over him. Perhaps his expression had conveyed the message to the pianist, whose hands were trembling. "Can't you suggest anything at all?"

There was a long pause. "Well, you might talk to old Uncle Samuel about it. He's always eager to help worthy causes. I would have thought he might find the idea intriguing, in view of the young man's concert ambitions."

"Yes, that already occurred to me, but I don't know how to reach Samuel these days. It's been a very long time." Mark watched Kaverin, who looked puzzled.

There was another silence. When his voice returned, Sharpe sounded cheerful. "I seem to think I have his number somewhere in my address book. Did you want me to give him a call for you?"

"Yes." As an afterthought, Mark added, "Please. It would be greatly appreciated."

"Why should I?" Sharpe's voice had suddenly hardened.

"For old time's sake. I think you owe me a favour."

"Perhaps." He sighed audibly. "We're never that keen to involve Samuel in family business, but I suppose that doesn't apply in this particular instance. Come to think of it, he might enjoy the idea. What's your number?" Mark read it off the dial. "I'll see if I can find him, and let you know. Will you be there for a while?"

"Until we hear from you. When you call, ask for Viktor Kaverin. It's his room."

"Very well." He chuckled softly. "You should be careful, Mark. You could end up owing me a favour instead."

"No, I think this one wipes the slate clean."

"Perhaps. Now, you'll have to forgive me. My friend is getting quite impatient."

"Yes. Thank you again, Quentin. Please apologize to your friend for me. Tell her I'm sorry to interrupt."

Quentin chuckled again. "Her?" Before Mark could reply, he hung up.

Viktor stood very close. There was a thin film of sweat on his face. "What did he say?"

"He can't help. I'm afraid he's not interested."

"Oh God!" The young man sat on the edge of the bed.

"He's going to talk to some American friends. They're very influential."

Kaverin turned pale. "Americans? I'm not sure that—"

"They might help you, Viktor. They're more liberal than the English, and they're more interested in the publicity. Perhaps your press statement in Moscow will prove to be useful after all."

Kaverin was silent.

Quentin Sharpe called back an hour later. "This must be your young man's lucky day, Mark. Our American colleagues were very pleased to hear from me. They always like to think we're in this together."

"Are you alone?"

"Yes. Your call rather spoiled the mood of my lunch. Anyway, Uncle Sam would like to hear the young man play the piano. He'll want to talk first."

"And his sister?"

"She can keep him company. They like gestures of this sort. He used some sort of odious expression like 'bring her along for the ride'! Have you any ideas about how we arrange a meeting?"

"Yes. Can I call you back later tonight? I want to check a couple of flights first."

"I'll be here."

"It may be quite late."

"I'm a light sleeper. Tell me, what's your interest in all this?"

"I want to help. I'm a sort of unofficial sponsor, and as a matter of fact, I'm considering managing his career."

"I thought it might be something of the sort. Anything else would be rather out of character for you, wouldn't it?"

Mark's voice was heavy. "I hope so."

"And the young man does have a flair for publicity, doesn't he?"

"He's a very talented musician."

"That's reassuring." Quentin's voice was soft. "I'd say he was a rather fortunate young man. With someone like you to vouch for him, he's well spoken for."

"I'll call you from Geneva, when I'm home." Mark hesitated. "And thank you again."

"No trouble, really. My Yankee colleagues feel they owe me a favour now, so everyone's happy. No guarantees, though."

Mark hung up, turning to Viktor. "I think you're going to be all right."

"You mean it?"

He nodded. "Some American friends in London want to meet you. Provided they are satisfied, they'll arrange for both you and Irina to stay."

"But how?"

"They have the authority to help. I told you my friend was influential."

Viktor shook his head slowly. "I can't believe it! Mark, you don't know what you are telling me. But how will I go to London? My ticket is for Moscow."

"Leave that to me. Flights can be rearranged. Can you call Irina later?"

"Yes. What shall I tell her?"

Mark smiled. "I think you'd better start by telling her not to worry. She's probably going out of her mind! I want to speak to her myself, if you'll tell me a good time to call."

"I still don't understand how you are going to do all this. We cannot just—"

"Don't worry about anything." Mark looked at his watch. "I suggest you try and rest for a while."

"I don't think I can."

"You should at least try. See if you can reach Irina, and tell her I'd like to call her very early tomorrow morning."

"Yes. There is a telephone in her bedroom. She will not mind if you wake her." Kaverin was silent. When he spoke again, his voice was halting. "Mark, I do not know what to say to you. For a while, up there on the mountain, it was as though we were in another world, cut off from reality, talking about a dream, but not believing that it could come true. Now, it seems that the dream is reality, and I am frightened."

"Are you having second thoughts?"

He shook his head slowly. "No. It is what I want, what we both want."

"Then I suggest you rest and prepare yourself for the concert. It's very important that you don't make Yuri suspicious. Presumably, he's in touch with our watchful friends this morning. If they suspect anything, they could move in closer."

"Yes. I will try to rest for a while." He laughed suddenly, like a small boy. "I will give a performance of the Chopin sonata that will surprise everyone!"

"I don't doubt it."

Mark closed the door and walked slowly down the thickly carpeted corridor to the lift. He was conscious that his heart seemed to be beating faster, and wondered whether it was with a sense of foreboding rather than excitement.

Geneva

6

Mark arrived deliberately early at Geneva's Cointrin Airport. It was another grey, overcast morning, and as the taxi approached the terminal building, the impenetrable wall of the Jura Mountains, their upper slopes still white with snow, formed a dark backdrop to the misty expanse of the runways.

He had called Quentin Sharpe again from his apartment in Geneva, late into the night.

"I'm sorry to wake you, but the drive from Lausanne took an hour."

"No problem. Anyway, we're an hour behind you. I hadn't gone to bed." Quentin's voice was unfriendly. "Frankly, Mark, we're not very happy with this whole arrangement."

"I don't see why not. They're not asking you for asylum from the Russians."

"I know that, but one of them is doing a bunk out of London, which is hardly going to endear us to our Russian friends."

"Friends?"

Quentin was irritated. "It's just an expression. Let's put it another way: if we are going to ruffle them, we'd rather choose something that's more advantageous to us."

"Well, at least that sounds a bit more true to life!"

"That's of little consequence either way. The point is that you're dragging us into CIA business."

"Then you can blame them."

"I intend to, but we're still going to be seen as aiding and abetting. How are you coming in?"

"Our first stop will be at about one-thirty, at Paris. We'll be on Swissair 724."

"Why Paris? There are plenty of direct flights from Geneva to London."

"I know, but the timing's wrong. We'll fly to de Gaulle and change there for London."

"Damn! That means we have to pull the French in too."

"Why?"

Quentin took a deep breath, as though talking to a small child. "Because you can't wander from country to country with a Russian national on your hands. I'll have to arrange for someone to meet you, which means using up a few precious Brownie points with the Deuxième Bureau. Do you remember young Bailey from here?"

"Yes."

"He'll meet you at the gate in Paris and walk you through."

"It shouldn't be necessary. We'll be in transit, which means we don't have to pass through French immigration. We can just as easily find our own way."

"I'm sure you can, but we'll do it my way."

"Why?"

"Because I prefer to see you on to the premises—and off again. That way, I'll know exactly what you're doing at all times. How long do you need to pick up the girl?"

"I said I'd collect her from the Royal Opera House tomorrow night after the performance, so we ought to be able to take a plane the following morning."

"Then why come in so early?"

"Because Kaverin's supposed to board a plane for Moscow at eleven fifty-five tomorrow morning. Do you think you could lend me a car while I'm in London?"

"I'll tell the Americans to find you one. They can put it on their expenses!" He was silent for a moment. "I'm just writing down a few details for them. You can have twenty-four hours, Mark, after which we want you out of here. Bailey will take you through immigration, but that's as far as we go. Officially, we're not involved."

Mark smiled into the phone. "You don't sound very happy about it."

"I'm not. We're trying to be a bit more companionable these days, and this sort of thing doesn't help."

"Then why have you agreed to do it?"

"Because we have a 'special relationship' with our great American allies, and they're as eager as ever to score points." He sighed. "God knows why some lousy pianist and his dancing sister should be considered so damned important, but ours is not to reason why. Anything Uncle Sam wants, Uncle Sam gets. I suppose that's what makes the relationship so special! Anyway, we're not going to help you more than that."

"You won't need to."

"I hope not. We've got our hands full of Middle Eastern characters these days. I've had to recruit half a dozen agents who can speak Arabic. It's only the Americans who remain so paranoid about Russia." He paused. Perhaps he regretted the last outburst. "Look, if anything goes wrong in London, we don't want to know. Your Mr. Kaverin will be on his plane to New York in the care of his new-found friends, with or without his sister. Do I make myself clear?"

"Lucidly."

"Very well." His voice softened. "You know, I'm curious. Why are you doing this? I thought you'd hung up your cloak and sheathed your dagger long ago."

"I have. To be honest, I'm not very enthusiastic about the whole idea myself. My own dealings with the Russians have been perfectly friendly during the past few months, and this is going to change all the goodwill there may have been. There's no way I can disguise what I'm doing."

"Obviously."

"But Viktor's a fine artist. I believe he may prove to be a great one. If I don't do something now, he may never have the chance to get out again. I promised I'd help."

"And his sister is part of the deal?"

"Yes."

Quentin chuckled softly. "She wouldn't happen to be pretty, would she?"

Mark kept his voice impersonal. "Yes, but that has nothing to do with it."

"Of course not, but it helps. Look for Bailey when you get to Paris." Quentin hung up.

Early in the morning, Mark had telephoned Irina at her London hotel. When she answered, her voice was sleepy.

"Irina, it's Mark. I'm sorry if I woke you."

"Mark!" Her voice was immediately alert. "Where are you?"

"In Geneva. Can you talk?"

She sounded puzzled. "Yes, I think so."

"Have you spoken to Viktor?"

"Yes. He told me that everything will be arranged. How is it possible?"

"I'll explain later. Are you sure this is what you want?"

She hesitated before replying. When she spoke, her voice was calm. "I am sure. It is what we both want."

"All right. We'll be in London this afternoon."

"But how can Viktor—"

"He'll be there. Don't worry."

"Where will he be?"

"I don't exactly know. Friends in London will look after him. Are you dancing tonight?"

"Yes. It is *Swan Lake*, but I don't understand—"

Mark spoke quickly, interrupting her. "Irina, I can't explain now. You'll have to trust me for the next twenty-four hours. It's very important."

"I do trust you, Mark. Viktor told me the same thing. What am I to do?"

"How quickly can you change at the end of the performance?"

"In a few minutes, if necessary." She laughed nervously. "Once, when I was in a hurry, I put a pair of jeans and a shirt over my costume, and—"

"Good. I'd like you to do that tonight. Can you bring a case to the theatre without causing attention?"

"Yes."

86

"Then do so. Pack whatever you can into it. You won't be returning to the hotel."

He heard a quick intake of breath. "Oh."

"At the end of the performance, I want you to go to the right side of the stage. There's a small electrician's control room there. Do you know where I mean?"

"Yes, I think so."

"See if you can leave your case there during the second act. Then, as soon as you've changed, go back there and wait. There are a few steps down to a door leading into the auditorium. Quite a lot of people use it to go backstage after a performance."

"I have seen it."

"Good. I'll be coming through that door."

"Why not come through the stage door?"

"Because I can't park a car in the street by the stage door. It's too narrow and there's never any space around there. Besides, that's where the rest of the company will be leaving from. If you tell them you're meeting a friend, they'll expect you to be a few minutes late."

"I see." She was silent, and he pictured her, a grave expression on her face, awaiting his next instruction.

"You and I will leave the theatre by the front. Hopefully, they'll be watching out for you at the stage door."

"I do not understand. Why should they—"

"Because, by the time I arrive, Viktor will be missing. I am gambling that they will not know where he has gone, but it may occur to Moscow that you planned this together. You'll need to be very careful."

She did not reply for a moment. "I think I am frightened."

"Don't worry too much. My experience of your countrymen is that they're usually strangled by endless bureaucratic delays. By the time a message reaches London, you will be gone. Try not to worry. If my plan works, they won't know where to look for Viktor, and the people in London won't have been warned that he's disappeared. The most important thing is for you to act completely normally. Tell your friends that you've got an admirer."

"I will try."

"I'm sure you will." He lightened his voice. "Perhaps you have. I'm looking forward to seeing you again. After all, I promised I would."

"Yes." She hesitated slightly. "I am looking forward also."

"Then I'll see you tonight. If anything goes wrong, I'll find a way to contact you." He wondered how.

"You think something might go wrong?"

"No. I simply wanted you to know that I'll be in touch. I'll see you tonight."

"I will be there."

Mark used the additional time to buy the tickets he had reserved earlier. The airport was moderately busy with the normal traffic of a Monday morning, and the lines at the check-in desk moved steadily. It was too early in the year for the tourists, and ski parties arrived and departed over the weekend. Most of the queues were occupied by impatient Swiss businessmen. To his relief, Agnes arrived, as requested, some time before the two Russians. She was carrying a large manila file.

"Good morning, Monsieur Holland. I have brought the files you asked for. Will you be away from the office for a long time?"

"I'm not sure. Something unexpected came up last night."

"It is not so important, but I noticed that you had one or two appointments later this week. Shall I postpone them?"

"Yes, please. I'd forgotten about them. You're very efficient, Agnes. I don't know what I'd do without you to look after me." She treated him to a warm, metallic smile. "If there's anything urgent, Rudi can look after it, and I'll be calling in regularly. Were there any reviews from last night?"

She looked concerned. "I did not see the newspapers yet. I forgot to buy them. Shall I go and get them?"

"No, not yet." He spoke sharply, causing Agnes to look at him curiously. Forcing a smile to cover his tenseness, he said, "Why don't you wait until the others arrive? You and Yuri Schedrin can find them while I check Viktor in. I'd better look through those appointments now."

"Oh yes. Monsieur Kaverin was wonderful! I have never heard the Chopin sonata played with such passion. It was very moving. I can understand why Yuri—Monsieur Schedrin, I mean—is so proud of him."

"Yes. I expect we'll be seeing a lot of Yuri in the next few months."

Agnes blushed slightly and produced Mark's desk diary from a briefcase. "I brought this from the office in case you wanted to see all your arrangements." Mark nodded. It seemed that some of Rudi's efficiency had brushed off on Agnes, but she did not make it so patently obvious. "Monsieur Schedrin was supposed to see you this afternoon, to discuss plans for Viktor. He told me that he would stay in Geneva an extra day before going on to Brussels."

"That's all right. I explained last night that I might have to leave town." He smiled. "I don't expect he'll mind having to spend an extra day in Geneva."

"Ah." She seemed to examine the diary very carefully. "Monsieur Schedrin has a very busy life, representing all those artists. It must be hard on his family."

Mark watched her. "I don't think he has a family."

"Really?"

"I had the feeling he was divorced some years ago."

"Oh." She consulted the diary further, avoiding his gaze, and it seemed to Mark that Agnes was suddenly very relaxed.

Viktor and Schedrin arrived a few minutes later. The Gosconcert man was dressed as impeccably as ever, with a new-looking Burberry raincoat draped over the shoulders of his business suit. Viktor, on the other hand, was pale and dishevelled, his hair tousled and uncombed.

Yuri grasped Mark's hand. "You should have joined us for supper last night. Agnes took us to a little café where, I understand, all the theatre people like to go. It was excellent."

"I'm sorry I couldn't be with you, but there were some urgent messages on my answering machine."

"No matter. We were well looked after." He turned to Agnes and leaned forward to kiss her on each cheek.

Viktor nodded his greeting without speaking. He was very nervous.

"I'm sorry to have to cancel our appointment this afternoon, but this trip is unexpected. I hope we can arrange another meeting."

"Of course. I will consult with Mademoiselle Muret." He had not yet let go of her hand.

"Have you seen the reviews?" Mark had already read them earlier. They were unanimously good in a cautiously Swiss way. The Lausanne critic had noted that Viktor had seemed a little uneasy in the Mozart and had not really settled down until the Chopin.

Viktor spoke. "We did not have a chance to see them. I'm afraid I overslept this morning. I did not sleep very well."

Schedrin nodded. "Too much excitement and too much coffee. You should try vodka. It's better than a sleeping tablet!"

Mark turned to Agnes. "Why don't you and Yuri go and find the papers while Viktor and I check in? There's a news-stand upstairs, at the far end of the shopping centre."

The Gosconcert man smiled. "Excellent! Viktor, do you have everything?" The pianist nodded. "In that case, Agnes and I will buy newspapers." He put an arm around her shoulders, to guide her, and Agnes shyly slipped her arm around his waist. Schedrin smiled. "If there is to be a moment of truth, I could not ask for a nicer companion to share it with me!"

Mark nodded. "We'll meet you upstairs when we're finished here. Why don't you order us a coffee."

As they joined the shortest line at the check-in desk, Viktor whispered, "What do we do now?"

Mark handed him a ticket. "We check in together for the Paris flight." Without looking round, he added, "Is there any sign of our friends from yesterday?"

Kaverin surveyed the busy terminal floor. "I don't think so."

"Then we may be clear. Keep watching, but try not to be too obvious about it." He nodded towards the imitation leather hold-all the pianist was carrying. "Is that all your luggage?"

"Yes."

"Good. We'll check it through to London."

"But we are going to Paris."

"And straight on to London. I've allowed enough time to change planes." The pianist looked puzzled, but Mark smiled, trying to remain calm. "Once we pass through immigration, Yuri won't see which gate we leave from. Your Moscow flight departs at eleven fifty-five, and the Paris flight goes at twelve-fifteen. That's why I chose it. It makes sense for us to leave together."

"But I don't have papers—"

"Don't worry. We'll be met off the plane at Paris. From there on, we'll be looked after. The only part that matters is that we make the flight without being spotted." Viktor was silent, but his jaw muscles twitched.

A cheerfully impersonal girl at the check-in tore tickets and stamped them. It occurred to Mark that it was fortunate that Geneva airport did not have separate check-in desks for different airlines.

"Do you want to send you baggage directly to London?"

"Yes, please."

"Smoking or non-smoking?"

"Smoking."

"Very good. Your flight will leave from Gate Thirty-four on time. It will be called at about eleven forty-five."

Schedrin and Agnes were already sitting at a table in the café at the head of the stairs, the newspapers spread before them. Yuri looked up with a broad smile. "Wait until you hear what they have to say about you! You are a hit, Viktor! The Swiss critics think you may be another Richter. My God, I haven't read reviews like this for a long time. Come and sit down. Your coffee's getting cold."

It seemed to Mark that the Gosconcert man was exaggerating, but he smiled and patted Viktor on the back. "My congratulations. I expected good reviews, but it's always nice to have one's opinions reinforced."

Schedrin turned to Mark. "It's a great pity about our meeting this afternoon, but I will make a point of coming back soon." Agnes looked pleased. "Surely, you are going to represent Viktor after this?"

"Yes." Mark smiled. "I think I had better!"

"Wonderful! I promised you it would be worthwhile." He raised his coffee cup. "Let's drink to a successful partnership!"

After a while, Mark looked at his watch. "They'll be calling your flight soon, Viktor. You might as well go through immigration early, in case you want anything from duty-free."

Kaverin looked puzzled, but Schedrin nodded. "That's a good idea. They have some excellent shops inside. Why don't you take Irina some champagne truffles? They are unbelievably delicious!"

Mark stood. "I may as well join you. My flight is only a few minutes after yours." Turning to Agnes, he said, "I expect I'll call you later. Tell Rudi I'll be in touch."

At the glass-fronted immigration booth, Schedrin hugged Viktor affectionately. "It starts well, Viktor. I will talk to you next week." He turned to Mark, grasping his hand. "Thank you again, my dear friend. I will send these reviews to Moscow immediately. They will be delighted. I hope we can talk again in a few days."

"I'm sure we will."

"Meanwhile, I will look after everything here." He placed a proprietary arm around Agnes's waist.

The uniformed Swiss in the glass box scarcely looked at their passports, and they entered the international departures hall. Mark walked Viktor to the far end, where the chocolate shop and the supermarket for cigarettes and alcohol were crowded. Only one man, of Middle Eastern appearance, was being served at the Swiss watch counter. Presumably, he was the only one affluent enough to buy the expensive goods on display.

"Do you want anything?" Viktor shook his head silently. "Then keep watching for any unwanted company. They may have booked themselves on your flight."

"What will I do if they have?"

Mark led him to the windows overlooking the misty runways. Several circular buildings about fifty yards away were surrounded by aircraft. "I don't know whether you remember the layout of this airport. The departure gates are over there," he pointed to the buildings, "and we walk out to them by underground passages. I'm pretty certain that your Moscow flight is from a different building. If our friends show up, let them go out first, if possible, and make sure they're well ahead of you. There's a security check at the entrance to each building, and once they pass through it, they'll have trouble trying to find you if you don't show up."

Kaverin was uneasy. "I am not sure—"

"As a further precaution, as soon as we reach the departure lounge, go into the lavatory and stay there as long as possible. I'll come and get you just before the plane leaves. All right?"

"Yes." Looking past Mark's shoulder, Viktor stiffened suddenly. "They are here."

Mark did not turn his head. "Where?"

"Standing in front of the departures board, by the stairs."

"All right. Go and have a look at the duty-free."

"I don't want—"

Mark's voice remained calm but firm. "I know, but it's suitably busy. They're not likely to bother you there. If they do, I'll have to think of some sort of diversion. With any luck, they don't plan to speak to you at all."

Leaving Viktor, he wandered casually towards the two men, who had now seated themselves on chairs facing the stairway to the subterranean passages leading to the departure gates. Both men were heavily built, with broad shoulders and slightly ill-fitting clothes. Presumably, their rank did not call for a clothing allowance like Schedrin's. The larger of the two men was wearing a raincoat and sat staring into space. His companion had removed his coat, revealing a dark brown business suit with shiny elbows, and was reading a newspaper. They seemed to ignore each other.

Mark walked past them to the newspaper stand and bought a copy of *Time* magazine. Then he rejoined Viktor, who was hovering by the supermarket, watching intently. "Let's go and sit behind them."

The young man was startled. "Why?"

Mark spoke casually, sure that his smile appeared false. "Because they obviously know we're here. The last thing you want to do is to make them suspicious." He turned in their direction, adding in a low voice, "Do whatever I tell you." They found two seats behind the Russians, who did not appear to notice their arrival, and Mark lit a cigarette.

Several long minutes passed. Mark engaged Viktor in conversation, discussing possible future engagements, and the pianist answered with monosyllables. He probably did not trust his voice to say more without revealing his growing anxiety. At one point, Mark placed a hand on Viktor's arm, as if to emphasize what he was saying, and the pressure seemed to reassure him. The Russians said nothing.

At length, the departure of the Aeroflot flight to Moscow was called, and after a slight pause the two Russians stood slowly without looking round. Mark followed suit. Viktor stared at him, a puzzled expression on his face, but he smiled and said, "I think that's your flight. I'll walk you some of the way." He led the way, staying at the Russians' heels.

At the head of the stairs, still close behind the two men, Mark said, "Wait. You've forgotten to buy Irina's chocolates." For a moment, he thought one of the men in front hesitated, and added, "It's all right, you still have plenty of time. The flight won't leave for a while."

He wondered whether either of the two men would stay behind, but they continued forward. The smaller man looked towards his companion briefly, but the other shrugged his shoulders very slightly, and they continued down the staircase.

Mark took Viktor's arm, urging him across the hall. Almost under his breath, he said, "Give them plenty of time. They won't worry for the moment. There's still another twenty-five minutes to departure." He smiled briefly. "We may as well buy some of those truffles Yuri recommended. They're as good as he says!"

Ten minutes later, they returned to the staircase. The two Russians were not visible, and Mark started down. He spoke quietly. "So far, so good. Their flight leaves from a different building from ours. If they've already passed through the final security check, they'll have trouble getting back."

They continued down the long walkway until they approached the exit leading to their gate. Two or three travellers were queuing by an X-ray machine, handing over their briefcases and passing through an electronically controlled doorway for their security check before entering the lounge containing the departure gates. Mark slowed down, putting a restraining hand on Viktor's arm. "Give the others time to go through. I don't want to wait in a line." He looked farther down the passageway, but the Russians were not there. By the time they reached the security check, there was no delay. Climbing the stairs into the departure lounge, he whispered, "There's a lavatory on your right at the top of the stairs. Lock yourself in one of the cubicles and wait for me to call you. Be ready!" Viktor nodded quickly and ran up the few remaining stairs. He moved like an athlete.

Mark entered the airy circular lounge, its glass walls revealing the various aircraft waiting to take on passengers. It was not very busy. The last of the duty-free shops were unpatronized, and the girls behind the counters chatted quietly together. A number of men were seated around a bar serving coffee and drinks. Mark selected a chair facing the stairway and opened his magazine.

The minutes ticked slowly by. Glancing at his watch, he saw that it was nearly eleven-fifty. He wondered whether the Russians would leave on their flight or return to the terminal to call Moscow. In the old days, under similar circumstances, either he or his partner would have remained behind.

At that moment, one of the Russians appeared at the head of the stairs. He was the more heavily built of the two. Mark looked up, and although their eyes met, he gave no sign of recognition. The man glanced at him, then stared round the room. His head turned slowly, but his body was immobile. Mark had the fleeting impression of an animal, tensed and ready to move suddenly. Then the man looked at his watch uneasily and returned down the stairs. Mark continued to read, wondering whether the Paris flight was on time.

In the distance, he could hear departures being announced with monotonous regularity, and the lounge began to fill with new arrivals. They congregated close to the exit doors of Gate Thirty-four, as if intent on being the first to board. It was odd that they still competed for a place when the seats had already been assigned.

After what seemed an eternity, a smartly uniformed young woman announced that the flight was ready for boarding, and the passengers converged on the glass exit doors. Mark remained seated, watching as they slowly filed through to the tarmac, walking the few yards to the mobile stairways attached to the aircraft. There was no further sign of the Russians. Fighting temptation, he hesitated longer. This was the critical moment.

The last of the passengers had departed, and the girls at the gate were standing together, checking a passenger list. Something seemed to be wrong. Suddenly, Mark realized that they might call his name and Viktor's over the loudspeakers, and he moved quickly toward them, catching the eye of one. Holding up a hand to ask them to wait, he jerked his head in the direction of the lavatories and indicated with sign language that his companion would be coming shortly. The girl nodded reprovingly, tapping her watch.

He ran into the lavatory and moved to the cabins, his voice harsh in the enclosed tiled space. "Viktor—now!" A door opened, and Kaverin appeared. His face was very pale, and his forehead glistened with sweat. "To your left, as you come out. Don't look around. Just go!"

They ran to the exit gate, oblivious of the lounge, and the stewardess greeted them with mock severity. "We thought we had lost you!" She glanced at Viktor and turned to Mark. "Is your friend ill?"

He smiled. "No. Hangover. Too much entertainment last night!"

The girl clicked her tongue and tore their tickets. "Please hurry. We are ready to leave."

They dashed across the tarmac, Viktor leading, and raced up the stairs two at a time. The stewardess awaiting them looked surprised. "Do not worry, messieurs. There is still a moment."

Mark glanced round. Behind him, they were already moving the stairway back. He placed a hand on Viktor's shoulder, gently urging him into the cabin. "Let me take the window seat. We're in row twenty-two, on your right."

By the time they were seated, the engines were already revving, causing a slight vibration through the fuselage. A recorded announcement in several languages was explaining how to fit life-jackets. As the plane slowly edged forward, Mark looked casually out of the window towards the glass exit gate. It may have been his imagination, but he thought he saw one of the Russians behind the window. The man was gesticulating angrily at one of the uniformed attendants, who seemed to be making soothing gestures. The aircraft gathered speed and taxied across the tarmac, cutting off his view.

At his side, Viktor had closed his eyes, his face white. He was breathing heavily. If they had been seen, it was better not to mention it. In any case, it was too late now.

London

7

Despite its comfortable proportions, the room in the airport hotel looked small, probably because it was dominated by the very large man standing in the centre, next to the double bed. He was unmistakably American. The broad cut of his lightweight suit, the rimless glasses, the beefy, pink-faced fleshiness of his jowls, and the disastrously loud colours of his tie made him look like any one of a thousand commuting business executives who emerged from the depths of Grand Central Station in New York every working day. His close-cropped hair, thinning rapidly, was an indiscriminate shade of brown and grey, and his fingernails were buffed to the same high gloss as his shoes. Mark hoped he was not an undercover man. He was hardly going to blend with the English scenery. On the other hand, it would be hard to miss him. He was a giant of a man, almost a head taller than Mark. Viktor and Bailey, hovering by the door, eyed him uncertainly.

He raised his hand to greet them jovially. "Hi! Jack Murphy. Welcome to London." His voice boomed and his smile was broad, revealing perfect teeth, but his eyes were cold. "How was the trip?"

"No problems." Mark felt a little like a spokesman addressing an alien being. "Mr. Bailey met us at the gate in Paris and guided us through."

"Good." Murphy's eyes never left Mark's face. "Anyone see you?"

"I don't know, but if they know what they're doing, they'll calculate that Viktor was on the Paris flight. It was the closest. There wasn't enough time to change names or try anything very subtle."

"Why not?"

"Because there's always the possibility that an official will want to check the name on the passport against the name on the ticket." Glancing towards the pianist, he added, "Twenty-four hours isn't much warning for preparing false documents. It's not my line of business."

"I guess not." Murphy now addressed himself to Viktor, extending his well-manicured paw. "Welcome to you, my friend." His voice was not very warm, but Viktor nodded silently, his hand disappearing inside Murphy's. "You feeling OK?"

When Viktor said nothing, Mark spoke again. "It's been a pretty nerve-racking day." He described their departure from Geneva, and the American nodded occasionally, his eyes now fastened on the Russian. There was something slightly awe-inspiring about the way he concentrated his attention. As he listened, he did not bother to smile further. When Mark reached the point where Bailey had met them, Murphy's eyes slid in the direction of the young Englishman, and he nodded again. He gave the impression that they had already met, perhaps for a briefing that morning.

They were still standing, and Murphy suddenly relaxed. It reduced the tension in the room. "Why don't you park yourselves." He indicated two armchairs and a hard-backed chair placed by a desk at the window, then slumped on the bed, which sagged beneath him. Viktor started towards the desk, but Murphy again raised his hand. "I wouldn't sit by the window if I were you. Try that easy chair in the corner." He spoke casually, but the command was implicit. On a side table, there were several bottles and glasses and an ice bucket. "Like a drink?" He grinned. "There's Scotch and bourbon—no vodka!"

Viktor sat on the edge of the armchair. "I think I would like a Scotch, with no ice. Please, Mr. Murphy, I am worried about my luggage . . ."

Bailey spoke for the first time. "It should be along shortly." He looked at Murphy. "I gave the baggage tickets to . . ." He had forgotten the name and hesitated uncertainly.

"Figlio?" Bailey nodded gratefully. Murphy shrugged. "No sweat. He'll be along later."

"You are sure?" Viktor was patently unhappy.

"Sure I'm sure." The American frowned. "What's the problem, Viktor?" He was not concerned with surnames.

"I suppose to you it is nothing, but the case contains everything I own. It is the only possession I could bring out of Russia with me . . ." He relapsed into silence.

For a moment, Murphy stared at Viktor. His expression was not friendly. Then he shrugged again. "That was your decision. Mike will bring your things up in a few minutes. He was probably held up waiting for them to unload. This goddam airport takes forever." To Bailey, he added, "Mine's bourbon—with ice." It was not a reprimand, but the instruction seemed to indicate to Viktor that he should adapt himself to his new surroundings.

It had been a tense, uncertain journey, despite its lack of incident, and Mark still felt the strain. Viktor slept during the one-hour flight to Paris. Nervous exhaustion following a sleepless night had left him drained. At de Gaulle Airport, Bailey had been waiting by the exit ramp into the *satellite*. There was a slightly unreal air of *déjà vu* to their arrival. The circular waiting-room was almost a reproduction of the one they had just left. It was hard to imagine what was going on in Viktor's mind. Perhaps he feared that they had played some nightmare trick on him and were about to return him to his Russian keepers.

Mark remembered Bailey from a previous occasion. He was a slightly built man in his late twenties, sporting an old-fashioned pencil moustache, with the irritating habit of shifting his accent from Oxford to Cockney and back in an effort to bolster some inner sense of insecurity. For their meeting, he had borrowed a British Airways uniform and, as they appeared, had led the way through a side door to a small, empty waiting-room, leaving them alone. Mark could not be sure, but thought he had heard the sound of a key turning in the lock. Bailey had not spoken.

"What will happen?" Viktor had surveyed the room, whispering nervously.

"Nothing. I assume he'll come and collect us when the London flight's ready. It leaves in about fifty minutes, so they'll probably start boarding in half an hour."

Bailey had returned in exactly thirty minutes, this time dressed in a blazer and grey slacks with a pale blue open-necked shirt. He looked like a casual tourist and was carrying a plastic duty-free carrier bag containing a bottle and a carton of cigarettes.

"OK?"

"Yes."

He handed them two boarding passes. "First gate on your right as you come out. Make your own way." For a moment, he had glanced at Viktor. "Good luck!" He had followed them on to the aircraft, sitting two rows behind.

After take-off, Viktor had whispered, "Who was that man?"

"An employee of my friends in London."

Viktor was pensive. "Your friends are . . . influential?"

"Yes, but not necessarily in our case."

"The French police were not there."

"They wouldn't need to be. We never left the transit area. I suppose he just borrowed a waiting-room."

"But how could he do such things? It is a breach of security!" Viktor sounded outraged by the thought.

"I suppose so. Nobody bothers to question a man wearing an airline uniform."

"In my country, he would have been arrested immediately."

Mark felt irritation growing. The journey had taken its toll of his own nerves. "It's no longer your country, Viktor. That's why we're here."

Viktor had been silent.

Murphy raised his glass. "Here's to you." He drained it quickly.

At that moment, there was a single rap on the door. Moving surprisingly quickly, the big American left the bed and stood next to the door, his hand reaching casually towards an inner pocket of his bulky jacket.

Mark noted that he kept his body next to the wall, leaving the wooden door exposed. If anyone outside fired a gun, the bullets would miss him. Murphy was a professional.

"Yeah?"

He could not make out the voice on the other side of the door, but the American, apparently satisfied, turned the handle to open it. Mark recognized the small, sallow man who entered. Bailey had spoken to him briefly as they had passed behind the immigration desks, and had handed him their baggage tickets. This was presumably Murphy's assistant, Mike Figlio.

For a moment, Murphy blocked the doorway. "Where's their stuff?"

"Downstairs. I told the porter to put it next door."

"Why didn't you bring it up yourself?"

For a moment, Figlio looked angry. He had dark, Sicilian features, with a heavy aquiline nose. Then he shrugged. "It's a bellboy's job. What's the big deal? I didn't want to draw attention to a couple of bags."

Murphy considered this. "OK, but be there when they arrive." He opened a door connecting the two rooms, and Figlio departed without comment. He had not glanced in the direction of Mark or Kaverin, but Mark suspected that he had already memorized their features to the last detail. It was reassuring to find oneself in the company of professionals.

Viktor stood. "Please, Mr. Murphy, when can I see my sister?"

A slight frown crossed Murphy's face, and he glanced in Mark's direction. "I wouldn't exactly know. We'll get around to her later. Before that happens, you and I have some talking to do."

"I don't understand."

Murphy's smile returned, but his eyes remained cold. "We're going to need to have a little heart-to-heart, Viktor—sort of get to know each other, if you see what I mean. There's nothing to worry about, but we'd like to know a little more about you—your background and all that kind of stuff. You're taking a big step, you know, but so are we. You can't expect to just walk in."

Viktor's nervousness increased. "What do you have to know? I don't have any documents, except my passport, which Mr. Bailey already took from me. I am a musician. What do I need?"

The big American smiled patiently. "You'd better leave the questions to me. There's a whole lot of stuff I have to go through, and a bunch of

100

paperwork that has to be filled out. When we've processed that, you can talk to your sister. Her name's Irene, isn't it?" He pronounced it I-reen.

"Irina."

"Well, I guess it's the same thing. We pronounce names the way they're spelled in the States, except for the Indian ones." He grinned. "There's only one exception I can think of—Fuchs." He pronounced it Fewkes.

"How long will these questions take?"

Murphy's smile had disappeared, but his voice remained friendly. "Until I'm satisfied."

Viktor was silent for a moment. "And if you are not satisfied?"

The American shrugged. "I guess you'll have to make alternative arrangements." Viktor was about to speak, but Murphy continued, "I wouldn't worry about it. I'm sure everything's going to work out just fine. They tell me you play great piano." He walked to the side table and picked up the bottle. "You want to freshen up your drink?"

"No." Viktor sat in the armchair again, looking towards Mark. There was an uneasy silence.

Murphy's voice became brisk. "OK, I'll tell you what: we're going to have to wait a few minutes until our London friend arrives. Why don't you go next door and rest a while? You've had a busy morning. We have a long wait on our hands . . ."

"How long?"

Murphy's voice hardened slightly. "I told you—until I'm ready. You run along next door and rest. If there's anything you need, just tell Mike, and he'll look after it for you. In a while, it may even be OK for you to call Irene, but it may be better to wait until she's out of the way of any . . . interference."

Viktor moved to the connecting door. His voice was stubborn. "I want to speak to her."

Murphy placed a beefy hand on his shoulder. "Sure you do, but you wouldn't want to stir up any suspicion right now, would you? The moment you didn't board that plane to Moscow, a whole lot of people must have been pretty concerned, wouldn't you say?" Viktor nodded. "Well, it's not going to help any if you start making phone calls, is it?" He spoke soothingly, urging Kaverin firmly through the door. "We'll get together in a while, Viktor. Meantime, just relax. I'll look in later." Viktor passed into the other room without speaking further.

Closing the door, Murphy turned to Mark with a grimace. "Jesus, that kid seems to think he's on a church picnic!"

"It's all happened very quickly for him. It's only just beginning to sink in."

The American slumped on the bed again. His voice was angry. "I don't like it. This guy Sharpe's giving us twenty-four hours," he looked at his watch, "and not even that, after which Kaverin goes. Washington's up my ass, telling me to clear him; you're supposed to deliver his sister, and the whole lousy operation has to be finished by tomorrow! Who do they think they're kidding?"

"Do you need much time?"

"I need more than they're giving me. Christ! The goddam State Department's talking about a press reception at JFK tomorrow afternoon. I told them it's too soon, but some jerk went and spilled the beans to the White House as soon as they heard about it, and the press secretary thinks it's a great story!" He scowled. "Great story! Shit, the whole thing's a lousy PR operation!"

"Have you told them that?"

"Sure I've told them, but they're not interested. The President's replaying *Shane*, riding into town to save the farmers! Public relations!" He swallowed his drink. "Give me a good old cautious, crooked politician any day!"

"What happens if you don't like Kaverin?"

Murphy shrugged. "He's out, unless I'm overruled."

"Out?"

"Sure. He can go any place he likes, just so long as it's not US territory. If the British don't want him, he'll have to try someplace else. If he strikes out, he goes back to Moscow."

"Do you realize what that would mean for him?"

Murphy was angry. "I'm not involved. I didn't make these goddam deadlines, and I frankly don't give a shit. As far as I'm concerned, he's just another Russian, and one less suits me just fine!" He stared out of the window in silence.

At that moment, the telephone rang. The sound was startling. Murphy lifted the receiver irritably. "Yeah?" He listened for a moment, then spoke with an effort to remain calm. "Why don't you just come on up? You know the room number? Right." He replaced the receiver with a thump, turning to Mark. "It's your goddam friend Quentin Sharpe,

102

being very British!" He essayed an English accent. "What's he making phone calls for, for Christ's sake? He knows where we are!"

"Natural caution, I suppose, and since you mentioned it, he's no great friend of mine."

"Really?" The American's eyes narrowed. "I thought he was an old working buddy of yours."

"No." Mark kept his voice calm. "I called him on behalf of Viktor, because I thought he could help. Quentin and I never worked together, and I certainly wouldn't describe him as a buddy."

Bailey stared out of the window without speaking, but there was the ghost of a smile on his lips.

Quentin Sharpe had aged surprisingly since Mark had last seen him. It was not so much the grey that was spreading rapidly through his dark hair as the deep lines on either side of his mouth and the blue-veined patches beneath his eyes. He had been a very handsome younger man whose boyish good looks belied his real age. Most handsome men age well, but too many nights without sleep, coupled with the pressures of the job, had given him a pinched, slightly aggrieved expression. He was dressed in a light grey pinstripe suit whose narrow waist indicated that he stayed fit. Mark remembered that he used to belong to a fashionable health club.

Quentin nodded to Mark and extended his hand to Murphy. "Hello, Jack." Bailey was ignored.

The American smiled briefly. "How are you? Listen, you're putting me on the spot with this Russian kid. I can't debrief him in the next eighteen hours, and I won't get to see his sister until just before she boards the plane. Give me a break, Quentin!"

Sharpe's smile was professionally smooth. "I'm sorry, but it's all I can allow you. We want him away from here by tomorrow morning—sooner, if it were possible."

"Why the hurry?"

"Because we'd like him out before the Russians even realize he's been here. For all they need to know, he could have flown directly from Switzerland to New York. I warned you when we first discussed this: we're not involved."

"The hell you're not!" Murphy's complexion had darkened. "What about the sister?"

Quentin looked at Mark. "We're relying on Mr. Holland to remove

103

her quickly and quietly, giving the impression that she ducked out on her own initiative to join her brother. That's one of the reasons why I want them kept apart until the last minute. I'd be happier still if you'd put them on different flights."

Murphy shook his head. "That's a waste of manpower, especially for a pianist and a dancer." His voice was scornful. "I want Mark to ride with me and the two of them tomorrow. If I start putting them on different flights, it means bringing in extra operatives. Hell, I don't see why you're making such a federal case out of it. I thought we were supposed to be on the same friggin' side."

Quentin sighed. "We are, Jack, but we're in the middle of some delicate negotiations of our own, which we've had to set aside because of this little emergency." Murphy's bushy eyebrows were raised, but Quentin did not elaborate. His smile was slightly forced. "We're pleased to have been of help, but I can't stretch the co-operation any further. I'm sorry."

The frosty silence was broken when Mike Figlio entered by the connecting door to the bedroom. Murphy snapped at him, "What's he up to?"

Figlio looked hurt. "Nothing. He's sitting on the bed, listening to a transistor radio he took out of his bag." He chuckled. "He looks like a teenage kid, with the thing stuck against his ear. I showed him how to work the TV, but he said he'd rather listen to music." He pulled a face. "Some sort of classical crap."

"How is he?" Murphy had relaxed, and his voice was more friendly.

"Seems OK, now that he's got his goddam case. He grabbed hold of it like a long-lost child as soon as he saw it. You need me any more?"

"I may. Stick around for a while." Murphy glowered at Quentin Sharpe. "I'm going to be up most of the night, talking, though God knows what I can learn in the time I have."

Mark spoke for the first time. "What exactly do you need to know?"

"For starters, just who the hell he is, and why the hell he should be given entry to the United States of America. All I've gotten thus far is that he wants to leave home and that he plays the goddam piano. It's not a hell of a lot to go on!"

"If it's of help, I can vouch for his talent as a pianist. He's one of the finest young artists I've ever heard."

"Big deal! We've got plenty of great young piano players of our own.

If it weren't for Washington getting in on the act, he wouldn't be here at all."

Quentin's voice was cool. "But he is, so there seems little point in discussing it further. If your people weren't interested in offering Kaverin and his sister asylum, they should have said so. It's a little late to start quibbling now, and as Mr. Holland has pointed out, there's really not that much to know about him." He smiled slyly. "For our part, we can vouch for Mr. Holland. Despite certain differences of opinion in the past, his credentials are impeccable. I expect his musical evaluation is equally sound."

Murphy drained his glass, thumping it down on the bedside table. His voice was subdued. "Sure." He stared moodily into space.

Sharpe turned briskly to Mark. "Everything seems to be in order. Are you staying at this hotel?"

"Yes. I have two connecting rooms on a different floor."

"And you've made the necessary arrangements with Miss Kaverin?" Mark nodded. "In that case, I suggest you travel separately with her to the terminal in the morning."

"All right. I have one small favour to ask. When I pick her up this evening, it would be very helpful to have a car with a driver at my disposal."

Quentin's eyes narrowed. "I thought Jack had arranged your car." Murphy nodded.

"He has, and I'll be using it, but when we leave the opera house, I'd prefer to be unencumbered. There's nowhere to park, and I'd rather not have to walk her along the street." He smiled. "I'd also like to leave my hands free, in case of emergencies."

Quentin frowned. "Are you expecting trouble? I've already warned you—"

"I don't know what I'm expecting. If it goes as I'm anticipating, we'll simply leave, but I'd like to be covered in case Irina is being watched."

Murphy put a hand on his shoulder. His voice was friendlier. "That makes a lot of sense. Someone round here's doing a little straight thinking. Do you want Mike?"

"It depends how well he knows London." Mark looked at Figlio, who shrugged uneasily. "Perhaps I'm being too cautious, but I'd prefer someone who knows a few back streets, if necessary. I wondered whether Mr. Bailey could lend a hand. It won't take long."

105

Quentin glanced at Bailey. "Very well. Where do you want him?"

Mark spoke directly to the young man. "Outside the front of the Opera House, at the end of the performance. There's usually a long queue of Rolls and Bentleys waiting to pick up their owners, unless you can persuade the police to let you sit outside their station on the opposite side of the road."

Bailey smiled. "That can be arranged. I've got a couple of friends over there. I'll be waiting for you, but don't expect me to wear a chauffeur's cap!"

"Thanks."

Quentin looked at his watch. "I'm expected back in town, so I'll leave you. You're on the Pan Am flight at eleven tomorrow?"

"If I'm satisfied." Murphy was not conceding anything.

Quentin ignored the comment. "Bailey will meet you at the check-in just before ten and see you through. Good luck." He hesitated as though deciding whether or not to shake hands, then moved to the door. Bailey joined him.

When they had gone, Murphy gestured to Figlio with a grunt. "It's great to have friends when you really need them! You'd better go sit with Prince Charming for a spell."

"He's not doing anything."

"I know, but there's a phone in that room. I don't want him trying to call his sister. I'll come through in a couple of minutes."

"Do you need me after that? I could spell you later."

"Nah. I'll keep him talking as long as I can. The kid looked out on his feet to me. He's not going to last long." Figlio nodded, and returned next door, and Murphy gave an exaggerated sigh. "It looks like it's going to be a long night." His ill temper seemed to have passed, and he poured himself a short drink, gesturing with the bottle towards Mark. "What are you going to do?"

"I'll be in my room, making a few phone calls, until it's time to pick Irina up."

"Who are you calling?" His voice was wary again.

"My office. I wasn't expecting to fly on to New York until you suggested it. Frankly, I was expecting to leave Viktor and Irina in your care."

"I'd appreciate your coming with us."

"It's not a problem, and I'd like to be there for a few days after they

106

arrive. I'm also concerned with what might happen to them if you decide not to pass him on to New York."

Murphy gave a gruff laugh. "I guess I was making too much of that. I'll process him through unless I discover he's KGB in the next twelve hours, which is unlikely." He hesitated for a moment. "I got the impression Quentin had a high opinion of you."

"It wasn't mutual."

"How come?"

Mark smiled. "It's a long story, and I won't bore you with it. Let's just say I disagreed with their methods."

"You bucked the system?"

"Something like that. Why were you so concerned with Quentin's time limit?"

"Because I don't like being pushed around. I'm a professional, and I do things by the book. The guy who wrote it knew what he was about. I don't like rubber-stamping a deal because some shit-headed ass-kisser in Washington thinks he'll score points with the President. You calling anyone else?" He spoke casually, but his eyes were cautious.

"Abe Sincoff, my partner in New York. He's a manager there, and we share a number of artists."

"Why?"

"Because I'd like to forewarn him of what's going on." Murphy started to speak, but Mark continued. "Don't worry, he'll be completely discreet. In fact, he could be helpful if you want to keep things quiet in New York until the Kaverins are settled in. Abe's a friendly, roly-poly little man with a winning smile and a mind like a steel trap. I'd trust my life with him. If you're at all concerned with their anonymity, I would have thought he'd draw less attention to them than any army of official-looking agents waiting by the arrivals gate."

Murphy was thoughtful. "You could be right at that, and it's unconventional enough to work." He smiled crookedly. "You wouldn't happen to be protecting your investment, would you?"

"Certainly. If I'm going out on a limb for Viktor and Irina and spoiling my new-found friendship with the Russian government, I might as well enjoy the benefits. Poor Agnes!"

"Who's she?"

Mark smiled. "It's not important. I was thinking about something else."

"Tell you what: hold off calling your friend in New York for an hour or so, and I'll come back to you when I've cleared Washington. They're waiting for me to check in."

"All right. Do you want me to bring Irina to you?"

"No. She's not going to tell me anything I can't get out of Viktor. We may as well play it Quentin's way. Keep her on ice until tomorrow morning." He reached into a back pocket. "You may as well take your air tickets now. We asked Quentin to share the costs, but he didn't want to know."

"That sounds like Quentin."

"I guess so. He muttered something about departmental budgets. It seems our special relationship doesn't go that far, but these operations are costly."

"Who covers them?"

Murphy grinned. "Uncle Sam and the American taxpayer. Don't they always?"

8

Mark found the parking place he wanted, and stopped the car. Above him, a man in shirt-sleeves opened a window and leaned out, eyeing the vehicle resentfully.

"I hope you're not planning to leave that here all night."

"No, I shouldn't be more than an hour." It was extraordinary how possessive people were about their frontages. He walked away, conscious of the man's disapproval, and took a taxi to Covent Garden.

There was still some time before the end of *Swan Lake*. It was a mild evening, and the street was crowded with pedestrians congregating by the many new cafés and restaurants that had sprung up around the tourist centre created in the old covered markets. Cars picked their way between the sightseers, stopping frequently at zebra crossings, and the traffic moved slowly. It was not going to make a hasty departure easy.

Mark strolled up Bow Street, pausing to light a cigarette outside the police station. As he did so, a large Mercedes pulled up, with Bailey at the wheel. Their eyes met for a moment, and the young man winked. He reached down to the co-driver's seat and produced a smart grey chauffeur's hat, which he set on the back of his head at a jaunty angle. Mark smiled and nodded recognition, then crossed the road. Minutes later, the doors of the opera house were opened, and the audience began spilling out across the pavement.

He stood back, withstanding the temptation to go in immediately. The first people to leave were almost certainly hurrying to catch trains and buses, and there would be some delay before the final curtain calls were taken. After that, Irina still had to change and find her way back to the stage. As he entered the foyer, Mark could hear waves of applause coming from inside, and he walked slowly towards the carpeted inner corridor that circled the auditorium. The last of the applause died away, and the narrow space was suddenly filled with people. Moving against the flow of the crowd, he edged his way towards the small, inconspicuous door leading backstage, and waited.

Irina was standing in the shadows at the side of the stage. She was wearing a raincoat, under which he could see a dark sweater and a pair of jeans. She ran forward, taking both his hands in her own. Her eyes seemed very large. He had forgotten how beautiful she was.

"Did you bring your case?"

"Yes. Over here." She reached down.

"I'll take it." For a moment, she hesitated. "Quickly! It will make you less conspicuous if I carry it. I'll go first. Keep behind me, but stay within reach."

"Yes." Her face was very pale in the half-light. He had the impression that she was trembling.

For a moment, Mark took her hands again. "Are you all right?" Irina nodded silently, apparently unwilling to trust her voice. He smiled, looking past her shoulder towards the army of stagehands storing scenery. "Don't worry, nobody's watching you. Just follow me out of the theatre and across the street. There's a car waiting."

The corridor was less busy, and Mark walked slowly, moving in pace with the stragglers from the auditorium. He did not look round to see if Irina was following. Outside, Irina drew level, and he nodded towards the Mercedes. "Don't hurry."

He stood at the kerb, watching as she crossed the road, edging between two cars, then followed. Bailey remained at the driving wheel, and as soon as they were in, the big car slid forward smoothly, joining the line of traffic. Irina sat crouched in a corner, silent, her head down and her eyes closed.

As the car gathered speed, Bailey looked round with a broad grin. "Where to, guv?"

"Head over to Kingsway and up to the Marylebone Road." Mark took Irina's hands. "It's all right. We're on our way." She nodded, still saying nothing, leaning her body against his.

After several minutes, Bailey spoke again. "I don't want to worry you, and it may just be imagination, but I think we might have company."

"Are you sure?"

"No, but there's a car at the back of the one behind me that seems to be following the same route. Shall I double back?" As if sensing Irina's nervousness, he spoke casually. Mark wondered whether he might be enjoying the situation.

"Yes." He did not risk looking out of the back window. "What makes you think it's the same car?"

Bailey turned left at the next corner. "One of his headlights is slightly out of kilter. It caught my attention when we stopped for a light." After a moment, he added, "He still seems to be with us." He sounded cheerful.

Mark kept his hand on Irina's. She had not spoken, but her hand now gripped his tightly. "Keep circling."

Bailey manoeuvred the car through several more streets until they returned to their starting place. His voice had lost some of its lightness. "It's still there."

"How far?"

"Twenty yards, maybe less. They're keeping their distance, but there's nobody between us. We lost the other cars."

Mark settled back in the seat, gently moving Irina with him. "Why don't you see if you can lose them too."

Bailey chuckled. "That's what I had in mind!" He slowed the car slightly as approaching traffic lights changed. The driver behind would see his brake lights go on. At the last moment, he accelerated suddenly, and the big car leapt forward with a screech of tyres. Mark could feel the back of his seat pressing against his shoulders. At his side, Irina gave a sharp intake of breath.

"Damn!"

"What is it?"

Bailey's voice was tense. "He guessed what I was up to. Hang on." He cornered suddenly to his right, and the car skidded across the line of oncoming traffic. Irina was half thrown across Mark's lap, but she did not cry out. He put his arms around her shoulders, and she buried her face in his chest. Several car horns sounded behind him.

"How are we doing?" They were travelling fast down a darkened street towards the Marylebone Road.

"Not too well." Bailey spoke through clenched teeth as he braked heavily for the next set of traffic lights. "I can't throw them off yet. Maybe, if we can get out on some open road . . ."

"That'll take too long. The question is what they plan to do next." Irina pressed more tightly against him. Partly for her benefit, he added, "They just seem to be following us for the moment."

Bailey nodded. They had stopped for a red light, and his eyes met Mark's in the rear-view mirror. "They're holding their distance again. If they have anything else in mind . . ."

"Right." Mark cut across the young man's voice before he could elaborate further. Irina was shaking. "Make a left here, and I'll give you directions." The light changed to green, and Bailey moved off quickly. "You can slow down. There's no chance of losing them here, and I don't want to interest the local cops unless it becomes necessary." He smiled grimly. "Quentin would never forgive you!"

"What are we going to do, then?"

"I'll show you when we get there."

They were travelling west along narrow roads to the north of Oxford Street, and Bailey was forced to reduce speed. Mark gave occasional directions, keeping his voice calm. After a while, Irina stopped trembling.

"Are they still well behind us?"

"Yes. They seem to be on a surveillance job more than anything else. They must be at least twenty to thirty yards back."

"Good. Coming up towards the end of this street, there's a right-hand turn into a mews. It's quite a narrow opening."

"I think I know where you mean."

111

"My car's parked in there. If you'll stick in the entrance for a minute or two, we'll switch and leave at the other end. Kill the lights when you stop. I'd rather not perform in a spotlight!"

Bailey laughed. "Gotcha!" He swung the car into the narrow opening between the walls and braked to a sudden halt, blocking the entrance to the mews. Mark threw the door open and, grabbing Irina's case in one hand, pulled the girl after him. They were running across the darkened cobblestones of the mews by the time a pair of bright headlights appeared behind Bailey's car, throwing long shadows across the white-painted walls of the houses.

Mark had left his car unlocked, and within seconds they were inside. The engine started immediately, and he raced to the far end of the mews, where a similarly narrow exit led to the next street. He paused at the corner, watching in the rear-view mirror as the car behind Bailey slowly backed out into the street again, and waited until its headlights had disappeared round the corner. It gave him a brief moment out of the other's sight. Mark steered his car right, in the direction from which they had come. With any luck, his pursuers would assume that he had continued west. Resisting the urge to accelerate away, he drove slowly, at an almost stately pace. Five minutes later, after several changes of direction and constant checks in the rear-view mirror, he turned to Irina. "It's all right. I don't think they're with us any more."

She nodded slowly, watching the road in front. "Is Viktor in London?"

"Yes. He's at the Skyliner Hotel, near the airport."

"Are we going to him?"

"No, we can't. I was going to take you there, but the fact that we were followed from the opera house means that they know he's disappeared. We can't risk leading them back to him."

"But you said we were not being followed."

"We're not, but there's the chance that they could spot us again. We'll go to Viktor in the morning. Don't worry; he's quite safe."

Irina was silent, and Mark turned the car west again, following a route through quiet suburban streets, empty of traffic, where any other vehicle would make its presence immediately apparent.

After a long silence, Irina asked, "Where are we going?"

"To a country hotel, somewhere between Heathrow Airport and Windsor. I made a reservation there this afternoon."

112

"Why? Did you know that . . . ?"

"No, but it never hurts to have an alternative."

She watched his face. "You are very good at this, Mark. I would not have thought of such a thing."

"It seemed logical at the time. The hotel's very quiet and undisturbed. You'll be able to get a good night's sleep."

She smiled ruefully. "I do not think that is possible."

"You'll be surprised, once reaction sets in. It won't be a very long night, I'm afraid. I want to be at the airport hotel by eight."

"I do not mind. I want to be with Viktor. We are doing this together."

The hotel was set in several acres of carefully tended garden and parkland. It was a large country house that had been converted some years earlier, and it specialized in providing comfortable accommodation for sales conventions and marketing seminars held by various multinational corporations. Its proximity to the airport made it an ideal meeting-place. Mark suspected that it also offered a suitable hideaway for amorous couples anxious to avoid publicity. The pretty receptionist did not even appear to notice that although he had reserved two connecting rooms, they only had Irina's small travelling case between them.

"I'm afraid the dining-room's already closed, but room service can arrange some drinks and sandwiches for you."

"Good." He suddenly realized he was hungry. "We'll be leaving early in the morning."

"Really?" Glancing from Irina to Mark, she momentarily lost her composure.

"We have an early plane."

When they had eaten, Irina seemed at last to relax. A half-bottle of wine had brought colour to her cheeks, and she settled back in her chair, nursing a brandy glass. "I cannot believe what has happened to me, Mark. I am sorry I was so frightened. I could not say anything." She spoke with childlike solemnity. He had forgotten how appealing it was.

"You did very well."

"I do not think so. How did they know I would run away?"

"They must have guessed, as soon as Viktor went missing in Geneva. I was hoping there would be a longer delay before the news came through."

113

"What will happen now?"

"Hopefully, very little. In the morning, we'll drive over to the hotel so that I can collect my things. We're supposed to meet Viktor at the airport. He'll be at the Pan Am desk at ten o'clock."

"Why not sooner?"

"We thought it would be safer to wait until the last minute. In view of what's happened this evening, I'm sure that's right. Don't worry. He'll be there."

"Can I not even telephone him?"

"No. The American who is looking after him thought we should take every precaution possible not to make contact." He decided not to mention Murphy's planned "debriefing" session.

"Yes." She was silent for a moment, watching Mark intently. "I put myself totally in your hands, Mark. I trust you."

"In that case, I suggest you change and go to bed. It's been quite an evening, and you have a very long day ahead of you."

She stood, like an obedient child. A smile crossed her face. "I am still wearing my ballet costume under these jeans, and I did not take off all my make-up. I will have a bath. I must look horrible!"

"You look beautiful, Irina. I'll be next door if you need me."

Half an hour passed, and he tapped lightly on the connecting door as he opened it. To his surprise, Irina was sitting on the edge of the bed, the telephone held to her ear. When she saw him, she replaced the receiver.

"Who the hell are you calling?" His voice was harshly abrupt, startling her.

"The operator. I asked her to wake me tomorrow at seven o'clock. Did I do something wrong?"

"No." For a moment, he felt foolish. "I'm sorry if I shouted at you. I suppose my nerves are on edge. Please forgive me."

"There is nothing to forgive." She smiled. "In the ballet, I am accustomed to being shouted at!" She was wearing a simple cotton nightdress, and the contours of her body were clearly visible through the thin material. "You do not think we were followed here?"

"No."

"But you are not absolutely sure?" She walked to him.

"I'm as sure as I can be, Irina. If they followed us after we changed cars, they must have been experts. Did you lock your door?"

114

"Yes." She hesitated, moving closer. "Are you going to sleep, Mark? You have not changed your clothes." A thought struck her. "But all your clothes are in the other hotel!"

He smiled. "I'll manage."

Her voice was softer. "You promised we would see each other again, when you were in Moscow. I do not think you believed it would be like this."

"No, but I'm glad we have." He was conscious of a delicate perfume.

"And I am glad also." She drew closer, so that their bodies touched. "I have been waiting to see you again. For a while, I did not believe it would happen. I thought that you were being kind to me that evening." She smiled. "And you were a little drunk!"

"I seem to remember I was a lot drunk!"

"I did not mind. You were very polite." She watched him. "You will be in the room next door?"

"Yes."

Her eyes avoided his. "You would not prefer to . . . stay in this room?"

Mark smiled, putting his arms around her, and she clung to him for a moment. Her arms were strong. "I would prefer to, but I think it would be better for you to sleep."

"You do not want to be with me?" Her words were almost inaudible.

"I do, Irina, but this isn't the right time." He led her gently to the bed. "Tomorrow, when we meet Viktor and take the plane . . ."

"You will come with us?" Her hands still held his.

"Yes."

"Then I am happy. I thought we would say goodbye tomorrow morning."

"No. I'm going with you." He lightened his voice. "Now, you must sleep." She nodded slowly, then put her arms around his neck. Her mouth was warm, and her lips parted over his. She was no longer child-like, but a passionate woman. For a moment Mark held her tightly, feeling her body pressed against his, then he released her. She turned to get into bed, and he was again reminded of a small, obedient child. At the door, he said, "I'll be here, if you need me. Try to sleep."

In his room, he dialled the airport hotel, asking for Murphy's room. After a short pause, the operator returned.

115

"I'm sorry, but Mr. Murphy has asked not to be disturbed until eight o'clock tomorrow morning."

"Are you sure?"

"Yes, sir. He called a few minutes ago. Would you like to leave a message?"

"No, I'll try again in the morning."

Mark sat on the bed, his back resting against the headboard, staring at the empty screen of the television set facing him. It was odd of Murphy to refuse calls. Perhaps he intended a longer cross-examination of Viktor than he had indicated. Glancing at his watch, Mark saw that it was a little after one o'clock. He lit a cigarette. As the American had predicted, it was going to be a long night.

The morning was grey and overcast, with a light rain drifting in the wind. The neatly trimmed gardens surrounding the hotel looked damply forlorn, and a clump of late daffodils hung their heads sadly. As if reflecting the mood of the weather, Irina was subdued, seemingly preoccupied. She refused coffee, and Mark quickly signed the bill, using a credit card. He wondered whether she regretted her offer the night before or was perhaps offended by his rejection. He knew so little about her. They drove in silence through the misty countryside.

They reached the hotel slightly after eight. At the front desk, Mark used a house phone to call Murphy, but there was no reply.

"Has Mr. Murphy checked out?"

The clerk looked at his register. "Not yet, sir."

"There's no reply from his room."

"Perhaps he's having breakfast. The dining-room's over there, to your right."

"It doesn't matter. I'll try again later."

In the lift, Irina watched Mark's face. "What is the matter? Is something wrong?"

"I'm not sure."

"Has anything happened to Viktor?"

The doors of the lift opened, and Mark led the way to Murphy's room. He was about to knock on the door when he noticed that it was not fully closed.

The big American was lying flat on his back on the bed, fully clothed. He might have been asleep, but for the stillness of the body, the pallor

116

of the skin, and the eyes that stared blindly at the ceiling. The strange angle at which his head was tilted indicated the cause of his death. His neck had been broken.

Mark heard Irina's sudden cry of horror as he ran to the connecting door, throwing it open. The bedroom was empty. Viktor's case lay on the bed and some of his clothes were spilling from it. He looked in the small adjoining bathroom, but it, too, was empty. There was no sign of Viktor. From a radio built into the wall next to the bed, canned music was playing softly.

9

Waiting in Viktor's room for Quentin to arrive, Irina sat close to Mark on the edge of the bed. She huddled forward, her chin resting on clenched fists whose knuckles were stretched white. There were tears on her cheeks. "I told him we should not try, but he wouldn't listen to me. Oh Mark, they have taken him away. I will never see Viktor again!" She began to cry, and Mark held her in his arms.

"There's still a chance we can get him out. They can't force him to leave England, especially if we can find where they're holding him. After what they've done to Murphy, Quentin may offer him asylum. I wish to God we knew what happened here."

"Isn't it clear?"

"I'm not sure. Why did they kill him?" He held her by the shoulders. "Irina, I need to know. Is there anything about Viktor that he hasn't told us?"

"What do you mean?"

"Why is it so important that he should be returned to Russia? Why kill a man just to force Viktor to return?"

"Mark, I don't know anything."

"You're not keeping information back?"

"No." Suddenly, she was angry. "He is my brother, Mark—my little brother. That is all I know about him! You talked to him, Mark. You know why he wanted to leave the Soviet Union. He had been forbidden to travel again, and he wanted freedom—for both of us." Her eyes brimmed again. "What is this information that you are talking about?"

"I don't know. I'm sorry, Irina. I didn't intend to bully you. It's just that I don't understand . . ."

"That man, the American, he must have tried to stop them." Her face was set. "You don't understand my people, Mark. You have only seen them when they are showing their best behaviour for Western visitors. At heart, they are animals—murderers! You don't understand what it is like to live in my country. Viktor and I used music and ballet to escape from the reality of our lives. But we knew. That is why Viktor wanted us to leave. He was prepared to take the risks, even when I told him we would never escape. Oh God, I will never see him again!" She was hysterical, and Mark held her close, whispering in her ear to soothe her.

When there was a sharp rap on the door, she started, her face fearful. Mark silently motioned to her to go into the bathroom, and walked to the door. He felt vulnerable without some form of weapon. "Who is it?"

"Sharpe."

Quentin Sharpe and Mike Figlio were outside. As he entered, Quentin said, "I called Mike and picked him up on my way here. Where's Murphy?" Mark led the way to the connecting door, standing aside to let them enter. "I haven't touched anything, except to put a DO NOT DISTURB card on the door." He remained behind. He had no wish to see the American again.

Quentin returned a moment later, closing the door and leaving Figlio inside. He had paled slightly. "Broken neck." Mark nodded. "Whoever did that must have been pretty strong. He was a big man."

"There could have been more than one, and they could have pulled a gun on him. I had the impression he was carrying one himself."

Sharpe shook his head. "I wouldn't know. We can check with Figlio later. Where's Kaverin's sister?"

"In the bathroom. She's terrified."

"I'm not surprised. You'd better get her out." For a moment, Quentin's self-control lapsed. "Damn it, Mark, why the hell did you call me?"

"Who else could I call? I don't have a bloody security directory!

With Murphy lying there and Viktor missing, you were the only contact I had."

"I suppose so. This whole thing's turned into a bloody mess! I don't know why the hell I let you talk me into getting involved!"

"Oh, come off it, Quentin! You were only too pleased to score a few points with the CIA in return for future favours. Your whole disinterested party act didn't fool anyone, including the late Mr. Murphy."

Quentin eyed him coolly, in control again. "You'd better bring out Miss Kaverin before she suffocates in that tiny loo, or this place will end up looking like a morgue."

When Irina joined them, she seemed to have made an effort to hold back her hysteria. Her face and hair were damp, presumably from cold water in the hand-basin, but she had applied a trace of lipstick. She shook hands gravely with Quentin, who motioned her to an armchair. She appeared calm, but Mark could see her fingers digging into the fabric of the chair.

Quentin perched on the edge of the bed, crossing one well-tailored trouser leg over the other. "I'm very sorry about the circumstances surrounding your brother's disappearance, Miss Kaverin. Can you offer any ideas?"

She looked surprised. "It is clear. They have taken him away. That is the only explanation possible."

"Yes, I suppose so, although I don't think he's shown up at any of the usual locations."

"What does that mean?"

"We try to . . . monitor the movements of your countrymen, Miss Kaverin, and nothing unusual has been reported. So, unless they are using a house we haven't yet found out about, I can at least tell you that your brother has not been seen entering any buildings that are occupied by members of the Russian government." Irina looked at Mark questioningly, but his face gave no response. "So, we must assume either that they have him hidden away somewhere or that they're riding around in a vehicle, waiting until the next flight to Moscow." Irina's hands moved to her mouth, but Quentin continued smoothly, "However, that doesn't necessarily mean that we'll permit them to take him. He may very well be a material witness to what happened to Mr. Murphy," he gave a slight nod in the direction of the other room, "in which case, he will have to stay here to give evidence, if necessary."

Irina grasped at the thought. "Please, you must not allow them to take Viktor back to Russia. You do not know what that would mean for him."

"I have a pretty good idea, Miss Kaverin. If it's at all possible, we will not allow him to leave, even though he's never officially entered this country. It's a rather delicate situation." He leaned forward. "What interests me more, Miss Kaverin, is why anyone would want to go to the length of killing a man in order to recapture your brother." He stared at Irina, who looked helplessly towards Mark. "Why is your brother so important to them?"

"I don't know! Mark has asked me the same question. Viktor is just a pianist—a great pianist. He has never been interested in politics or . . ." She searched for words. "He is just my brother."

The room was silent. In the distance, Mark thought he could hear the sound of jet engines through the double-glazed windows. Then he noticed that they were not completely closed. Turning to Quentin, he asked, "What happens now?"

Sharpe looked at his watch. "Alan Grunfeld should be here shortly. He said he would make it before nine." He looked up at Irina and smiled. "Alan is a colleague of Mr. Murphy's. In view of the fact that you were with Mr. Holland yesterday evening and all last night, I see no reason to keep you here. So I've suggested to Mr. Grunfeld that he accompany you on the eleven o'clock flight to New York, as arranged."

"No!" The word was like a cry.

"What do you mean?"

"I do not leave without Viktor."

Quentin flushed slightly. "I don't think you understand the situation, Miss—"

"You cannot make me leave." Her jaw was set. "Until I know where Viktor is, I am staying here." She turned. "Please, Mark, explain to him!"

Quentin stood up. "I don't think you have much choice in the matter—"

"Yes, I have a choice!" Irina's eyes blazed. "You cannot make me leave without Viktor! You cannot do it! I am here legally, with the Bolshoi Ballet. You cannot make me fly to America."

"But that's ridiculous! As for your being here legally—"

"I have done nothing wrong, and I will not leave before I know where

120

Viktor is. If you try to make me take an aeroplane to New York, I will tell them that you kidnapped me!"

"Don't be a fool!" Quentin was ruffled.

Irina looked from Quentin to Mark. She was like a trapped animal. "You cannot force me to go. Until you find Viktor, I will stay!"

Quentin was angry. "In that case, we hand you back to the Russian authorities. Is that what you want?"

"If necessary, yes. I will tell them you kidnapped me and tried to smuggle us both into America. I will tell everyone it was a plot to discredit my government. It may help Viktor if I do!"

There was a long silence while Quentin walked to the window and gazed across the rain-streaked fields. "Very well. Until we have news of your brother, you may stay. I think you'd better calm down. When we know something more definite, you will have to decide what you want to do. I should warn you, however, that if the Russian authorities make representations to us, we are not in a position to grant you more than a temporary stay in Britain." He turned to Mark. "Have you any suggestions?"

Mark was about to reply, when Figlio re-entered the room. The American said nothing, but he was visibly moved. Returning to Quentin, Mark said, "I can't tell you anything. I tried to call Murphy a little after one this morning, to say we were safe. I chose a different hotel after we were followed . . ."

"Bailey told me what happened. Go on."

"I was very surprised when I called here. Murphy had told the hotel operator to hold all calls until eight o'clock this morning." Quentin's eyebrows were raised. "That was the only call I made. First, you had made it clear that you wanted to be left out of things. Otherwise, I might have tried you. Secondly, I didn't want to risk revealing my cover, no matter how remote the chance. It was late, and I decided to wait until this morning."

"Then you didn't speak to him?"

"I couldn't. The operator wouldn't put me through."

"I see. That's odd." Quentin was thoughtful. He turned to Figlio. "Is that a normal practice for your people, Mike?"

Figlio shrugged. "Under normal circumstances, no, but it was an abnormal situation. He had to debrief Kaverin overnight, which didn't give him much time. Maybe he didn't want to be disturbed."

"I see."

Figlio's anger came to the surface. "Jack knew what he was doing, and he could look after himself. I hope I find the bastards who fixed him!"

Mark watched him. "Why do you think they killed him?"

"I don't know, for Christ's sake! He knew how to handle himself."

Quentin's voice was hard. "Not this time, it seems." Figlio glowered at him, but said nothing. "What do you think, Mark?"

"I don't know. We spoke for a minute or two after you left, and he gave me the impression that the whole matter was little more than routine as far as he was concerned. If you must know, he just about confessed that he was overplaying his irritation with you for giving him so little time with Viktor, more out of frustration with Washington than out of any real need to debrief a runaway pianist." He avoided Irina's gaze.

Her voice was soft, in strong contrast with the way she had previously been speaking. "But that is all my brother is."

Quentin frowned. "Then why kill Murphy?"

"Because my people can be very brutal." Her voice was sad. "You do not really understand them. If Mr. Murphy tried to fight them, they would not hesitate to kill him."

"You're probably right. He might have been careless. He was drinking when we saw him yesterday afternoon."

Mark looked directly at Figlio. "I noticed the Scotch bottle this morning. It's almost empty." Figlio glared at him.

Quentin nodded. "Perhaps he took on more than he could manage. Then again, he might have stumbled across something unexpected. I wonder if we'll ever know."

There was a brief knock on the door. Quentin opened it, ushering in a thickset man in his early forties who had disguised his receding hairline by brushing the hair across his forehead. He was dressed in a dark blue blazer and slacks, with an open-necked shirt. Quentin introduced Alan Grunfeld and, after a moment, led him into the other room. Figlio followed, closing the door behind him.

Irina ran to Mark, her arms grasping his waist. "Please, Mark, you will not let them make me leave? I was telling the truth when I threatened to say that they kidnapped me. I cannot leave before I know about Viktor."

"What will you do if the Russians are holding him? If Quentin refuses to let him stay, they'll take him back to Russia."

"I know."

"And you?"

She shrugged helplessly, sitting on the edge of the bed. "I cannot think about it until I know what has happened to my brother." She seemed to retreat within herself.

The three men returned, leaving the door open. Quentin was speaking to Grunfeld. "I think it would be better if we kept the police out of this for the moment. I can lend you some people from the Department, if . . ."

"Thank you. I believe we have specialists who can look after it, if it's all the same with you. I'll make a call in a few minutes."

"As you wish." Quentin smiled at Mark. "You were right about the whisky bottle. I might not have noticed that."

Grunfeld approached Irina, eyeing her cautiously. "Miss Kaverin, I've spoken to Quentin here, and he's indicated that he's prepared to let you stay on for a while, until we learn the exact location of your brother." She nodded, her eyes lowered. Grunfeld was embarrassed. "I just wanted to say that the United States is still prepared to offer you a home if you so wish. However, before we do, I think we have to come to some sort of signed agreement that it is your express wish to be granted entry and that you're doing so of your own free will and not as the result of coercion on the part of any person or persons known to you." Irina stared at him, slightly puzzled. It was apparent to Mark that, somewhere in his past, Mr. Grunfeld had taken a law degree. "Now, Mr. Sharpe here tells me that you're not prepared to leave London immediately, so—"

His speech was interrupted by the persistent ringing of the telephone in Murphy's room. Figlio said, "I'll get it." Grunfeld was about to begin again, when the American reappeared in the doorway. The urgency in his voice made them turn towards him. "Mark—it's for you."

"Who is it?"

"He says he's Viktor Kaverin, and he'll only talk to you, but you have to make it fast. He's at a public phone."

It seemed to Mark that, for an instant, everyone in the room froze. They came to life with a babble of voices. As he ran towards the phone, he was conscious of Irina calling to him.

"Viktor?" The line was crackly.

"Yes, Mark."

"Where in God's name are you?"

"At the London airport. Didn't Mr. Murphy tell you what happened?"

Mark hesitated. Irina was standing anxiously at his side, waiting to speak. Beyond her, Quentin was watching from the doorway. "No, he didn't say anything. Why are you at the airport?"

"It is as we arranged when I ran away last night."

"Ran away? What are you talking about?"

Viktor sounded impatient. "Mr. Murphy will explain it to you. I am surprised he has not done so already. Is Irina with you, Mark? Is she safe?"

"Yes."

"Thank God! May I speak to her?"

"In a minute. Viktor, what happened last night?"

There was a pause. When he continued, Kaverin kept his voice low. "Some men came to the hotel."

"What men?" At Mark's side, Irina gestured to be allowed to speak, but he waved her away irritably. Quentin watched impassively, leaning against the door-frame.

"They were representatives of my country."

"How do you know?"

"Mr. Murphy told me so. There was a call on the telephone from downstairs. He told me there were two men from my country on their way to see him. Didn't he tell you this?"

"Not yet. Go on."

"It was a great shock, Mark, and we had to make a quick decision. You see, we didn't know whether they were looking for me, or whether they had discovered that Irina had disappeared. You are sure she is safe?"

"She's standing here with me. What did you do?"

"Mr. Murphy said it was too dangerous for me to hide next door, so I told him I would find a way out of the hotel and call him from the airport in the morning. He did not like the idea, but there was very little time to discuss it. The men were already coming to his room. He gave me some English money and told me to go. I was very frightened. I do not understand why he has not told you."

124

Mark ignored the comment. "How did you escape?"

"We waited until they knocked on the door of Mr. Murphy's room. He told me he would steal them. I think that was the word." Mark did not bother to correct him. "Then I went to my room and climbed out of the window. It was not difficult. It is only one floor up, and there was a ledge from which I could hang. It was quite easy for me. I used to jump from much higher when I was training." He was silent for a moment. "I think I will need more money soon. How long do these calls last?"

"I don't know. Do you have more coins?"

"Yes, I have many. I will put them in." After another frustrating pause, he asked, "Do you hear me?"

"Yes. What happened next?"

"I was frightened, Mark."

"Yes. You said that before."

"I was also very tired. It made me panic."

"How do you mean?"

"I realize I should have waited and returned to my room when they had gone. When they saw that Irina and I were not with Mr. Murphy, the men would have left again. I should have watched the entrance of the hotel."

"Perhaps."

"But I was afraid they might wait. It all happened very quickly, and I was confused."

"What did you do?"

"I lay in the dark by the wall of the hotel for a long time. Then I ran round to the other side of the building and crossed the road into a field. I was afraid they might see me from a window."

"You seem to have been thinking very clearly."

"Maybe it was not necessary. I ran through more fields until I came to the edge of the airport, where there is a wire fence. I walked along a path by the fence until I found the road that goes into the airport. There is a long tunnel there. I ran through it as quickly as I could." He paused again. "I think that was the worst moment of all, Mark. I was sure that at any moment a car would come after me. It was like a bad dream. But nothing happened. It was too late."

"Go on." Irina had approached him again, and Mark cupped his hand over the mouthpiece. "He's all right, but I must talk to him. I'll let you speak when I've finished." She nodded, biting at her lower lip. Behind her, Quentin watched but made no move to interrupt.

"The airport was very quiet. There was nobody anywhere. I did not realize it would be closed at night."

"Where did you go?"

"To the car-park that is next to Terminal One."

"The car-park?"

"Yes, Mark. I hoped I could find a car that was not locked. It was cold. When I left the hotel, I pulled a leather jacket from my bag, but it was still very cold in the night. All the cars I tried were locked, but I found an old van with the back doors tied together with some rope. It was better for me. I was able to lie down and sleep."

"Is that where you've been until now?"

"No. I awoke at seven o'clock."

"What did you do?"

He laughed nervously. "It was difficult to sleep and very uncomfortable." It seemed to Mark that Viktor's accent had become more pronounced. Perhaps it was tiredness. "When I saw new cars arriving and people going into the terminal, I went inside to find a telephone. It must have been about seven-thirty. I telephoned Mr. Murphy, but the operator said he would not take any calls until eight o'clock. Then I called you, Mark, but they told me you were not there. I was very worried. Are you sure Irina is safe?"

"Yes. You can speak to her in a moment."

"Thank God! When the hotel said you were not there, I did not know what to think. I was afraid you had been stopped, and that . . . Please, can I speak to her?"

"Very soon. I must know everything that happened."

"Yes. I understand. As soon as it was eight o'clock, I called Mr. Murphy again, but they told me there was no reply. I asked them to try three times! They thought maybe he was eating breakfast, and said I should call back later. Then I tried your room again, but there was still nothing."

"No. We were out." Viktor must have telephoned Murphy within minutes of his arrival. "What did you do?"

"I knew I must wait, so I went to the men's lavatory." He laughed again. "It was like Geneva, Mark, but they have machines which sell razors and toothbrushes, so I was able to wash and shave quite well. At

126

first, I was worried to be in the airport, but I saw that Terminal One is only for British Airways. The men who came to see Mr. Murphy know he is American, and I took the risk that they would not look in this building. I am still very tired, Mark, and I was hungry and cold. I ate some breakfast while I waited. Now, please can I speak to Irina?"

"Yes. One more question, Viktor. How did these men know where to find Murphy?"

There was a long silence. "I do not know, Mark. Perhaps they watch him every day and were suspicious when he went to the hotel. Has he not discussed any of this with you?"

"No." Mark hesitated. "Not yet. We only arrived a few minutes ago." Irina was watching him curiously. "I'll put Irina on now, but I'll need to speak to you again. Can you call me back in about ten minutes?"

"Why?"

"Because we have to decide what to do next."

"But I thought we were leaving. Mr. Sharpe said that we must—"

"I know, but I have to make sure that all the plans are the same. Besides, we have to arrange a rendezvous. Will you call me back?"

"Yes, in ten minutes. I will have to change some more money. I have used all my coins."

"All right." He turned to Irina, keeping the mouthpiece covered. "Don't tell him about Murphy." She looked puzzled. "I don't want to upset him further, Irina. He's all right, but he's had a very bad night. We can explain everything when we see him. OK?"

She nodded. Grasping the phone, she turned her back on the room. "Viktor?" She listened in silence, then spoke softly in Russian.

From the doorway, Quentin beckoned to Mark. "You'd better bring us up to date. Where is Kaverin, and what the hell's going on?"

Mark closed the door on Irina and faced the three men. He started to recount Kaverin's story, trying to remember every detail. When he described how Viktor had climbed through the window, Figlio and Grunfeld exchanged glances. Watching their faces, Quentin interrupted. "That's somewhat unconventional, isn't it? The man was supposed to be in his care, but he let him jump out of a window, with a hasty arrangement to talk again in the morning. Then he told the operator to hold all calls until eight o'clock!"

Mark nodded. "Always assuming that he was the one who spoke to the operator. I have the feeling your people are going to need to talk to the staff about what happened last night."

Figlio grunted. "It's crazy! Jack was a pro. What the hell got into him?"

"A large amount of whisky, by the look of it." Quentin was enjoying himself. "I'm curious also to know why Murphy didn't have a partner. Isn't that unusual?"

Grunfeld cleared his throat. "Under normal circumstances, yes. Kaverin arrived at the wrong moment. We're a little below full operational power at the moment, and it seemed like a pretty routine situation." He looked uncomfortable. "I authorized Jack to look after it. Mike was to stand by if Jack wanted him."

"I did stand by." Figlio was defensive. "Jack said he didn't need me."

Mark continued without further interruptions. When he had finished, the others were silent.

Quentin eyed him thoughtfully. "Why didn't you tell Kaverin about Murphy?"

"Because he sounded stretched as tight as a drum. Look, he jumped ship yesterday morning in Geneva. Since then, he's been chasing across unknown countryside at night, dossing down in an empty van, expecting at any minute to find Russian agents bearing down on him, and going half out of his mind because there was nobody here to answer the phone when he called in. You seem to forget that he's a young concert pianist on the run, not some sort of hardened criminal. He was scared stupid and terrified that his sister was in trouble, because he couldn't reach me. I didn't add Murphy to the list because I didn't want him running amok in the London airport before we retrieved him."

"I suppose you're right." Quentin stared at Grunfeld. "If you'll forgive my saying so, Alan, this whole business is a bloody mess!" Grunfeld looked fixedly at the carpet. "What exactly are you expecting me to do about Jack Murphy?"

"I would have thought the strongest protest—unofficially, of course—was in order."

Quentin was contemptuous. "On what grounds? What proof do we have? If Kaverin is to be believed, he wasn't a witness to anything. All we know is that Murphy *said* there were two Russians on their way up to see him, after which Kaverin did a bunk and showed up this morning in Heathrow. I'm not saying it didn't happen, but we can't prove a damned thing! Anyway, we can hardly call Kaverin as a witness. Officially, he was never in this country."

"That was your decision, not ours."

"I'm fully aware of it. I'm simply stating that, on the face of it, we have no grounds for complaint, no matter what we know or think we know."

Grunfeld tried another approach. "We thought you'd be keeping an eye on this hotel—"

"I made it patently clear that we weren't involved."

"Nevertheless—"

"No. I meant what I said. I gave you twenty-four hours, during which you were supposed to clear Mr. Kaverin, collect his sister, and see them on their way. Hopefully, you still can, but Mr. Murphy's your problem, not mine." He walked over to the window and gazed out. Figlio watched with a look of pure hatred, and it occurred to Mark that he would not be a good enemy to make. There was too much Sicilian in his genes. Quentin apparently did not care. True to form, he was ensuring that the Department was not involved. It was a convoluted but familiar method of maintaining a clear conscience.

Grunfeld shrugged slowly. "I think we touched on this earlier, before we knew what had happened. A couple of our people will be around later to take Jack out of here. I seem to remember your offering help, but let it pass."

"Very well." Quentin might have said more, but Irina re-entered the room.

"Poor Viktor! He has had a terrible night. Please, can we go to him soon?"

Mark looked at Quentin. "I told him to call back in ten minutes. Have you decided what you want to do?"

"I've made it very clear. We want both of them out of here as soon as possible. Where they go is partly up to Alan. Are you still prepared to take them?"

Grunfeld nodded. "I guess we'll have to do any processing after they've arrived." Looking at Irina, he added, "I'll still need your signature to the document we discussed. My government does not wish to . . . to find itself accused of abducting foreign nationals against their will."

Irina bowed her head. "I was hoping you would forgive me for what I said earlier. I did not know what had happened to Viktor, and I was frightened."

Grunfeld softened his voice. "I understand."

Quentin seemed relieved. "That's settled, then."

Grunfeld smiled thinly. "Everything can be resolved quite amicably." He relaxed for a moment. "Would you believe it, but a White House spokesman has already contacted us to say that the President thinks it would be a great gesture if Viktor plays that recital for him. We thought he'd wait a while and ask for a White House recital, but he wants him to play Carnegie Hall as a kind of curtain-raiser to the Statue of Liberty celebrations." He spoke with reverential awe.

Mark smiled. "That's a bit premature, isn't it? I thought the festivities weren't supposed to take place until July. They're going to have to keep Viktor under wraps for three months."

"I guess they thought it would be appropriate because he's an immigrant in the centennial year."

Quentin's voice was cool. "He's not exactly arriving with the steerage on Ellis Island!"

"Maybe not, but it's an important gesture. That newspaper piece seems to have stuck."

"Maybe so. I had the impression he made the statement as a gesture of international goodwill towards all men and that sort of thing. Under the circumstances, it's hardly going to generate much of that!"

Irina was angry. "That is not fair! Viktor was speaking from his heart when he said that. You are distorting the truth!"

Quentin looked at her pityingly. "I think, Miss Kaverin, that when Viktor chose to leave Russia this way, the goodwill ceased to apply. It also seems reasonably clear to me that, had he not said it, he would not find himself being given such an enthusiastic welcome, so you'll have to balance one against the other."

"But they are using him!"

"And vice versa." He looked at his watch. "He should be calling back in the next minute or two. I suggest you tell him to stay inside Terminal One until exactly ten o'clock. Then he's to go downstairs to arrivals and wait near the taxi rank. Alan will pick him up there. All right?" Grunfeld nodded. "In the meantime, I suggest that Mike here drive Miss Kaverin and Mark to Terminal Three, where Bailey will be waiting."

"Our baggage," Irina interrupted nervously. "Viktor reminded me that we must remember to bring his bag to the airport."

"Of course. We'd hardly leave it behind."

Figlio was contemptuous. "He's always so goddamned concerned with his baggage!"

"You don't understand. It contains the only possessions he could bring out of Russia. It is very important to him."

"Yeah. He told us so before."

Quentin's voice betrayed his impatience. "Let's get this sorted out before he rings, for goodness sake! Miss Kaverin can take her luggage and Viktor's. Bailey will have someone standing by to look after it. None of you will be going through immigration. At the risk of repeating myself, with the exception of Mr. Grunfeld, you have never officially been here." He permitted himself a fleeting smile. "Neither, officially, have I!"

The rain was falling steadily as Figlio drove them in silence to the terminal. Seated in the back of the car, next to Irina, Mark watched the hypnotic swing of the windscreen wipers.

"I'm sorry about Jack Murphy. Had you known him for a long time, Mike?"

The American shrugged his shoulders, keeping his eyes fixed on the road. "Not long—three, four years maybe."

"Did he have a family?"

"I wouldn't know." His voice was resentful.

"I'm sorry I brought up the matter of the whisky."

"Forget it. He goofed, and I guess he paid for it. I'd seen him drink before. It was a dumb thing to do. I guess I'm still surprised. I always thought Jack knew how to take care of himself."

"They could have caught him off guard—a sudden whiff of mace or God knows what else. There are some pretty sophisticated devices around. I suppose your people will be able to tell later."

"Maybe." Figlio relapsed into silence, unwilling to talk further, and Mark settled back against the seat. He found that Irina's hand was in his. She clasped it tightly.

They were in a small, airless waiting-room, somewhere near the international-departures lounge, when Grunfeld brought Viktor in. The young

131

man looked pale and tired, with dark patches beneath red-rimmed eyes. Caked mud spattered his shoes, and his trousers were creased and stained. With a small cry Irina ran to him, throwing her arms around him, her cheek pressed tightly to his. Standing together, holding one another, their eyes closed, they looked like reunited lovers. At length, Viktor released his sister and walked over to hug Mark.

"Thank God I am here! There were times during the night when I wondered whether I would ever see any of you again." He laughed. "I wondered what would happen to me if the owner of the van came back to the car-park. I imagined myself being arrested by the English police!" Irina rejoined him, and he put an arm round her shoulders. "She has told me about your own adventures last night, Mark. Thank you. We both owe you our freedom. Where is Mr. Murphy? I wanted to thank him too."

"He couldn't be here, Viktor. I'll explain later."

"I will write to him as soon as we reach New York."

Alan Grunfeld stood at Mark's side. He appeared to have cheered up considerably. "I guess we'll be boarding shortly. Mr. Bailey will come for us when the plane's ready." As if to prove this, he produced boarding cards from an inner pocket. "I have a whole bunch of papers for you folks to fill in, but we can do all that once we're airborne. We can switch seats while I fill in the various documents and questionnaires. That way, we can process everything the moment you land." He smiled apologetically. "I guess every country has its red tape."

Viktor nodded solemnly. "Thank you, Mr. Grunfeld. We are both very grateful to you too. It is a very important moment for us, to be starting a new life. From now on, we are in your hands!"

Grunfeld looked delighted and beamed at Mark. Viktor had turned on his boyish charm with great facility, throwing off the tension and pressures of the previous twenty-four hours. The American patted him on the shoulder happily. "Don't you worry about a thing from here on in. You're among friends."

Bailey put his head round the door. "All set?"

Mark smiled. "Thanks again for last night."

"Any time." He grinned mischievously and from behind his back produced the chauffeur's hat, which he set squarely on his head. He saluted. "New York coming up!"

New York

10

"I must say, Mark, you sure have a talent for picking 'em!" Abe Sincoff reached into a humidor on his desk and selected an illegally imported Cuban cigar, sniffing its length with pleasant anticipation. "For an aspiring young pianist, hoping to make his mark on the American musical scene, Viktor Kaverin makes Greta Garbo look like a topless starlet at the Cannes Film Festival! I never saw anyone so camera-shy."

"He's nervous, Abe. I think he also believes he should be judged by his talent rather than his notoriety."

Abe busied himself with a match, going through the ritual of lighting the Havana. "He's also anonymous at the moment. The only picture anyone could come up with was taken five years ago, when he was wearing his hair like a convict. We'd better arrange a photo session this week."

Mark nodded. "Viktor's becoming accustomed to his new life, Abe. After all, he only arrived two days ago, and he had a pretty frightening time getting here. Coming from the sort of totalitarian world he's known, he finds everything new and unexpected, and I don't think he's ready for it yet. You forget how awesome New York is for anyone the first time. His only experience of the West so far has been Bergen and Lausanne, with some very unpleasant memories of Geneva and London airports. It's not surprising that he should retreat into a shell."

"I'm not complaining, kid. Most of the young hopefuls we meet can't get enough publicity. This is the age of overexposure." He sighed. "Why do you think there are no more Hollywood legends? In the good old days, you only saw Clark Gable or Spencer Tracy when you paid your nickel and went to the movies. Now every actor, author, musician, politician, or whoever is there at the flick of a switch, doing the rounds on radio and TV, plugging whatever it is they're trying to sell." He scowled. "And a lot of them aren't so bright or articulate when the microphone's switched on. I like the idea of surrounding Viktor with a little mystery for a change. I just hope to God he delivers when he sits down to play."

"He will, Abe. I can guarantee that. I've heard him four times now, and he seems to get better every time."

"Yeah, so you said." He inhaled smoke, coughing slightly. "Let's hope a couple of critics agree."

They were sitting in Abe's small office, high above Fifty-seventh Street. The inner sanctum of Sincoff Presentations, Inc. was quite sparsely furnished with a small desk, which Abe left bare, and several comfortable leather armchairs. Only the walls were crowded, covered with photographs of musicians. They were mostly formal portraits, with the artists posed against pianos or holding instruments, and they were all signed. There was hardly a square inch of wall space left, and Mark had often wondered in the past whether some of the older pictures were discreetly removed to allow room for newcomers. It was unlikely. Abe was very loyal.

Slanting sunlight filtering into the room heralded the first breath of spring, although Mark knew that it might be short-lived. He remembered times in late March when seventy-degree balminess had been followed within twenty-four hours by two feet of snow or a heat wave. The weather was as changeable as the city, and at this time of the year, one never knew what to expect.

"I still can't figure how they got on to him—or me—so quickly." Abe frowned. "The goddam phone hasn't stopped ringing for two days— almost as soon as he landed. *Time* wants to do a piece about him, the *Village Voice* asked for an interview, and NBC wants him for the 'Today' show. Merv Griffin's office called twice this morning. Christ, in the ordinary way you couldn't get to first base with a classical pianist!"

"But not, apparently, one who wants to play for the President."

"Right. I wonder if he realized what he was doing when he said that."

"So do I. I'm beginning to think that little speech is going to haunt him."

"Yeah." Abe's normally cheerful face was sombre.

"What's the matter, Abe? It's not like you to complain when the world comes knocking at your door. I would have thought you'd be delighted."

"I don't know, kid. I don't feel good about it, and I can't even tell you why. I guess I'm beginning to feel old."

"Never!"

Abe sighed again, staring at the thin, straight line of smoke ascending from his cigar. "I guess it comes to all of us in the end. These days, I find myself remembering the past with a kind of terrible regret, wishing they still wrote lyrics like Ira Gershwin or Lorenz Hart, if that makes any sense to you." Mark nodded silently. "Yesterday, in the car, they were playing *Der Rosenkavalier*, and I'll be goddamned if I didn't start crying, right there on the corner of Lexington Avenue and Seventy-third!" Abe shook his head in wonder. "It's the same with TV. I'm watching some God-awful soap opera, and suddenly I'm choking back tears because the kid with the big jugs has discovered she's got multiple sclerosis just when they picked her for the softball team!" He blinked. "I'm ageing, and I don't like it."

"That's not age, Abe. You're mellowing."

"Yeah. Well, it's bad for business." He looked at his cigar gloomily. "I'm supposed to give these up too. Myra talked to Dr. Frascati, and he finked on me." He grinned suddenly. "I must be the only Jew in New York who goes to a guinea doctor!" Abe affected an unbridled racism as part of his hard-boiled New York persona, embracing all ethnic backgrounds, colours, and creeds, although Mark knew him to be a generously kind man who had never shown any form of discrimination in his life. It was part of his New York façade. Still, it was disquieting to see him so morose. Perhaps it was just the end of a long winter and another busy season.

"Never mind, Abe. I'm sure you'll snap out of it. I've been here half an hour, and you haven't even told me a joke."

"You're right." He brightened. "Did I tell you about the guy who was standing on the corner of the street, beating a kid around the head?" Mark shook his head dutifully. "So, someone goes up to him and says, 'Hey, mister, why are you beating up on that kid?' The guys looks at him and says, 'I'm a double-bass player, and he loosened one of my strings.' 'Yeah, but why are you hitting him so hard?' " Abe scowled, fully in character. " 'He won't tell me which one!' "

135

Mark laughed. Abe always had a new joke. "That's better."

"I guess so." He smiled. "This is the toughest, cruellest, feistiest, most exciting city in the world, and I love it. And if you ever breathe a whisper of what I just told you, I'll break every bone in your English fairy body!" Mark laughed, relieved to see him back in his normal form. "Speaking of Jews, what the hell's got into Viktor over the New York Israel Foundation? They offered to sponsor his career, but he turned them down."

"Really? Why?"

"Who knows? Arnold Silverman spoke to them, and they offered to take him to Israel on a tour. Arnold said he'd persuade Avram Gutman to play a recital with him. That's a hell of an opportunity for a young pianist, but he said no. He wants to stay here for a while and won't play Israel for the moment. Arnold was offended. He could be very influential."

Mark nodded. Arnold Silverman, one of the world's leading violinists, gave much of his time to sponsoring young musicians and helping their careers, and his many ties with Israel made him one of the most powerful figures in both of the world's two largest Jewish communities, of which Israel was the second biggest. A sponsorship offer from Arnold was like a royal command. One did not treat it lightly.

"Is Viktor Jewish? I hadn't thought about it."

Abe smiled again, regaining his normal good humour. "All musicians are Jewish, especially Russian ones! Otherwise, turning down Arnold would be a real insult! Don't you know the definition of a Jew, Mark? It's somebody who doesn't have to be more anti-Semitic than absolutely necessary! Listen, maybe you should have a quiet talk with Viktor about this foundation offer. It's a hell of a starter for his new career. Forget Russia. Besides, I'd sooner he didn't get on the wrong side of Arnold, and he can't trade on his defection for ever. Talk to him, will you? He'll listen to you."

"Yes." Mark was thoughtful. "I'll take it up with him when I see him."

"Good. I've arranged a meeting with the City Ballet, to talk about Irina."

"Can you help her?"

Abe nodded, his eyes half closed, and shrugged with that combination of omniscience and *Weltschmerz* that characterized his people, indicating that there was nothing he could not do. There were few people in the New York world of music and the arts that Abe did not know, and his list of contacts was encyclopaedic. "I can't promise anything sensational, but they'll certainly give her an audition. The name Bolshoi is still good for a few points. These days, I'm told Kirov would be better, but we'll see what can be done."

"Thank you, Abe. I don't think they realize how lucky they are to have you on their side."

Abe scowled. "Better they should have Arnold and the New York Israel Foundation!"

A few minutes later, Shirley, Abe's elderly and devoted secretary, announced that a Mr. Craig Sherman was waiting to see him.

"Sherman? I don't know any Sherman."

Shirley looked ruffled. She was a large, motherly woman who had worked for Abe for more than twenty years, adhering to the theory that every successful man had a wife who told him what to do and a secretary who did it. "Sure you do, Mr. S. He's the one from the State Department who spoke to you about Mr. Kaverin."

"Oh, that Mr. Sherman. OK, send him in."

"Mrs. Sincoff said you're not to smoke."

Abe smiled at her acidly. "It'll be our little secret, Shirley!" She sniffed disapprovingly.

Watching her departing figure, Mark asked, "Who's Sherman?"

"Says he's State Department, but that covers a lot of territory."

"You mean he's more likely CIA?"

"Or FBI. Now that Viktor's here, they'll want to take him over if they can. There's always a lot of rivalry going on."

Sherman was a tall, sandy-haired man dressed in a conservatively dark suit. His rangy, raw-boned appearance suggested that he might be more comfortable in casual clothes. When he had first visited New York, Mark had played a private guessing-game whereby he tried to identify Americans' national backgrounds. Their names were no guide, because so many of them had been changed. However, judging by his appearance and his first name, Mark guessed that Sherman was of Scottish ancestry. On the other hand, knowing New York, he was just as likely to be a descendant of Lithuanian or Polish immigrants. That was what made the game amusing. The man shook hands with both of them before settling in an armchair.

"You'll be pleased to hear that Viktor Kaverin and his sister have both been granted full residential status. We've already provided social security numbers, and we're sending round their green cards later today." He sounded pleased with himself. "As of now, they're both fully entitled to live and work here."

Abe grinned. "And pay taxes! I guess you people can work fast when you want to."

"We do our best, Mr. Sincoff." He hesitated. "We are a little concerned at the moment."

"What's the problem?"

"It seems their arrival has caused a negative reaction in certain quarters. We've been monitoring phone calls at the Dorset Hotel—with their permission, of course." He was quick to justify the intrusion. "It seems there are one or two groups who object to their being given asylum here. Naturally, we didn't want to trouble them with this kind of thing, but I thought I should pass it on to you."

Mark was puzzled. "Who are these people?"

Sherman shrugged. "They claim to represent various Mideastern causes. I'm told one caller was from an extreme right-wing Jewish group." He looked apologetic. "You can never satisfy everyone."

Abe stubbed out his half-smoked cigar. His voice was cheerful. "That's New York for you. The city's full of nuts! As soon as you help one person, somebody else is out there, bitching about it. I tell you, if Jesus Christ himself were to come back to earth tomorrow, there'd be a demonstration outside the United Nations within twenty minutes!"

Sherman appeared uncertain whether to find the analogy amusing. "Anyway, I thought we would pass the information on so that you'd understand why we're leaving one of our people in the hotel for the moment to keep an eye on the Kaverins."

Abe sighed. "So, if the muggers don't get them, the nut cases will!"

"Have any of these callers made threats?"

Sherman looked at Mark. "Not in so many words, Mr. Holland, but we thought it wiser to make sure they don't speak to them in person. These situations usually pass quite quickly. The splinter groups move on to the next target. As a matter of fact, we're disappointed that Mr. Kaverin turned down the offer from the New York Israel Foundation. It might have eased things for the moment."

Abe sat forward. "You heard about that already?"

"Yes. Mr. Kaverin told us himself, and my director had a call from Arnold Silverman, who was a little concerned." Abe exchanged a knowing look with Mark. "It seems Mr. Silverman took a personal interest in the situation."

"Mr. Sincoff and I were just discussing the same thing. I'm hoping perhaps to persuade Viktor to change his mind."

"That will be appreciated, Mr. Holland." Something seemed to be troubling Sherman, and he hesitated before speaking again. "To be honest, gentlemen, we have a slightly more pressing situation on our hands and we're looking to you to co-operate, in view of the time span. I guess you know that the White House has been following this story closely."

Abe smiled. "It didn't go by unnoticed!"

"Well, it seems the President's been looking at his schedule, and he's going to be pretty well tied up for the next few months."

"We expected that."

"Except for this Saturday."

"What?" Abe barked the question.

Sherman looked startled. "I know it's short notice, but we've checked Carnegie Hall, and it appears they're actually free, which we hadn't expected . . ."

"You're crazy! You can't put on a concert with two days' notice! Who the hell's going to be there?"

"That shouldn't be a problem. As soon as it's announced, the house will sell out in a few hours. You seem to forget that this has been one of the major news items of the week. The press secretary is making the announcement in Washington at noon, and I assume all the media will carry it." He smiled nervously. "After that, we believe it will be one of the hottest tickets in town. After all, it's not often the President goes to Carnegie Hall . . ."

Abe brushed the argument aside. "I'm not concerned with tickets alone. The kid's not ready, for God's sake! He hasn't prepared a programme." Abe searched further. "He hasn't even picked a goddamned piano!"

Sherman smiled. "I guess these things can all be looked after in the next day or two. As for a programme, I'm sure he can select items from the repertoire he's been playing over there in Europe. As I understand it, he only just gave a recital in Switzerland last weekend. He won't have forgotten all that music by now, will he?"

Abe shook his head. "You guys don't understand how the music world works. That was a recital in Lausanne, Switzerland, and we're talking about Viktor making his début in the most important city in the Western world! These things have to be prepared properly."

Sherman's voice had cooled considerably. "I'm afraid you don't understand how the presidential schedule works, Mr. Sincoff. Now, it may be . . . inconvenient for Mr. Kaverin to play a recital with only two days' notice, but we're telling him, not asking! He should be reminded that he's been granted permission to settle in this country under very special circumstances, in which the President himself was consulted, and he's going to be given the opportunity to fulfil what he claims to be a lifelong ambition. I doubt that there are many pianists in the world who would turn down an opportunity like that, so I see no point in quibbling over a few minor details—"

"Minor details?" Abe stared at Sherman as though he had temporarily lost his senses.

"Minor, Mr. Sincoff." Sherman was emphatic. "My colleagues are in touch with the television networks, and we fully expect one of them to participate. You know, I really can't understand your objections!"

Before Abe could reply, Mark interrupted. "Has anyone spoken to Viktor yet?"

Sherman smiled comfortably. "One of my colleagues is with him right now. I've no doubt Kaverin will be calling you here shortly. Personally, I imagine he'll be pretty excited with the prospect."

"In that case," Mark looked at Abe, "I suggest we wait for Viktor's reaction."

"We're reasonably certain he'll agree. Under the circumstances, he could hardly refuse, could he?"

"No." Mark ignored Abe's glare. "I think he'll do it. I'm not so worried about the way he'll play. Once he steps on to the stage, I don't think he'll be concerned with where he is or who is listening." He smiled at Abe. "Viktor's strong and probably tougher than most of us suspect."

Abe shook his head slowly. "I hope you're right. The whole thing sounds totally irresponsible to me."

Sherman stood. "I feel you're overreacting to the situation, Mr. Sincoff. As we understand it, Viktor is a fine young pianist who'll be a credit to his profession. We'll give you and him every kind of support he'll need. Now, if you'll forgive me, I have a meeting I'm already late for." He reached into a pocket for his wallet. "I'll give you my card, in case you want to get in touch with me. I can always be reached through this number. You can probably guess that the security arrangements are going to be something of a headache for us. Most recitals like this take place at the White House, but the President expressed the particular wish that this one should be in New York, which has been the landing place for so many Russian immigrants in our history." He smiled briefly. "At least we're not giving anyone else much warning, which could have its advantages. I'll stay in close touch from now on." He shook hands with Mark and nodded cordially to Abe.

When the door had closed, Mark looked at Abe. "Why such strong objections?"

"Because." Abe was reaching into the humidor again, then changed his mind. "We're in the business of managing, Mark. On the face of it, this concert's the answer to our prayers, but it won't do Viktor any good if it goes off half-cocked. I don't think two days is enough time to prepare. I'm against seven-day wonders, from Russian defectors to twelve-year-old whiz-kids who are discovered on a Sunday and forgotten by the following Saturday. We're trying to build Viktor on a firm foundation, no matter how good you say he is. I'd rather see it all put together in a package. Anyway, you were the one pleading for him to be given a little peace and quiet."

"I know, but Sherman's right. It may be inconvenient, but Viktor has to play. I'm not worried about his readiness. If he plays half as well as I've already heard, he'll still be outstanding. You worry too much. Anyway, you can't turn down the President of the United States."

"I don't see why not." Abe grinned. "I'm a registered Democrat!"

At that moment, Shirley buzzed the intercom with a call from Viktor. Abe grimaced, then smiled as she connected him. "Good morning, Viktor. How are you? . . . Yes, we heard the news, too. Are you sure you're ready to go ahead at such short notice?" He listened, frowning. "OK, but I wouldn't want you to feel railroaded. What about your piano?" He listened again, and his frown deepened. Putting his hand over the mouthpiece, he said, "Those interfering jerks have arranged to take him over to Steinway Hall and choose one. I wonder if they're planning to play the frigging recital for him!" Returning to the phone, he forced a smile. "Yes, that's very helpful. Maybe one of us should meet you there. About half an hour? Fine! Do you want to talk about your programme? OK, why don't we get together when we meet? We also have to arrange a photo session." He listened further, occasionally nodding his head. "Listen, do you want to talk to Mark? He's right here with me. I'll pass you to him." He handed the phone across the desk.

Viktor's voice was intensely excited. "Mark? Is it not wonderful news? I could not believe my ears when they told me! What a fantastic country!"

"Yes. Abe and I were a little worried that it might be too soon."

"No. I am ready to play. I feel I have been preparing for this all my life! There are still two days, and they have already arranged with Steinway's to let me practise there for as long as I want."

"Have you chosen your programme?"

"I would like to play the same as Lausanne, finishing with the Chopin sonata." He chuckled delightedly. "You remember, Mark? I said I would make it my special piece."

"I remember." His enthusiasm was touching. "How is Irina?"

For a moment, Viktor hesitated. "I think she is a little unhappy, Mark. Everything has been happening so quickly for us, and I think she is feeling—what is the word?—disorientated."

"That's understandable."

"Do you think you could talk to her, Mark? She is very restless." He lowered his voice. "I cannot say very much, because she is in the room next door. My sister is depressed. I think it is because she is accustomed to a very regular routine in her life. She already misses the ballet."

"I was going to tell you about that. Abe is in touch with people who may be able to help."

"That's wonderful! Thank you again, Mark. I do not think we will ever know how to repay you for what you have done."

"Don't worry about it. Tell Irina I'll come round to see her. Perhaps we can talk when you and Abe finish with Steinway's."

"You will not be there too?" In his excitement, Irina seemed forgotten. "I think of you as my manager, Mark."

"I'll join you later. Before you make a final decision about the programme, Viktor, talk to Abe. He understands American audiences and can advise you better than I can."

"All right, but we will meet soon?"

"Of course. I also want to discuss the offer from the New York Israel Foundation." Abe nodded encouragingly. "I think you should consider it carefully before making any final decisions."

"Yes, Mark. If you believe it would be good for me, then I will do it. I only said no because I wanted to stay in New York. It is such an exciting city!"

"We'll talk about it when we meet."

"Good. I will see you later today." He hung up.

Mark handed the receiver back to Abe. "He'll do whatever we recommend. It looks as though Arnold Silverman will get his way, as usual!"

Abe winked. "Nobody refuses Arnold. He's a good friend, but he's a bad enemy."

Before Mark could reply, the door opened and a flustered Shirley entered. "I'm sorry, Mr. S., but Mr. Laufer and another man are outside, and he says he's not leaving until you see him. He's very insistent."

"What does that little creep want?"

"He didn't say. Only that it can't wait."

Abe looked at his watch. "Viktor won't be at Steinway's for another twenty minutes. You'd better show the jerk in."

Mark had noted more than once in the past that, although Abe despised Gregory Laufer of Magnum Records, he still received the man cordially, basically out of respect for the power and sales distribution of the multinational corporation for which he worked. As vice-president of artists and repertoire, Laufer was something of a joke in New York's musical community. His many *faux pas* and malapropisms created a folklore of their own; managers and their artists exchanged the latest "Lauferisms" gleefully, marvelling that a man so ill informed and ill mannered could have risen to such an influential position in classical music, but they could not deny the enormous commercial strength of his corporate organization. Laufer, undaunted, laughed all the way to the bank.

He entered the room briskly, in his best vice-presidential manner. Having read numerous books on body language, corporate politics, and accounting, Greg exuded executive self-confidence. He was a small, compact man in his early fifties, with a high forehead, hollow cheeks, and a protruding jaw. He was dressed, as ever, in very expensive clothes which, in the combination he chose, managed to look cheap: a three-piece tweed suit, a custom shirt and silk tie whose colours made one's eyes water, and Gucci loafers that had been polished to a high gloss. Mark suspected he bought them all from a man who gave special discounts.

Seeing Mark, Greg Laufer interrupted his prepared greeting to grasp him by the hand, welcoming him with a warmth that was patently insincere. "Hi! I didn't expect to find you here. I'm glad we were able to work out that deal with Steigel. How is Konstantin?"

Mark winced inwardly. No one called the conductor by his first name, including Laufer, but absence bred familiarity. "He's very well, thank you."

"Great!" Laufer, smarting over the loss of *Wellington's Victory*, had grudgingly accepted Steigel's counter-proposals. "Be sure to give him my best when you next talk. If we'd known you'd be here, Larry"—he indicated his partner—"would have brought the new contract along." He made it sound as though it was Mark's fault for not informing them that he would be present. "You remember Larry?"

"Of course." It was impossible to forget Larry Austerklein, Laufer's vice-president of business affairs. Nearly everyone at Magnum was a vice-president of something. A small, sleazy little man whose fingernails and shirt collars were perennially grey, Austerklein was the archetypal New York lawyer whose mission in life was to pull a fast deal on his fellow man. He specialized in "boiler-plate" fine-print clauses in contracts that would whittle a few pennies off a royalty, deliberately misleading phrases that could later be misinterpreted to the advantage of the company, or any other sharp practice that would find a way legally to cheat the unsuspecting musician of his income. Everything was fair game in his book, and his reputation was even worse than Laufer's, if only because encounters with him did not generate humorous anecdotes. Austerklein's weakness was that he was not very astute; his transparently dishonest efforts were foiled in the first reading of one of his draft contracts, to be followed by acrimonious correspondence in which the lawyer, who was timid in person, was arrogantly offensive in print. Mark still bore the scars of past exchanges. Fortunately, Larry Austerklein did not shake hands. He always had wet palms.

Abe smiled thinly. "Well, Greg, what's so desperately important that it can't wait?"

Laufer arranged himself in an armchair, making sure the language of his body was suitably aggressive. "You don't really have to ask that, do you?" When Abe was silent, he gave a slippery smile. "A certain Russian pianist who just defected. I hear he's really good."

Abe nodded silently. One had to admire the man's streetwise business sense. "Where did you hear that, Greg?"

"Switzerland. Our man in Zurich called this morning. He says Viktor Kaverin is terrific. He gave a fantastic recital in Lausanne a few days ago."

Abe looked at Mark. "News travels fast."

Laufer smiled contentedly. "Come on, Abe. Don't hold out on me! I want him under contract. You owe me."

"I do?"

"Sure. Ever since I agreed to take that lousy French soprano's recital."

Abe's expression darkened. "She's not lousy, and you didn't have to take it. Considering she paid all the costs herself, you had a pretty good deal."

"You deliberately misled us, Abe. It was supposed to be favourite arias by Puccini."

Abe took a deep breath. "No, Greg, it was always Piccinni. We listed the titles. Puccini didn't compose *Roland* or *La Buona Figliuola.*"

"I assumed it was a typo in the contract. Anyway, we still put it out, so I consider you owe me a favour."

Abe glanced towards Mark again. "We haven't made any commitments on his behalf yet. Viktor's only just arrived. Why don't we wait for a few days?"

"No!" Laufer leaned forward, lowering his voice. "I had a call this morning from Steve Kalman in our video division. We already know about the recital, even if we're not supposed to talk about it until it's official." The efficient Swiss representative of Magnum Records was set aside. "Anyway, if Magnum gets the TV show, we'll have them include the record as part of the same deal."

Austerklein added smugly, "Our usual terms." He avoided Mark's eyes.

Abe opened the humidor and reached for another cigar. Before he could close it again, Laufer had helped himself. "If that's the situation, why are you asking us?"

Laufer waved the idea aside. "I'm not talking about that record.

Recitals don't mean a thing. What I want is a follow-up. We need something we can really move." He raised his voice slightly, a sure indication that he knew he was on thin ice. "Listen, does Viktor know 'Midnight in Moscow' and a couple of the other big Russian hits? With a synthesizer backing and a picture of him standing in front of Red Square, we could sell a million!"

11

It was only a short walk from Abe's office to the Dorset Hotel. Mark crossed Fifty-seventh Street, dodging between taxis and trucks, and strolled down to Sixth Avenue, past the building that used to house the old Horn and Hardart automat. Many years earlier, when he was an impecunious student, the self-service restaurant, with its hinged pigeon-holes housing all sorts of instant meals at surprisingly low prices, had been his chief source of food. In those far-off days, it had been his centre of operations. There was something slightly disconcerting about the way establishments and whole buildings in the city disappeared, seemingly overnight. New York was constantly changing, but that was part of its attraction.

It was a glorious day. Sunlight sparkled on the tall glass buildings that ranged along either side of the Avenue of the Americas. He was never sure why New Yorkers insisted on calling it simply Sixth Avenue. Was it laziness or their constant preoccupation with facts and data? Even the sports commentators spent their time listing statistics, almost ignoring the action. He could remember, not so long ago, when the only tall building on the Avenue had been Radio City, and it had been a street of shabby three- and four-storey houses, filled with unusual little shops—pen repairs, numismatists, back-date magazines, party jokes and tricks. They had all gone, and the steady stream of one-way traffic pushed its way uptown in the glass and concrete canyons, jockeying for position to the accompaniment of car horns and traffic cops' whistles. Everyone was competing.

The Dorset Hotel was a quiet, conservative building between Fifth and Sixth Avenues, on a relatively calm section of Fifty-fourth Street. It sat next to the garden of the Museum of Modern Art, whose newly added storeys of horrendously expensive apartments now loomed over it. Mark liked the Dorset. When he could not reserve a room in the Mayflower on Central Park, handy to Lincoln Center, he preferred it for its unostentatious comfort. It seemed to have a European atmosphere, away from the gaudier razzmatazz of the Hilton and some of the more recent hotels which now challenged Miami Beach with their outrageous splendours. It was a wise choice for the Kaverins.

He called Irina's room on the house phone, giving his name. There was only the slightest hesitation and connecting click before he heard her phone ringing. Apparently, his name was on an approved list vetted by Mr. Sherman. "Hello, Irina? It's Mark. I'm downstairs."

"Mark!" She sounded delighted. "Come up. Do you know where we are?"

She was standing in the open doorway as he left the elevator and scampered down the corridor to meet him. "Mark!" She flung her arms around his neck, and he held her tightly, lifting her off the floor. They walked, as close as lovers, to her room.

"How are you feeling?"

"Still a little tired. Everything is upside-down! I am finding it hard to adjust to the change in time and I keep waking very early in the morning, but there is nothing for me to do. If I was at home in Moscow, I would begin exercising. There is a barre in the apartment. Viktor put one on the wall of my bedroom. It is not the same here." She led him to a large, spacious room, decorated with cheerful floral patterns. Irina kept her arm around Mark's waist. "I'm sorry. I should not call Moscow my home any more, should I?"

"It will take a while to get used to the idea. Don't worry about it. Has Viktor left?" She nodded. "The news of the recital is exciting, isn't it?"

"Yes." She laughed. "This is an unbelievable country, I think. I cannot imagine anywhere in the world where the President himself would arrange a recital for Viktor! He was so astonished when he heard the news that I thought he was going to cry." She smiled at the memory. "I did! Everyone has been so friendly. Viktor has gone to the Steinway house to choose a piano and practise for a while. He said that we should go to him later so that we can all be together again."

"Good. In the meantime, what have you been doing?"

For a moment, her face clouded. "Not very much. There has been no time to do anything. It's strange. I have been here for only two days, and sometimes I feel it has been a very long time. At other times, I am afraid to put my head out of the door so I sit in this room and listen to all the noises. They are so . . . different. I have heard car horns and sirens and bells. Early this morning, there was a terrible rumbling. I think it was a truck to take away rubbish. It woke me." She sighed. "Sometimes it is the same, and sometimes it is all completely different from what I expected. When we came here in the car from the airport, I thought I was in the middle of a strange dream. I recognized the skyscrapers from pictures I have seen." She smiled. "Even in Russia, we know what New York looks like! But once we were inside, looking upwards everywhere, it was so different!"

"New York is only one town, Irina. It's a very big country, with every kind of scenery you could imagine. I'm sure you'll see a lot of it as time passes."

"Do you mean that we can go anywhere we like? I did not think of that. In Russia . . ." She hesitated, unwilling to continue.

"Wherever you want to go and whenever you like. I met Mr. Sherman this morning, who told me you've already become bona fide residents."

She laughed. "That is the man who took us everywhere yesterday, in a *huge* car." Her eyes were wide as she described the vehicle. "A family could live inside it! He drove us to offices, where we filled in more and more papers. I have never answered so many questions in my life! They took photographs and fingerprints," she grimaced, "and showed us so many places—uptown and downtown and midtown. It was very confusing." They were still standing close to each other, and she put her arms around his neck, nestling against him. "I am glad it is all finished."

Mark kissed her gently. For a moment she responded, and he could feel her body tightly against his. He was surprised to find how much it pleased him. Then she drew slightly away, her face serious. "I wanted to apologize to you for the way I behaved in London. I am ashamed."

"Why? You behaved very well." For a moment, he thought she was referring to the night in the hotel.

"No. I was very frightened and I acted like a child. When I told that Englishman—I have already forgotten his name . . ."

"Sharpe?"

"Yes. When I told him I would say I was kidnapped as part of a political plot, I should not have spoken like that. I behaved very badly. It was because Viktor was missing, and when I saw the other one, the man lying on the bed . . ." She faltered.

"They understand, Irina. You have nothing to apologize for."

"I was afraid they were going to take me away, without Viktor."

"They understood that. Anyone would have said the same things."

"But it was stupid! Do you know if Mr. Grunfeld is still here?"

"No."

"I could apologize to him in person."

"There's no need. Anyway, now that your papers have gone through, he's probably flown back to London."

"I feel very foolish."

"You don't have to. It was self-preservation. I'm sure they understood that. It was cruel of them to suggest taking you out of London before Viktor was found." She nodded, her head down. "Anyway, that's all past history. You don't have to talk about it any more." Mark looked round. "I like your room."

"It's beautiful!" Something of the childlike quality had returned to her face. "I did not know that hotels could be so luxurious."

"Didn't Viktor tell you about the one in Lausanne?"

"Yes, but I thought he was exaggerating." The child took over again, and Mark found himself smiling at her. "He always claims to know more than I do. Sometimes, he makes me angry."

"Never mind. What would you like to do? I told Abe we would meet him and Viktor at four, so we have plenty of time. Shall we have some lunch?"

"Yes, but not very much. Everyone eats so much here! If I do that, I will never dance again!"

"Speaking of which, Abe Sincoff may have some interesting news for you."

"Which one is he? The little fat man who smiled and made jokes?"

"I'm not sure he'd like all the description, but that's the one. Abe's made an appointment with the City Ballet, to talk about you. I think he'll find you a place in the company."

"Really?"

"Yes. Abe knows everyone in New York. He's the unofficial mayor!"

"But the City Ballet is very famous."

"So is the Bolshoi. Abe said he couldn't promise anything, but if I know him, he'll get what he wants."

"Why should he do this for me?"

Mark smiled. "Fifteen per cent for starters, but mainly because he's a friend and wants to help." He watched her expression. "You look sad, Irina. Is anything the matter?"

She shook her head slowly. "No, Mark. I am just surprised by everything that happens here. It is not what I had expected." She was silent for a moment. "It is as though there is a whole part of my life I do not understand . . ." She seemed uncertain what to say next.

"I don't understand you."

Her smile was brief. "I cannot explain. Everything is happening too quickly." Suddenly, she was nervous. "Oh, Mark, I should be exercising. I have done nothing for two days. They will want to audition me, and I will make a fool of myself!"

He smiled, taking her hand. "Two days aren't the end of the world. Besides, you're not going to dance for them today. You'll have plenty of warning. If Viktor takes up the offer to tour in Israel, you'll have time to work."

Irina looked surprised. "But I thought . . ."

"I talked to Viktor about it a little while ago. It seems a pity not to take advantage of Arnold Silverman's offer. He can be a very powerful friend, and he's promised to persuade Avram Gutman— What's the matter?"

"It is nothing. When we spoke about it, Viktor said he did not want to play with Gutman."

"Why not? It's a great opportunity for him."

"I do not know, Mark. You will have to ask Viktor." Her mood seemed to have changed.

"We'll talk about it later. I'm sure he's much too preoccupied with the recital to think about it."

"Yes. After the concert, it will be different."

"In the meantime, let's go and find some food. What would you like? New York has everything in the world—even Russian."

"Can we walk first? I have not been out very much, except with Mr. Sherman. After the phone call, I was afraid."

"What phone call?"

"A man spoke to Viktor, the first morning."

"Who?"

"I don't know, Mark. He made threats."

"What sort of threats?"

"Viktor would not tell me what he said, but he was upset. He said that we must be very careful, and not to speak to anyone we did not know. We told Mr. Sherman about it."

"What did he say?"

She shrugged helplessly. "He said that one of his colleagues would answer the phone for us and that we should not worry!" Her voice was reproachful. "How do we do that? Mr. Sherman said that such things are quite normal in New York. Do you believe that, Mark? He said"— she seemed to be trying to recall his exact words—"that in a true democracy like America, one must accept the principle that any political group can ask for the right to be heard, even if its views are diametrically opposed to those of the majority. He said that there are political factions of every type in New York and that our being here would be certain to anger one group or another." She frowned. "He told us that, coming from Russia, we would find it difficult to accept such a principle. Viktor was a little angry. He felt that Mr. Sherman was treating us like children, but Mr. Sherman just smiled and told us not to worry. He did not seem very disturbed by the whole incident." Her face was grave. "I suppose I am not yet accustomed to living in a country where political opinions can be expressed like this, but we have done nothing!"

"Why didn't you tell me about this?"

"Oh Mark!" She held his hand tighter. "I have hardly seen you since we arrived! On the first evening, when we had dinner, I was so tired! We spent all of yesterday with Mr. Sherman . . ."

"I understand. I'll talk to Viktor about the call."

"There was only one. Since then, we have stayed in the hotel most of the time. The man who called Viktor spoke to him in Russian."

"But you don't know what he said?"

"No. Only that we should not be here and should go home to Moscow. He said other things, but Viktor would not tell me. I think he was trying not to frighten me. Since we told Mr. Sherman about it, there have not been any more calls, but we have tried to stay hidden." Mark nodded. "Mr. Sherman has put one of his colleagues in the hotel to be near us." Her face was sombre.

"That should help."

"I suppose so."

"You don't sound very convinced." He tried to keep his voice light. "Viktor and I will talk about it when I see him."

"It is not that I am ungrateful, Mark. So many wonderful things have happened to us since we arrived, and everyone we meet has been so kind. I do not like the feeling that Viktor and I are being watched all the time."

"Of course not. Try to think of it as being protected."

"Yes."

"After the recital, there'll be no more need to hide. Viktor will be so famous that nobody will dare come near him! Did you know that it may be televised from coast to coast?"

She nodded. "Viktor told me. After the recital, it will all be different."

"Don't look so sad about it!"

"No." She smiled suddenly, and her face was beautiful. Perhaps it was make-up, but her eyes seemed to taper to the edges of her temples.

"Come on!" He pulled her gently towards the door. "I think you're going stir-crazy!"

Irina looked bewildered. "What is that?"

"Just an expression, describing people in prison. We'll walk on Fifth Avenue, and I'll show you some of the city. The streets are so crowded that you'll find it easy to disappear. Nobody will notice you—except perhaps that you're very beautiful!"

"I will not be frightened if I am with you."

"You won't be frightened at all. In a little while, you won't even think about it. Now, what are we going to eat?"

"Do you think it will be possible to order a hot dog?" She said it so seriously that Mark laughed.

"Haven't you ever had one?"

"No. I read that everyone in America eats hot dogs and hamburgers. When I was in London, I ate a hamburger, but it was not very good."

"The English variety bears very little resemblance to the genuine American original!"

152

"They do not make them properly? The little food bar near Covent Garden had a sign that said REAL AMERICAN HAMBURGERS."

"They always do, but they rarely are. The English version of the hot dog is even worse, believe me!"

Her mood lightened. "I think maybe you are making fun of me. We are arguing about hot dogs and hamburgers!"

"Well, if we're going to argue at all, I can't think of a better subject! I know just the restaurant we need, and you'll have to trust me when I tell you it's one of the best!"

For a moment, Irina was serious again. "I do trust you, Mark." Her eyes were wide. "With my life."

Leaving the hotel with Irina, Mark was not conscious of being under surveillance. The man at the front desk nodded cheerfully as usual. Mark remembered him from previous visits to the city. Either the watchdogs were very discreet or they were more concerned with Viktor. The events of the past few days could have played havoc with Irina's imagination, but he was content to feel her hand clutching his arm.

Fifth Avenue was as crowded as he had promised, and they walked slowly uptown, pausing at every window for her to stare at the luxuries on display.

"I could never have imagined so much!" She was almost outraged. "It is more than anyone should need!"

He laughed. She was bemused by the opulence of the new Trump Tower. "It will take a while to get used to the idea that there's always something more in a consumer society. That's how capitalism works."

"You are laughing at me again!"

"Not really. After Moscow or even London, New York is a shock to the system. Besides, we haven't passed Tiffany's yet!"

At the entrance to Central Park at Fifth Avenue and Fifty-ninth Street, opposite the Plaza Hotel, a street-seller beneath a multicoloured golf umbrella was dispensing hot dogs and cans of drinks. Leaving the crowded pavements to the shoppers, Mark guided Irina to the stand. "I promised you one of the best restaurants in town. This is it!" She looked delighted. "Do you want it with all the trimmings?"

Irina tasted hers cautiously, wrinkling her nose. Then she smiled contentedly. "I think I am going to love America!" After a second bite, she asked, "Can I eat two? I promise to exercise tomorrow!"

They walked hand in hand through the park, and the brilliant light and unexpectedly warm sunshine affected her, driving away the fears and doubts. The trees were still bare, but there was a damp, earthy perfume coming from the soil and fresh young sproutings of grass. Irina stretched her arms and turned her face to the sun, inhaling deeply, then hugged Mark's arm again. The footpaths were crowded with pedestrians and joggers, and the benches were filled with office workers enjoying an alfresco lunch in the balmy spring weather. Walking past, Irina looked at them covertly, apparently fascinated. An elderly woman, leading a newly clipped miniature white poodle on a jewelled lead, made her giggle like a schoolgirl, and she buried her head against Mark's shoulder.

When they reached the exit to Seventh Avenue, he asked, "Shall we keep going or head back? There's a lot more park."

For a moment Irina was undecided, looking round. Then her eyes met his, and she was very still. "How long is there before we meet Viktor?"

"Plenty of time—about two hours."

It seemed a long time before she spoke, her eyes never leaving his face. In the background, impatient taxis on Central Park South maintained a constant chorus of horns. "Take me back to the hotel, Mark. I want us to be alone together." She held his arm, leaning close, and they walked in silence. At one corner, while they waited for the light to change, she reached up towards him, her mouth lingering on his.

The hotel room seemed shadowy after the brilliant sunlight of the street, but Irina moved quickly to the windows, drawing the curtains, and was silhouetted against the pale glow. She stood still, her arms outstretched, waiting for Mark to walk to her. As they touched, her body pressed close against his and her arms tightened about his neck.

"I still taste of hot dogs!"

"So do I!"

"How delicious!"

They kissed slowly, as though exploring, and her arms drew him closer. Somewhere, in the distance, a door closed.

Irina drew back slightly. "What was that?"

"I don't know."

She seemed suddenly alert. In the half-light, he saw her eyes flicker in the direction of the connecting door to the next room. "It sounds as though it came from Viktor's room."

Mark held her gently. "Could he have returned?"

"No." She was uneasy. "He said he would meet us at the Steinway house. We are supposed to go to him."

He wondered whether it might be one of Sherman's men keeping a watchful eye on them, but decided not to mention it. "Perhaps it's one of the hotel staff. There are always maids and housekeepers . . ."

"Perhaps." She bit her lip.

"Do you want me to look?" Irina nodded silently.

Mark opened the door slowly and entered the room. To his surprise, the curtains there had also been drawn and his eyes, already accustomed to the dark, could make out the items of heavy furniture. He turned back towards Irina, who had not moved. "It must have been somewhere . . ."

He sensed, rather than heard, the swish of sound behind him, but before he could move there was a sudden, crushing blow to the base of his skull. His legs buckled and he fell forward, putting out his hands to save himself. He thought vaguely that he heard Irina call his name, but a second, sickening blow struck the nape of his neck and darkness enveloped him.

He did not know how long he was unconscious. It was as though he was in a deep, peaceful sleep. A distant telephone bell rang insistently, and he opened his eyes slowly, aware that the sound was coming from the room next door. For a moment, tiredness engulfed him and he lay still, enjoying the sensation. The bell continued to ring, and almost regretfully, he started to rise. Then the violent, painful throbbing in his head began, and a nauseous dizziness made him collapse. He lay, breathing slowly, waiting for the waves of pain to decrease. The phone continued to ring.

Slowly, Mark rolled to his side, fighting the nausea and the hammering in his brain. Moving cautiously, he raised himself on one arm, massaging his aching neck with his free hand. His hair and skin felt dry against his probing fingers. As though detached from his body, he thought, "There's no blood." He waited again until his head felt clearer, then pulled himself upwards until he was half lying, half sitting on the bed. The phone had stopped ringing.

A pale light under a door on the other side of the room caught his attention, and he stumbled across the few feet of floor towards it. The effort seemed to drain all his strength, and he leaned heavily against the wall, waiting to recover. His senses were beginning to return. It was a small, tiled bathroom, and the light coming through the window was painful. Half closing his eyes, he filled the hand basin with cold water and then buried his face in it, holding his breath until it gushed out into the liquid, bubbling and boiling round his ears.

Slowly, everything came back into focus, and he stood straight, breathing slowly and forcing the pain to recede. He plunged his head back into the cold water and then leaned back, shaking droplets from his face. The back of his neck felt stiff and bruised. If his assailant had struck him any harder, it would have broken his neck. The light no longer hurt his eyes, and he reached for a towel to dry his face. Then he remembered.

"Irina!" His voice was a harsh croak, and he staggered through the darkened room to the pale rectangle of the connecting door. "Irina!"

Her room was silent. He reached the window and tore the curtains open. He felt one of them rip away from the pelmet as he dragged them apart, using the full weight of his body. Light poured into the room, harsh against his eyes and bringing another wave of pain. He turned inward, fearing what he would find.

The room was empty. The coverlet on the bed was undisturbed, the doors of the closets were closed, the polished furniture was shining mutely. Looking beyond the bed, he could see through the open door into another bathroom exactly like the one he had used. It, too, was empty, upturned tumblers standing on a glass shelf, plastic containers of shampoo and bubble bath neatly arranged. It was all as vacant and anonymous as a hotel bedroom.

Irina was gone.

12

Craig Sherman arrived first. Mark was sitting in an armchair, a damp face-cloth pressed against the back of his head, when the door opened without warning. Apparently, Sherman had a passkey. He halted briefly, surveying the room, then placed a hard-backed chair facing Mark.

"What's your version?" His voice was unfriendly.

Mark looked at him. "It's hardly a version. I was here when it happened!"

He nodded impatiently. "Very well. Describe it."

Mark spoke slowly. His head ached, and the bruising on his neck made it painfully stiff. He described his arrival, the walk through the park, and their return.

"What time are you saying you got back?"

"A little after two. We were supposed to meet Viktor and Abe at four."

"But you came back here?"

"Yes." When he mentioned Irina drawing the curtains, Sherman's expression did not change. If he drew conclusions, he gave no indication.

Mark described entering the adjoining room, and Sherman interrupted again. "You say the curtains were drawn there too and the room was dark?"

"Yes."

"Did you hear anyone doing it?" There was an edge to his voice.

"No. The only sound we heard was a door closing."

"Is that unusual in a hotel?"

"Irina was nervous. She thought the sound came from her brother's room."

"OK. Finish your story."

Mark continued, piecing together his actions. When he had ended,

Sherman remained silent. "Did any of your people see Irina leave the hotel?"

"What people?"

"She said you had posted someone here to watch over her and her brother. I assumed . . ."

"We have one man in the hotel. He went with Viktor to Steinway Hall. He's still there."

"Then nobody was looking after Irina?"

Sherman was angry. "We're not running a private detective agency! I asked the clerk on the front desk to make a note of any visitors, but that's it. How much of the taxpayers' money do you expect us to spend on this? The Kaverins claimed they'd received a threatening call, so we told the operator here to ask for names on any incoming calls. She had a check-list to work from. I don't consider the girl important, and when Viktor told me about the threat, I suggested moving her out of town, but she wanted to stay."

"Then nobody was watching her."

"She was seen leaving." Sherman was staring fixedly at Mark.

"When?"

"A little after two, with a tall blond man wearing a grey suit." His eyes took in Mark's clothes. "The clerk was busy serving someone at the time, but the description fits you well enough."

"That's ridiculous! I was . . ."

"He said he thought she was walking arm in arm with this man, as though he was a close friend." Sherman bore on. "He didn't pay much attention, but he thought it was the same man that came for her around noon."

Mark sat very still. "And you think the man she left with was me?" Sherman said nothing. "Why?"

"You tell me."

Mark turned his head. The movement was painful. "What the hell do you think this is on the back of my neck?"

Sherman shrugged. "That can be arranged. It depends who's working with you. It's worth being slugged on the back of the head if it will make a story stick."

"This is madness! Why should I abduct Irina Kaverin? I arranged her escape!"

"So I heard. It all went smoothly, did it?" His sarcasm was heavy.

158

"You known damn well that a man was killed in London!"

"Yeah. Tell me about that."

"I don't know. Quentin Sharpe is probably putting it together at the moment. It happened while I was with Irina. The night she left the theatre with me, somebody got to the hotel where Viktor was hiding, and killed Murphy, the man who was with him. Viktor managed to escape. You know all this!"

"Sure. Where did you say you were at the time?"

"I was with Irina at a different hotel, about five miles away."

"And she could confirm this?"

"I suppose so. She was sleeping next door."

Sherman's voice was soft. "But she can't vouch for you now, because she's disappeared."

Mark tried to stand, but the sudden pain in his head forced him to sit again. "I'll go through it one more time. A few days ago in Lausanne, Viktor Kaverin begged me to help him escape from Russia. He chose the moment for two reasons: first, it was his last chance to make a run for it outside the Soviet Union; and secondly, his sister was also outside the country, appearing with the Bolshoi Ballet company in London. When Viktor asked me, I told him I didn't know how to help, but I called Quentin Sharpe. He wasn't prepared to offer asylum, but he passed us on to the CIA. We switched flights in Geneva, and Viktor waited in London with Murphy while I went to collect Irina. Murphy died, Viktor met us at the airport, and we flew in with your friend Grunfeld. Today, when I came back here with Irina, someone knocked me out and took her away. If the clerk downstairs is to be believed, the man who did it was similar in appearance to me." He paused. "What the hell do you think has happened?"

Sherman was silent for a long time. He took out a cigarette, tapping the end against the back of his hand. "I had a long talk with your Quentin Sharpe yesterday. He told me you worked for British security for quite a spell."

"Yes."

"And quit with a chip on your shoulder."

"I wouldn't have called it that."

"How would you call it?"

Mark sighed. "Disillusionment, dissatisfaction . . . I'd lost faith in what I was doing and didn't like what I'd become."

"In other words, if not a chip, some pretty bad feeling?"

"Yes. What are you trying to say?"

"I'm getting there." Sherman put the unlit cigarette into the ashtray. He was probably trying to give up smoking. "You were a full-time field agent?"

"Yes."

"Involved in—what shall I call it?—close encounters with the other side?" Mark nodded silently. "To the point that they could identify you?"

"My cover was broken a few times, yes."

There was a long pause. Mark half anticipated the next question. "Then what the hell were you doing in Moscow last December?"

Mark hesitated. "I left the Department a long time ago. That part of my life ended when I did. Nobody has ever questioned my loyalty, and I had a clean record." Sherman nodded silently. "Last November, at a concert in Geneva, the Russian Gosconcert Agency invited me to hear Viktor play a recital and attend an international press conference. Now, maybe it was partly because I wanted to forget my years with the Department and maybe it was because I was flattered to be invited, but I accepted. Nothing questionable happened when I was there, and nobody approached me. What was wrong with my going there?"

"A hell of a lot, and you know it, otherwise you wouldn't look so damned guilty when you tell it!"

"All right. It was a calculated risk, but it was my risk and not the Department's. You won't understand, but I wanted to prove, to myself if nobody else, that I was no longer involved with the Department and that I'd finally made it into a sane, healthy world, where the only kind of serious crisis I would encounter would be a conductor who missed a plane connection! Does that make sense?"

"Maybe." Sherman took out another cigarette. This time, he lit it. Some of his aggressiveness had ebbed. "Until I have news of Irina Kaverin, I'll accept your story . . ."

"Thanks a lot!"

"But that's as far as it goes."

"What do you mean?"

The American paced the floor, pausing occasionally to stare at Mark. "I can think of another scenario. You remember the Russian sailor who jumped ship here a year or two back and then claimed the American government had kidnapped him?" Mark nodded. "It left a lot of people with egg on their faces. So, let's take the plan forward. How about a scheme that leaves the President of the United States with egg on his face, while the whole world watches and laughs?"

"I don't follow you."

Sherman continued pacing. "I think you will. Suppose a Western agent—one with a chip on his shoulder, who'd like to get back at his ex-employers—dreamed up his own sweet little plan. He persuades a talented young Russian pianist that fame and fortune await him if he changes sides, especially if he's sure to tell the world press that he's just dying to play a concert for the President of the United States of America! Pretty smart, eh? This agent offers a fantastic career—money, television, concerts. All the kid has to do is walk through a few doors the agent is going to open for him. So the pianist, who's a little naïve, agrees, and suddenly he's walking into freedom. Even better, the White House falls for the concert story and announces to the world that the President will attend. Wouldn't it be just great if, on the very day the announcement is made, the Russian pianist and his sister disappear and show up in Moscow claiming they've been kidnapped and fooled by imperialist American agents?"

"That's insane! For a start, Viktor hasn't disappeared."

"No, but if his sister has, there may be enough pressure to make him want to leave. They're very close. Maybe he and Irina really did want out of Russia. Once they're safely back in sunny Moscow, they'll say whatever they're told to say."

Mark shook his head. "Your story's full of holes. The agent has no guarantee that the President would even hear about Viktor's dream recital, so the whole plan falls flat."

"Perhaps. It didn't have to be the President. That was the jackpot, if it came off."

"You really believe all this?"

"I don't know what I believe right now. You asked me for an alternative story, and I'm looking at the facts I have." His voice hardened again. "A Russian pianist and his sister, with a little help from a man with connections, escape to New York. A recital for the President is arranged and the pianist says he'll play, despite the objections of his managers, who want more time. Time for what?" Mark was about to speak, but Sherman waved him to silence. "Meantime, there's a dead

161

CIA man in London, whose murder hasn't been solved. The agent claims he was several miles away when it happened, and the only witness who can testify to this is the pianist's sister. But the sister's disappeared, last seen in the company of a man who fits the agent's description." Sherman halted in front of Mark. "Now, maybe you're telling me the truth and maybe you went to Moscow to salve your conscience or erase your past or God knows what else, but until I have a few more facts and a few more satisfactory explanations, I'm leaving my options open, mister! This whole thing stinks!" He stubbed the half-smoked cigarette out angrily.

"What do you plan to do?"

"We wait. With Irina Kaverin gone, that's all we can do. The next move comes from them. If you want a doctor to take a look at the back of your head, we'll send for one." Mark shook his head. "Either way, we wait here, and we wait together. You're not going anywhere!" He slumped into his chair.

"Where's Viktor?"

As if in reply to the question, a key turned in the door and Viktor entered with a man Mark did not recognize. The pianist's face was pale. "Have you heard any news, Mark?"

"Not yet." He glanced at Sherman, who had joined the other man. "We're waiting to hear from them."

"You think we will?"

"I'm sure of it."

"Oh God!" He sank into a chair, his face in his hands. "My poor Irina! I should not have done this to her!" Looking up, he asked, "Do you know who it was?"

"No, but I must assume it was someone from your country."

"Why? I am not important. I am a musician."

"They don't want you to play that recital. My guess is that they're going to try to force you to return to Russia." Viktor became very still. "Mr. Sherman has the theory that they want to disgrace the United States by claiming that you were abducted from Switzerland. He thinks they'll force you to say that you and Irina were kidnapped." Mark turned to Sherman, who was now listening. "He thinks I'm part of the plot."

"I don't understand."

162

"It's a very complicated theory, Viktor, based on . . . a job that I used to have. You'd better ask Mr. Sherman to explain!"

Sherman looked uneasy. "I didn't say that. We were discussing various possibilities. There are too many loose ends in the story as I've heard it, and I'm not yet satisfied."

Viktor stood. "Mark is my friend. He rescued me! You do not suspect him? That is mad!"

Sherman held his ground. "Until I have a few more answers, I suspect everyone! How about you, Viktor? What do you plan to do?"

Viktor stared at the man helplessly. "I do not know."

"We'll offer you protection. It seems to me that an immediate press statement might be the best move. We have to fight fire with fire."

"But Irina . . ."

"She can't be very far from here. We'll do everything humanly possible to get her back. Listen, you've got that recital to play. That's the most important fact to hang on to. The President's going to be there, with the whole world watching. There's no going back now."

The pianist shook his head. "I cannot think until I know what has happened to my sister." Almost incongruously, he said to Mark, "The practice was good. I think I am playing better than ever." He shook his head as if to clear it. "That is no longer important. I must know what has happened to Irina!"

Sherman nodded slowly. "In that case, all we can do is wait."

Mark asked, "Does Abe know what's happened?"

"No. I told him we needed Viktor for a couple of hours to complete a few more documents." There was a sardonic smile on his face. "He was pretty mad! It seems we cut into his plans for a photo session!"

Mark moved to the phone. "I'd better call him."

"No!" Sherman's voice was sharp. "Until we hear some news, you don't speak to anyone. Sincoff can wait, God damn it! The fewer the people that know about this for the moment, the better. It needs handling carefully." He turned to Viktor, lightening his tone. "Why don't you and I go next door and talk? I'd like to ask a few questions."

"I have done nothing but answer questions for two days, Mr. Sherman. I have told you everything I know!"

"Perhaps, but I'd like to backtrack on a couple for my own benefit. It will pass the time." His voice softened. "Your answers may help to clear Mr. Holland."

"Mr. Holland is clear. He is my friend! If he hadn't helped me when I asked him, I would still be in Russia!"

"OK, in that case, you'll want to talk, just to satisfy any doubts." He motioned to the adjoining room, and Viktor, after a final questioning glance at Mark, accompanied him next door.

Sherman's assistant seated himself near Mark. As he made himself comfortable, he unbuttoned the jacket of his suit, revealing the butt end of a revolver tucked against his ribs. From time to time his jaw moved as he transferred chewing-gum from one side of his mouth to the other. The man stared vacantly into space, a bored expression on his face.

Mark took out a cigarette. "I assume I'm allowed to smoke?"

The man shrugged, his eyes on Mark's hands. "They're your lungs."

The call came less than an hour later. The abrupt ring of the phone in the silent room sounded harsh. Mark's keeper lifted the receiver. "Yeah?" He listened. "Hold." The door to Viktor's room opened, and Sherman appeared. Viktor was close behind him.

"Who is it?"

"Didn't say. They want to speak to Holland. The man says he won't talk to anyone else."

He was using the telephone on a desk by the window; there was a second phone on the bedside table. Sherman walked to it and gently lifted the receiver, placing his hand over the mouthpiece. Then he nodded to Mark.

"Hello?"

"Is this Mr. Mark Holland?"

"Yes."

"Irina Kaverin is in our keeping. She is perfectly safe, and no harm has come to her." The speaker sounded American, but with a distinctive accent.

"Can I speak to her?"

"Of course." There was a momentary silence.

"Mark?" It was Irina's voice. She sounded frightened.

"Yes. How are you?"

"They have not hurt me. Is Viktor with you?"

"Yes."

"Tell him not to be afraid. I—" Her voice was cut off, and the man returned.

"Are you satisfied, Mr. Holland?"

Mark looked at Sherman before replying. The American signalled to him to continue. "Yes. What do you want?"

"Viktor Kaverin." The man did not speak further.

"And if he says no?"

"He will never see his sister again."

"I understand." Mark was aware of Viktor, hovering by him. "What if he agrees?"

"We are prepared to exchange Irina for him."

"Why?"

There was a slight pause. "Because we are more concerned with Mr. Kaverin's return home. He is an important artist. May I speak to him?" At the other phone, Sherman shook his head.

"He's not available."

There was a slight chuckle. When the voice returned, it was pleasantly conversational. "I find that hard to believe, Mr. Holland. I will call back in ten minutes. By that time, you will have had the opportunity to discuss our proposal with the unavailable Mr. Kaverin. It is a simple exchange, and nothing will happen to Irina if you agree. You will receive another call, but I must warn you that it will be the last one that you will get." The line went dead.

Mark and Sherman hung up almost simultaneously. Viktor came forward. "Is Irina safe?"

Mark looked again at Sherman before he replied. "She's all right, Viktor."

"You spoke to her?"

"For a moment. She said you're not to worry. They haven't hurt her."

"What do they want?"

Sherman spoke from the bedside table. "You, Viktor. They want you." The pianist stood very still, his eyes closed. "They're prepared to make an exchange—you for Irina. He's calling back in ten minutes for an answer."

Viktor sat on the edge of the bed, staring at the floor. The room was silent except for the continuous low rumble of traffic in the street many floors below. Sherman took out a cigarette and lit it. "We haven't much time." When Viktor remained silent, he spoke. "I say we tell them to go to hell!"

Mark looked at him. "Why?"

"Because we have Viktor. If we refuse to negotiate and tell them we're going to put the story on the front page of every newspaper in the world, they won't dare hold her."

Mark thought about it. "You're probably right."

Sherman stood in front of Viktor, speaking to his bowed head. "Look at it this way: if Viktor plays the recital, with coast to coast TV coverage, he's going to make national and international news. They'd never dare hold her in the face of such publicity. We call their bluff."

Sherman's partner spoke. "It gives us a chance to get the girl back. They've still got to get her out of here."

Mark shook his head. "Don't offer too many guarantees. This is a big country."

"What do you mean?" The man looked angry.

Mark stared him down. "Be realistic. If they're the people we think they are, they're going to know a dozen ways of smuggling her out of the country, either directly or through Canada or Mexico. The chances of stopping them are going to be limited."

"Whose side are you on, for Christ's sake?"

"Viktor's—and Irina's and yours!" He turned to the pianist. "Mr. Sherman's right, Viktor. There's a chance you could call their bluff, but don't let them fool you into believing that it's going to be easy to find Irina. They're more worried about the White House and your recital than they are about Irina's safety."

Sherman flared. "You goddamned bastard! One more word out of you, and I put you behind bars and throw away the key! Viktor here had just about convinced me you were on the up and up before that phone rang. If you think . . ."

"Don't come all virtuous at me, Sherman! You forget I used to do this sort of thing for a living, and most of the time with men more ruthless than you because it was their daily bread and butter and they didn't have three thousand miles of Atlantic Ocean to hide behind! I've already said I think you're right. We call their bluff and challenge them to hold Irina, despite the bad publicity, but don't try to kid Viktor that you'll get her back for him!" He sat on the bed, putting an arm round Viktor's shoulders. "Listen to me. When they call back, I'll tell them you don't agree. If they don't release Irina immediately, we announce to the entire world what they're trying to do. OK?"

Viktor shook his head slowly, speaking quietly. "No. I cannot risk

Irina, Mark. She is my sister—the only family that I have in the world. I understand what you are telling me, but you do not understand my countrymen. They do not care about publicity! They will simply call it Western propaganda. None of you understand the power of my country. They are not afraid of anything the United States has to say. They are accustomed to it!" Sherman remained silent. "They will take Irina, and . . ." He did not finish the sentence. "I know them. I know their mentality. They will do it if only to punish me. I know how they think." Viktor sounded tired. Turning to Sherman, he said, "Don't blame Mark for trying to warn me, Mr. Sherman. He is a friend, and he wants what is best for me. I had guessed already that you could not guarantee to bring Irina back."

Sherman exchanged glances with his assistant. "Suppose we don't let you go?"

Kaverin smiled sadly. "You cannot really stop me. If I refuse to play the recital, what use will I be to you? For two days, everyone has been telling me that this is a democracy, where every person has the right to speak. If I tell the American newspapers what you are trying to make me do, then the situation will be reversed. You know I am telling the truth." Sherman said nothing. "I am no longer any use to either side." His face was grey. "I will go back, in exchange for Irina. Then at least one of us will be free." He turned to hug Mark for a moment. "Thank you for trying, my friend. I have told you many times that this has been like a dream for me. Now, it is time to wake up!"

"There's still an outside chance."

"How do you figure that?" Sherman's voice was bitter.

"The exchange. It depends what they have in mind. Look, we're not talking about bridges between East and West Berlin, unless they're going to fly Irina back before making the deal. We're inside the United States, and the nearest point in the Communist world is more than three thousand miles away. Even if they do have Viktor, we're going to be right on top of them from the moment they make the switch."

"You just spent two minutes telling him that we can't stop them from getting his sister out!"

Mark stood up. His head was beginning to clear. "That's the point. We don't know where his sister is, which gives them an advantage as large as the country. For all we know, that phone call came from next door or somewhere on the Canadian border." He looked at his watch.

167

"If they drove her straight to an airport, she could be anywhere by now."

"And?"

"Viktor's going to be with us right up to the moment we exchange him. Unless they plan something very sophisticated, which is unlikely as he's only been here for forty-eight hours, it's going to make it very hard for them to make him disappear."

Sherman was unconvinced. "What are you going to do—plant a direction finder on him and follow the little blip on a radar screen? You've been watching too many B movies on 'The Late Show'!"

"I don't think so. It's a long shot, but it's our only chance from now on. They're going to have to make an exchange somewhere, and that's the moment when they'll have to take their greatest risk. If we play along, there's the chance that they'll be overconfident—and careless."

Sherman was silent, thinking it over. "Maybe. There's not much else we can do." His eyes narrowed. "You're too goddamned eager to play along with them!"

Viktor spoke. "No, Mr. Sherman. I have to go back. I cannot take chances with Irina's life." His voice was sad. "I'm sorry I have failed you after all."

Mark smiled at him. "Not yet. You may still play that recital, Viktor." He turned to Sherman. "Will you try?"

Sherman scowled. "You haven't given us any choice!"

The phone rang again a few minutes later. Sherman said, "Wait!" and walked to the bedside table. He lifted the receiver in unison with Mark.

"Mr. Holland?"

"Yes."

"Have you had the opportunity to discuss our proposal?"

"Yes. We accept your conditions."

"Good. We thought you would."

"What do you want Viktor to do?"

"You will drive Mr. Kaverin to a location we have chosen outside the city."

"Will Irina be there?"

There was a pause. "She will be returned separately."

"No. That's not good enough."

The man gave a gruff laugh. "You're hardly in a position to bargain with us, are you?"

"I think so. We could still persuade Viktor to stay here and make a press statement on the situation. Would you prefer that?"

The man hesitated. "Please hold the line for a moment. I will discuss it with my colleagues." In the ensuing silence, Sherman covered the phone with his hand and said, "You might just be right!" He was smiling.

The caller returned. "We would like to propose a compromise, Mr. Holland. I am sure you appreciate that the exchange of brother for sister is going to be a delicate matter to achieve. If we synchronize our watches, would you agree to an exchange at exactly the same moment in two different places?"

Mark did not look to Sherman for approval. "Yes."

"Very well. You'll come alone."

"No."

"What do you mean?"

"I couldn't come alone, even if I wanted to, and you know it! I'm a visitor to this country, and the situation is outside my control." From his corner, Sherman nodded vigorously. "It's possible I could come with only one other person, but he would need to be an authorized representative."

There was another pause. "Very well."

"Where do we meet?"

The man laughed. "Come, come, Mr. Holland! I'm hardly going to tell you that now! What time do you have?"

Mark looked at his watch. "Five thirty-seven and thirty seconds . . . now!"

"Good." A short pause. "We are synchronized. At exactly eight o'clock we will deliver Irina Kaverin back to the hotel, provided her brother is in our custody. Is that acceptable?"

"Not without better guarantees than you're offering."

The man spoke patiently, as if to a child. "A car will be standing by, with Irina inside. As soon as I telephone the driver, he will stop outside the hotel and she will get out. That will be at the same moment that Viktor joins us. Well?"

"All right. If she's not there, Viktor stays with us."

"That is understood. It will be exactly eight o'clock."

"Where will we be?"

"There is a small town in Connecticut called New Milford. It lies due north of Danbury on Route 7. Do you know it?"

Mark looked at Sherman, who nodded. "Yes."

"Very good. It will take you approximately two hours to get there by car, if you leave shortly. I am making allowances for the evening rush-hour traffic."

"I understand."

"Just after you cross the bridge to enter the town, you will see a gas station on the left-hand side of the road."

"Yes."

"At exactly seven-forty, I will call that gas station and ask the attendant for you by name. Do you follow me?"

"Yes."

"When we speak again, I will give you further instructions where to go. We will be waiting nearby to make the exchange, and we expect only you, one other man, and Viktor. Is that understood? We will be watching, and if there are any others, you will not hear further."

"I understand. Suppose we are delayed and don't reach New Milford in time. What happens?"

"I have given you plenty of time, Mr. Holland, if you leave immediately. However, I am prepared to call once more, at seven forty-five. I will not call again after that."

"You're not allowing much leeway. Anything could happen between now and—"

"Please be there, Mr. Holland. I think we will all regret it if you're not."

Before Mark could reply, he had hung up.

13

"Shit!" Sherman glared at Mark. "Why the hell did you agree to everything like that?" He looked at his watch. "We don't have time to set up a goddam thing! You're playing right into their hands!"

"Not completely. They've already made their first mistake."

"Oh sure! How do you figure that?"

Mark stood. His head still ached, but the throbbing had ceased and his neck and shoulders moved more freely. "The delivery. I'm surprised they agreed to return Irina to the hotel."

"If they return her at all!" Sherman ignored Viktor's reaction. "What difference does it make?"

"Quite a large one. It gives you a better than even chance of spotting Irina long before she gets here. Fifty-fourth Street is one-way—so is Sixth Avenue—which means that you can see anyone approaching from at least two blocks away. Whoever drives her here either has to come up Sixth Avenue or cross over from Seventh. There's no other way. Have you got extra men?"

"A few." Sherman was thoughtful.

"Do they know what Irina looks like?"

"Most of them. There are photographs for the others."

"Good. It means you can post men on both the approach roads to the hotel. If they're lucky, they'll see her coming a block away. With walkie-talkies, they can signal ahead. There are lights on every corner and her driver isn't going to risk jumping any of them, which gives you a further advantage. Right?" Sherman nodded. "We've just agreed that the exchange will take place at exactly eight o'clock. If any one of your men sees her on the way in, it means they have her covered before Viktor leaves us."

"Maybe." Sherman was not prepared to be convinced.

"You can also close off the other end of Fifty-fourth Street, at Fifth

Avenue. Once her car turns into Fifty-fourth, for the hotel, it's cut off."
He frowned. "They're almost asking to get caught."

Viktor looked uneasy. "Please, Mark, nothing will happen to Irina? She will not be harmed?"

"No. Don't worry. If they bring her this far, she'll be all right. There's still the risk that they'll try to double-cross us, but it's one we have to take." He turned to Sherman. "Is there a two-way radio in your car?"

The American nodded. "And a telephone. This is the 1980s! You're right about those approach streets. That was a dumb choice. It makes me wonder whether they really plan to exchange her."

"We've got to hope they do."

"We also have to move now if we're going to make New Milford by seven-forty." Turning towards his assistant, Sherman added, "I need another five minutes to set things up this end. The rest can be done from the car." He spoke in a low voice, giving rapid instructions.

Mark walked over to Viktor and put a hand on his shoulder. The young man was pensive. "Do you want to take your bag?"

He shook his head. "I will leave everything here. I will have no further use for it."

Mark smiled. "Even that little transistor radio you take everywhere with you?"

"That too. I will not be permitted to keep it." His face was grave. "Please, Mark, you will look after Irina when I am gone? I will leave everything in my room for her, but she will be alone." He reached into a pocket. "There is also some money . . ."

"We'll worry about that when the time comes." He increased the pressure on Viktor's shoulder. "Don't give up now. A hell of a lot can happen between here and Connecticut!"

It was dark by the time they left the main highway just north of Danbury to join Route 7. Mark sat next to Sherman in front, watching the steady flow of evening traffic coming from the town. From time to time the American spoke into a hand microphone, maintaining contact with a back-up car a mile behind them. Viktor sat huddled in the back seat. He had hardly spoken since the journey began. The road along which they now travelled was narrower, making them reduce speed. It passed through a typical peri-urban strip—drive-in restaurants, soda fountains,

172

pancake houses, shops, and service stations, with isolated buildings and advertising billboards separating the road from open farmland and fields. To the left, a huge car-park surrounded a busy shopping centre where evening commuters collected last-minute items.

"How are we doing for time?" He half knew the answer, but conversation reduced the tension.

"OK. We don't have much to spare." The radio crackled with static, and an almost unintelligible voice droned a coded message. Sherman raised a microphone to his mouth and said, "Check."

Mark grinned. "I thought you were supposed to say 'Ten-four'!"

Sherman did not smile. "Only on television. If anything goes wrong with this goddam radio, we'll have to switch to an alternative system."

"Why are you using it?"

"To keep one hand free. I can't use a radio and a phone at the same time. There'll be a phone line open between the hotel and the back-up car. As soon as they see the girl arrive—*if* she arrives—they'll call in, and the car will radio me. If they should lose contact on the phone, they'll use mine." As the journey had progressed, he had become more friendly, but a veil of professional caution still separated them.

Mark lit a cigarette and offered the pack to Sherman, who shook his head. "I take it you're trying to quit."

The American smiled briefly. "Does it stick out that much? It could be that's what makes me so jumpy!" He accelerated past two slower-moving cars to the top of a hill. The bare skeletons of trees were picked up by the headlights. They passed a clump of graceful white birches whose brightly coloured trunks looked as though they had been freshly painted.

Mark glanced round. "This looks like an attractive area."

"It used to be good farming country. Now it's mostly fancy weekend homes for well-heeled New Yorkers. Lake Candlewood, over to the left," he jerked his head, "is more like Madison Avenue on a Saturday afternoon—nothing but rich bitches serving martinis in their designer jeans! Real estate round here needs a Wall Street income." His voice indicated his disapproval.

"How far do we still have to go?"

"A few miles. We should make it just about on time." He stopped for a lonely set of traffic lights, surrounded by a few darkened houses. "That goddam traffic on the Deegan slowed us up." It had been a long, frustrating crawl through heavy commuter traffic as they left Manhattan. About eight million people entered New York City every day, and the evening drive home was one of the penalties paid for the comforts of suburban living. There had been a breakdown on the Major Deegan Expressway, one of the main arteries to the north of the city, and the minutes had ticked away as they had impatiently edged their way north to Yonkers and the faster roads.

The wayside shops and buildings were becoming more scattered and Sherman was able to increase speed steadily, passing through open fields and farmland, occasionally hidden behind dark clumps of trees. It was pleasantly undulating land, and unlike in Britain, the road cut a straight path through the landscape. Far to his left, Mark thought he could distinguish the outline of tall hills. Solitary lights from distant farmhouses revealed the topography. He turned in his seat to look at Viktor, who remained curled in a corner, apparently lost in thought. If the Russian was aware of Mark's questioning gaze, he did not respond to it.

Crossing the brow of a hill, they were confronted by lights on either side of the road. A drive-in McDonald's restaurant, its forecourt crowded with cars, was busy; used-car lots, illuminated by strings of light bulbs that swayed in the breeze, displayed neat rows of vehicles at bargain prices; garages and filling stations trumpeted special offers with gaudy placards. Overhead street lights indicated the approaches of a town.

"We're coming into New Milford now. I make it seven thirty-seven." Sherman lifted his microphone and pressed a button on its side. "Hold before the traffic circle. I'll try to park in sight." The voice on the radio crackled a reply. Turning to Mark, he said, "We should make it by the first call, but only just. I'm still trying to figure where the exchange will take place. With fifteen or twenty minutes to go, the choice is wide."

"Are there many towns in the area?"

"Villages, mostly—Bantam, Marbledale, Lake Waramaug. I suppose you would call Litchfield a town. They could be anywhere round here."

"You seem to know the place well."

He shrugged. "I grew up in Bethel, Connecticut, which isn't so far away. I had an aunt who lived around here. My folks used to visit her and I got dragged along." Sherman seemed to relax slightly and grimaced. "I always hated her—a stuck-up, pretentious bitch with a voice like a buzz-saw. She spent her time bullying her old man and putting on

174

airs. He was some kind of cheap lawyer whose hobby was trying to screw the world. What a neurotic pair! I guess they deserved each other. The only part I remember with any pleasure was a great peach farm in the neighbourhood that made its own peach ice-cream. My folks used to talk about it all the way up in the car to make the rest of the day sound bearable. I don't know why we used to visit with them. My folks couldn't stand them either!" He steered the car round a traffic circle, driving over a darkened bridge whose metal girders gleamed in the headlights. Thirty yards ahead, amid the first cluster of houses marking the start of the town, there was a small, brightly lit filling station on the left side of the road. Sherman parked opposite and looked at his watch. "Seven-forty!"

Viktor moved forward so that his head was between their shoulders. "Ask if Irina is all right."

Mark nodded and stepped out of the car to cross the road. The night air was cold, and he hunched his shoulders against the wind. From the small office at the rear of the filling station, a radio was blaring rock music. As he approached, the sound was suddenly reduced and he heard a telephone ringing. He walked forward quickly.

A young man dressed in dirty dark blue overalls appeared in the doorway. Seeing Mark, he called, "Would you be a Mr. Holland?"

"Yes."

The man turned his head, indicating the office. "There's a call for you." He looked puzzled. "How come he knew you were here?"

"He knew I expected to stop here about this time. Otherwise, I would have called him."

"Oh." The young man looked suspicious. "This ain't a public utility. Do you need gas?"

"Probably. I'll check with my friend."

"OK." Honour was satisfied. "I guess it didn't cost!"

The telephone was a greasy, oil-smeared wall model. It slipped in Mark's fingers. "Hello. This is Mark Holland."

He recognized the voice. The speaker sounded genial. "Well done, Mr. Holland! You made it on time, I see."

"Only just. Where do we go?"

There was a momentary pause. "Tell your driver to continue in the same direction through the town, and turn north on Route 109 for a few miles. Just beyond New Preston, there's a right turn on to 47, to

175

Washington Depot. I want you to go straight on up the hill to Washington Green. Have you got all that?"

"Yes." Mark repeated the instructions.

"Good. As you enter the Green, make a half-right and stop. You wait there. A car will be on the far side of the Green. It will blink its headlamps twice. Remain exactly where you are and turn your lights off. Mr. Kaverin is to leave your car and walk across the Green to the other car. Understood?"

"Yes. What about his sister?"

"She will be on her way to the hotel, as promised. She is perfectly safe, if you're worried. Nothing has happened to her. Now, I will repeat those instructions if you wish." The voice was slightly bantering. "We wouldn't want you to get it wrong!"

Mark controlled his impatience. "I'll repeat the last part back to you."

When he had finished, the caller said, "Very good. I think I should warn you that you have just about enough time to get there, so you'd better hurry. We will not wait, and Irina Kaverin will not be returned. Understood?"

"Yes." He could not resist adding, "And you won't get Viktor. We'll be there on time."

"I hope so. Please don't try anything foolish, Mr. Holland. You'll only regret it."

"We'll be there. You'd better make sure that Irina is too."

"No problem, Mr. Holland." The bantering tone returned. "You'd better get going!"

As Mark left the office, the young mechanic called after him, "What about that gas?"

"We'll be back in about half an hour for some. There isn't time now."

"Yeah? Next time, use your own goddam phone!"

Sherman listened in silence as Mark relayed the directions word for word. He nodded and moved off. "I know Washington. We're going to have to step on it if we're to be there on time." Picking up the microphone, he passed the information to the back-up car. "Shit! If they do get away with Viktor, we don't have a hope of finding them. The whole area's a rabbit warren of country lanes and small roads between Washington and Roxbury, right over to Woodbury. They chose a good place!"

He accelerated up a hill past neat streets of houses, seemingly venting his irritation on the car.

"Don't go too fast. I don't want to arrive early."

"You'll be lucky to arrive on time. What are you getting at?"

"I have an idea. About how big is Washington Green? How far is it from one side to the other?"

"I don't remember." Sherman shrugged. "Fifty, seventy yards, maybe. There's a church in the middle. Why?"

"When we get there, they're going to call their man in New York and tell him to deliver Irina."

"Right, provided they keep their part of the deal."

Viktor started to speak, but Mark cut across him. "We assume they will. Viktor, you must wait until the last possible moment before you step out of the car. You still have to walk across the Green. It may just give us the time we need." He looked at Sherman. "That depends how fast your men spot Irina in New York."

The American was silent for a moment, concentrating on the road down which they were now travelling. They had passed the last of the houses on the perimeter of the town and were driving through open countryside. Occasional buildings, their windows like beacons in the darkness, stood sentinel on either side. Sherman smiled. "Maybe it's not such a long shot after all." He glanced at Mark. "You must have been a pretty good operator in your time. Too bad you quit!"

They found the turn-off to Washington Depot at seven fifty-four, and Sherman accelerated again. The dark country road was broad and there were no other vehicles. After a further message on his radio, Sherman settled back in his seat. "It must be twenty years since I was here, but I guess it won't have changed. Washington Depot's mostly new. The old town was washed away by a flood years back. You'd never think it, to look at the little stream that flows through the centre. The new part's OK. I guess it's what you English call the down-market end. The fancy part's the Green, on top of the hill. It's one of those New England showplaces, with big white clapboard houses and painted shutters. Some of them date back to the eighteenth century, but you can't tell which are the old and which are the new. Everything has to be built in the same style. Some of the snobbier owners put the date over their front door just so you'll know!"

"It sounds beautiful."

"Yeah, it looks like that old TV soap opera. What was it called? 'Peyton Place.' "

Isolated street lamps appeared, heralding a village. Sherman slowed for a corner and turned left. Mark glimpsed a group of houses and a small modern block of buildings. A supermarket at the end of the row advertised meat at special prices. It was closed for the night. The time was seven fifty-nine.

"How far do we still have to go?"

"This is the Depot." Sherman nodded straight ahead, where the road curved up a wooded hillside. "The Green's at the top of that hill."

"You'd better slow down, or we'll be early. Any word from New York?"

Sherman now kept the microphone in his left hand, steering with his right. He spoke into it. "Has she shown?"

The radio crackled slightly. "Not yet."

"Park at the bottom of the hill and wait there." They were climbing slowly, and the road rounded a bend between the trees. A house with darkened windows loomed out of the shadows.

The radio sputtered again. "They think someone's approaching now." Sherman braked, leaning forward. The voice returned. "False alarm. Just some old dame arriving at the hotel." He sighed, and eased the car forward up the steep incline. Mark held his watch close to the dashboard to read the time from the reflected light. It was seven fifty-nine and fifty seconds.

"It's time."

Sherman reached the top of the hill and steered the car to the right, entering the perimeter of the Green before coming to a halt. Almost under his breath, he said, "I guess we'd better start praying!" He lifted the microphone to his mouth. "What's happening?"

The voice at the other end was impassive. "No sign."

"How about the men round the block?"

"They're checking in now. Nothing yet."

"Shit!"

The broad expanse of the Green was dimly lit by a few street lights which illuminated the substantial-looking two- and three-storey white houses with their dark-painted window shutters. Lights shone in a few rooms, but most of the windows were darkened. To Mark's left, just off the centre of the Green, the large, square shape of the Congregational church, constructed with the same horizontal slats of white-painted wood, obscured the view of the opposite side of the Green.

"Anything?" Sherman's voice was tense.

"No."

Diagonally across the Green, about seventy yards away, a car parked in the shadows of a large house blinked its lights twice. Mark glanced round at Viktor, who was now hunched back in a corner. He kept his voice calm. "We're supposed to turn our lights off." Sherman moved his hand to the dashboard, and the white beam of light faded. It seemed much darker. Mark noted that he had left the engine running.

The radio was silent. Sherman stared at it. "Come on, you mothers!"

The car across the Green blinked its lights again. Mark looked at Viktor. "Are you ready?"

"Yes." He seemed to speak with difficulty.

"I don't think we can delay them much longer. When you get out, walk very slowly."

"Yes. Mark . . ." His voice was strangled.

"Yes, Viktor?"

"Thank you for everything you have done. I will always be grateful to you. Irina . . . will you look after Irina?"

"I will. There's still time. Move slowly. They're probably waiting to see you get out of the car before they pass on their instructions."

"I . . ." Viktor did not speak further, but opened the door and stepped out. As he turned to close it, Mark called softly, "Don't shut the door. You'll need it!" The Russian hesitated, then turned and began to walk slowly. As he did so, the car across the Green blinked its lights again.

Sherman watched him go. His voice was low. "I guess it didn't work. What now? Do we go after him, and the hell with the girl?"

Mark looked at him. He had anticipated Sherman's plan. "Not quite yet. They've only just seen him." Viktor was ten yards away. Light from a street lamp outlined him clearly.

The radio came to life again. "Something's happening." Sherman leaned forward, gently turning up the volume. He did not interrupt the call with his microphone. "They think she's coming in." The voice was calm, but there was a slight undercurrent of excitement. "The man on Seventh Avenue says a dark blue Buick, with a single woman sitting in the back, just turned east on Fifty-fourth Street. He can't make a positive identification. The car just stopped for the light on Sixth Avenue. Wait a minute! The guy on the corner of Sixth saw her too. He isn't certain, but it sure looks like her!"

"Jesus Christ!" Sherman peered into the darkness. Viktor was now thirty yards away, walking slowly, his head down. He had momentarily disappeared into a shadowy part of the Green.

The radio crackled. Mark could hear a second, faint voice, relaying the information as it came in. "The Buick's continued along Fifty-fourth Street, heading towards the Dorset. It's been held up at the corner. There's a taxi double-parked outside the Warwick Hotel, letting off a fare, and it can't get past!"

"Come on!" Sherman spoke through clenched teeth. "Get out of the goddam way!"

The radio suddenly faded, and Mark feared for a moment that they were losing contact. Then the voice returned, speaking with mounting excitement. "The Buick's pulling up at the Dorset! It's stopping now. The girl's getting out. It's her! It's her! We've got her!"

Mark heard himself shout, "Now!" Viktor was already fifty yards away, crossing the last part of the well-trimmed grass that formed the Green. He paused for a moment, looking back. As he did so, the other car turned its headlights on, illuminating him in the glare.

Sherman stamped his foot on the accelerator and their car heaved forward, slithering and screeching as its spinning wheels tried to grip the surface. The engine roared. He turned the lights on full, driving straight across the grass towards the solitary figure, now standing dead still, caught in the crossed beams of both cars.

The American wrestled with the wheel as the car lurched across the slippery grass, gathering speed. In front of them, the other car was moving forward towards Viktor. Sherman gained control of his vehicle as it raced after the Russian, now only yards away and in danger of being run down. He waited until the last possible moment, then expertly skidded the heavy machine round the stationary figure, placing himself between Viktor and the other car. The door had swung open, and as the pianist ran forward, Sherman braked to a sudden halt. The pianist threw himself across the back seat and Sherman pressed the accelerator again, making the car slide forward. Within seconds, they had reached the small road circling the Green. The tyres gripped the hard surface, and they gained speed with every second. The radio was still chattering with excited voices, but Sherman ignored them, concentrating his attention on the road.

Mark looked round for the other car, but it had turned and was now heading away from them at high speed. Presumably, its driver wanted to avoid identification.

Viktor's eyes met his. "Irina?"

"She's safe, Viktor. They've got her back!"

Sherman braked hard as he reached the corner of the Green and headed back down the hill. He glanced briefly in the rear-view mirror, but Mark guessed that he had already seen the other car's departure. As they descended the hill, he reduced speed. His face had relaxed but a thin film of sweat glistened on his upper lip. "Jesus H. Christ! How much closer did you want to make it?" He glanced back at Viktor. "You OK?"

"Yes." The young man was breathing in great gulps of air. "Thank you!"

"We'd better get the hell out of here, in case they have reinforcements, which I doubt. It looks like we were both bluffing each other. I'd sure like to go after that car, but it's too late anyway." He picked up the microphone, but before pressing the talk-button he looked at Mark. "Is this the way you used to handle things in the old days?" He was smiling.

"Not quite. We usually hoped for a little more . . . flexibility!"

"So how would you describe it?"

Mark grinned. "Like everything in the music world—a matter of good timing!"

14

Sherman drove to a small all-night diner somewhere near Danbury, to hold a hasty conference with his assistants in the back-up car. Mark and Viktor occupied a separate booth while the others talked. The pianist seemed to be in shock and scarcely spoke.

"Are you still going to play the recital, Viktor? They would understand if you cancelled."

"No, it is more important than ever that I do."

"You're not going to be in any shape to play. After—"

"I will be well enough. I will sleep. Tomorrow I will be well again. Is Irina safe?"

"Yes. She's a little stunned by it all, but they're looking after her. They called to say they'd given her a sedative and she's resting."

"Thank God!" He closed his eyes. "Can we leave soon?"

"I'll ask. You've had a bad time. For a moment, I thought it was all over!"

"At least it is finished now. Don't worry for me, Mark. I will play a memorable recital. I am stronger than you think!"

They arrived at the Dorset just before midnight. Sherman walked Viktor to the door, where two heavily built men awaited him. The agent returned immediately to the car.

"Do you want to go in? Irina's sleeping."

"I'll catch up with them tomorrow."

Sherman hesitated. "I'm sorry I gave you a hard time earlier. I guess I have to suspect everyone."

"It goes with the job."

"You did pretty well tonight. Did you really think we'd pull it off?"

"It was a gamble. They were careless, and we were lucky."

"They were plain amateur! I guess they thought they had us by the short hairs. How's your head?"

His head was throbbing, and his bruised neck had stiffened again. Nervous tension and exhaustion had taken their toll. "Terrible, but I'll probably survive!"

"I hate to do this to you, but I have to file a report."

"Can't it wait until the morning?"

"I'd sooner do it now, while it's still clear."

"Still suspicious?"

Sherman laughed. "No, but the book says make the report first and sleep after. I guess you remember the routine. We can do most of it with a tape recorder. OK?"

The agent delivered him to the Mayflower at two in the morning. As Mark turned to leave, Sherman handed him a small tablet. "Take that when you lie down. You'll sleep."

"I'll sleep anyway!"

"Just to be safe, but wait until you're lying down!"

There were various messages awaiting Mark at the front desk—two calls from Switzerland, three from Abe. The last thing Mark remembered was swallowing the tablet as he was reading them.

A phone was ringing insistently, forcing him back into consciousness. With an effort, he lifted the receiver to his ear.

"Mark, where the hell have you been?" Abe was furious. "I've been trying to reach you for twenty-four hours, God damn it! I rang the hotel yesterday and was told you weren't taking calls until two o'clock. I left three messages, but you didn't reply. I even stopped by, and you weren't in."

Twenty-four hours? Damn Sherman's pill! "Abe, I'm sorry—"

"Sorry? Listen kid, it may have escaped your attention, but we have a recital tonight, featuring that well-known Russian *émigré*, Viktor Kaverin, courtesy of Mark Holland Productions! How the hell can you drop out the day before a concert? The office has been going out of its mind; I've had Shirley calling every number in the book except the Missing Persons Bureau, and you're sorry! What is this, for Christ's sake? Have you gone out of your mind?"

"Abe, I'll explain it all later . . ."

"Later won't do! I couldn't reach Viktor until noon yesterday, and all he would say was the he'd slept late and was on his way to Steinway Hall. Irina couldn't talk and you'd disappeared! What's going on?" Some of Abe's fury had receded, but he was still angry. "Jesus, Mark, how could you do this to me?"

"I called back yesterday evening, but there was no reply."

Abe sounded calmer. "I had a concert yesterday evening. Some of us work for a living! Why didn't you call my home number?"

Mark hesitated. "Abe, I'm sorry I let you down. I haven't been very well."

"What?" Abe's manner changed immediately. "Why didn't you say? Have you seen a doctor?"

"It wasn't necessary." Abe's concern made him feel guilty. "It was some kind of fever. I'm all right again."

"Listen, are you sure? I can get someone to look at you. Why the hell didn't you call me as soon as you felt bad?"

"There was no need. All I had to do was sweat it out."

"You should have told me." His voice was suspicious. "Where were you when I stopped by the hotel?"

"I must have been walking it off. I went to the Dorset to make sure that everything was all right with Viktor and Irina."

"Oh. They didn't mention it. I called them too. You know, we're going to have to talk to Viktor. He can avoid the press if he wants to, but he can't play hide-and-seek with his manager."

"He'll be co-operative once this recital's out of the way. It's mostly reaction to the last few days. Everything's happened too quickly for him. I haven't told you the whole story of how he and Irina escaped. They had a frightening time. I'm amazed he's able to play at all. To be honest, I think it's the only thing that's holding him together."

"Let's hope it lasts through tonight! Listen, are you sure you're OK?"

"I'm feeling much better. Will you be in the office today?"

"Will I ever! Where d'you think I'm calling from? Saturday or no Saturday, I have three days' work to cover in the next twelve hours. I guess God will forgive me this one time. He understands the music business!" His good humour was returning. "I could sure use your help, Mark. I didn't sign the television contract yet, because I couldn't find you, and I gave Greg Laufer what Sam Goldwyn used to call 'a definite maybe' on the rights to the recording."

"That's fine."

"Good, but we still have to go through the contracts. Magnum was on my neck all day yesterday, wanting to know if they could install their goddam equipment backstage, plus a whole army of television people . . . Jesus, kid, you picked a bad time to drop out!"

"Give me half an hour to shave and have a cup of coffee."

"Nah, take your time. I can manage for the moment. You sure you can make it?"

"Sure. What's happening at the box-office?"

"Insane! Sherman was right. The whole place sold out in a little over two hours. I never saw anything like it since Horowitz made his come-back! They're going out of their minds, trying to print up programmes in time. To make matters worse, I had to waste two hours yesterday afternoon with a bunch of security guys from Washington. Why the hell couldn't they set this damn thing up in the White House?"

"You heard what he said: it's some kind of presidential gesture."

184

Abe grunted. "More like some kind of vote-pulling gimmick! Art and politics don't mix."

"It's funny Abe, but that's what Konstantin Steigel said."

"Yeah? Well that old buzzard's a sly fox."

"You're mixing your animals!"

"Kid, at this moment, I don't have time to mix a martini! I'll see you when you get here. Shirley will order you an extra cheese Danish!" He hung up.

Mark looked at his watch. It was just after seven-thirty. He had lost a complete day. Bright sunshine was streaming through the windows of the bedroom, and he walked over to draw the blinds. What he had told Abe had been partially true. The previous twenty-four hours had been a nightmare, and he still felt light-headed. He wondered how much of the whole story he would ever be able to tell.

He had slept for thirteen hours. Sherman's tablet had left him unconscious, and he had awoken in the middle of the following afternoon, dizzy and nauseous, with an unreal sense of detachment. After fifteen minutes under the shower, alternating between bursts of hot and cold water, he had emerged with his senses still reeling and, after pulling on some clothes, had staggered from the hotel to cross the road and walk in Central Park. He vaguely remembered a doorman taking him by the arm, a look of concern on his face. The man probably thought he was drunk.

He could not remember how long he had walked for, forcing one leg in front of the other, his eyes fixed, his mind blank, until the effects of the drug wore off. There were only blurred memories of paths through the park and clumps of tree trunks that seemed to spring up before him, forcing him to change direction. Slowly, his brain had cleared, and he had stumbled back to the hotel. By the time he had called Abe's office, there was no reply, and he had showered again before going to the Dorset. Sherman had met him in the foyer.

"I was just leaving. How're you feeling?"

"What the hell did you give me? I feel like a refugee from *The Lost Weekend!*"

"What's that?"

"An old film about an alcoholic."

"Oh. I guess I only go back as far as *Days of Wine and Roses.*" He grinned. "You should have gone on sleeping. There was enough in that pill to knock out a horse!"

"There was enough for an elephant! Why did you do it?"

"You looked like you needed it. Going to see Irina?"

"Yes. How is she?"

"Not bad—a little the worse for wear."

"Did she take one of your specials too?"

"Sure, but don't worry. By tomorrow, you'll both be as right as rain."

Irina had been listless and distracted, uneasy in the presence of the bulky guard sitting on the sofa facing the doors of the elevators. She had kissed Mark briefly, her lips brushing lightly against his.

"Did they give you something to help you sleep?"

"Yes."

"Me too. If it's any consolation, I feel just as bad. I don't know what they use here, but it's lethal! Where's Viktor?"

"Still practising, I think. I do not know."

"I met Sherman downstairs. He was the one who helped Viktor to escape last night."

"Oh. I did not realize. He came to give me our alien registration cards." Two small plastic-encased documents not much larger than credit cards were lying on the desk.

"The famous green cards. You should feel flattered, Irina. Most immigrants wait for months for one of those. They're very precious."

"I suppose so." She yawned. "Oh, Mark, I'm so tired! I can't think properly!"

"It's the sedative. Have some food sent up and go to bed. Tomorrow's a very important day. How is Viktor?"

"Viktor is indestructible!"

Mark dialled room service and ordered a large breakfast. He suddenly realized he was hungry. His last meal had been a hot dog in the park a day and a half earlier. He sighed, heading for the bathroom. It was going to be another long day.

Abe made the time pass quickly, explaining the intricacies of American contracts, organizing the distribution of the block of tickets he had acquired, arranging limousines, telephoning innumerable last-minute confirmations—piano tuners, florists, journalists, television executives, house managers, and many more. His address book was ever-present, and he left nothing to chance. Shirley maintained a steady flow of fresh coffee and food. Somewhere around two o'clock, he looked up solicitously from his desk, peering over the rims of his glasses.

"How're you making out, kid?"

"Hanging on, Abe, by my fingertips! I've learned more in the last few hours than I thought I knew over the past ten years! You didn't need me here!"

Abe looked pleased. "Sure I did. If anything goes wrong, I've got you to blame, schmuck! Didn't that asshole Greg Laufer teach you anything about decision-making in the corporate world?"

"I'd sooner deal with him than that creepy little man Austerklein."

Abe lit his third cigar, waving away smoke as he dismissed the vice-president of business affairs. "He's just a New York shyster. I eat them for breakfast! You simply have to persuade those goniffs they got away with one of their deliberately ambiguous clauses, and they're so pleased they don't notice you just upped the royalty a couple of points! Are you sure you're OK? You don't look so hot. Myra will kill me if I don't look after you. She already told me to order a carton of matzo-ball soup." Abe's long-suffering wife, who dominated his life with a fatalistic anticipation of the worst, believed that men survived by three things above all: a good job, a good Jewish wife, and a bowl of chicken soup. "Listen, there's not much else we can do here. Why don't you go back to the hotel and rest up? Do you want to pick up Viktor? He said to be at the hall by five-thirty."

"Right."

"Great." His secretary appeared in the doorway. "Shirley, you're a doll! Are you coming to the concert? You can get to see the President."

"No thank you, Mr. S. My sister and her family are visiting this evening. I'll catch Viktor next time. I reserved your usual table at the Russian Tea Room." She shrugged. "Besides, I already saw the President. He was on TV last week."

Mark lit a cigarette. "Abe, I still owe you an explanation about yesterday, as well as a lot of other matters. Viktor and Irina have had a very difficult time—"

"Not half as difficult as it's going to be if this wingding tonight turns out to be a hit, kid! That's when we really start working! We can talk about it tomorrow. Right now, you need a couple of hours with your feet up, and I need a shave, a clean shirt and thirty minutes with the

London *Times* crossword. I have it flown in every day, and it's the only way I get to relax. Come on, kid, let's get out of here. We can share a cab uptown. That way, we both claim it off our taxes!"

Viktor was waiting with Craig Sherman. He was dressed in a shirt and slacks, with the grey nylon windjacket that Mark had first seen at the Moscow reception. His eyes glittered with suppressed excitement. As Mark entered, the pianist greeted him with a warm hug, pressing his cheek close.

"How do you feel?"

"Wonderful! I still have another hour of hard practice, but I am ready!" Although he was perhaps a little paler than usual, he showed no other signs of his experiences.

"And Irina?"

"She is much, much better. Yesterday, she felt bad all day. She could not stay awake." Mark looked at Sherman, who winked. "She went out to choose a new dress for tonight." He lifted his hold-all. "Come. I have everything I need. I will wait in the hall until the concert begins. Will you fetch her later?"

"Of course."

As they entered by the stage door of Carnegie Hall, Mark noticed two men in dark suits standing with the uniformed guard. Seeing the direction of Mark's gaze, Sherman said, "The place is swarming with plain-clothes men. They've been here all day, along with metal detectors, sniffer dogs, and Christ knows what else!" He shook his head sadly. "To think there used to be a time when a President could do a whistle-stop tour across the country and all he needed was a campaign manager and a valet!" He nodded to one of the men, then turned back. "You'll be OK from here on in. Once those guys have seen you, they never forget a face!"

Viktor looked anxious. "Please, Mr. Sherman, it is very important that the hall should be empty for half an hour while I prepare myself for the concert. Can this be arranged?"

"That may not be so easy. Apart from the security men and the cleaners, there's a television crew setting up lights and cameras."

"It means a great deal to me. I cannot make myself ready if all those people are watching me. I only need half an hour. After that they can come in, and I will play for them if they need to make a camera rehearsal or adjust their microphones." He seemed very ill at ease. "Please!"

Sherman hesitated, then nodded. "I'll see what I can do. I guess the television crew takes a break somewhere around now. I'm not so sure about the security guys."

"But they will be doing a better job if they protect all the entrances. I will be completely safe inside!"

The American smiled. "I guess so. To be honest, Viktor, I think they have someone else's safety in mind! Wait here." He walked down the long, carpeted corridor towards the front of the building.

"Shall I take your bag up to the dressing-room?"

"No, I shall keep it with me." For a moment, Viktor looked guilty, then gave a conspiratorial smile. "I stole several towels from the hotel—but I promise to put them back afterwards. I will need them to dry myself while I practice."

Sherman returned a few minutes later. "OK, Viktor, the TV crew will take a break now, but you can only have until six-fifteen. They've been working all day, so they appreciate the suggestion."

"Thank you, Mr. Sherman. I will play for them when I am ready. What about the security men? I am sorry to insist. You see, I am a little nervous and very superstitious. This is the most important moment of my life, and I am going to play in one of the most famous concert halls in the world. This is the same stage that was used by Godowsky and Rachmaninov and Rubinstein . . ."

Sherman grinned. "Hell, Viktor, it was even used by Judy Garland and Benny Goodman! It's OK. They said to go ahead. The security's even better if nobody gets in."

"Thank you."

"Would you like me to wait outside too?"

"Yes, please, Mark, if you do not mind. I want to listen for a moment to the ghosts of all those past musicians. They will inspire me!"

There was a brief pause as a huge stagehand whose pot-belly hung ponderously over his baggy trousers stood on the stage shouting instructions in various directions. Viktor stood before him, next to the front row of seats, watching. Standing in the doorway, Mark glanced round the famous old building, which was due to be given an expensive face-lift. With its red carpeting and white and gold decorations, everything glowed in preparation for the evening, and there was a colourful array of spring flowers surrounding the presidential box. It had always been one of his favourite concert halls, not only for its excellent acoustics but also for the warm, friendly atmosphere it inspired. He wondered also whether he was not, like Viktor, influenced by its long tradition and history, and the many great musicians who had graced its stage for nearly a century. Avery Fisher Hall, in the newer Lincoln Center, was only twenty-odd years old. It did not have the same atmosphere. The auditorium slowly emptied and the stagehand, with a friendly nod to Viktor, waddled to the exit that led upstairs to the dressing-rooms.

Mark returned to Sherman, and they walked slowly along a corridor whose walls were decorated with framed originals of the manuscript scores of great composers. In front of them, many of the workers were making their way into the bar. Only the security men remained at their posts, standing with their backs to all the doors leading into the main hall.

Sherman lit a cigarette. "I guess musicians are almost as superstitious as sportsmen. I like the idea of communing with all those old greats before he plays. It has style."

"He meant it when he said this was the most important day of his life. If the concert goes the way I expect, he'll join that list of greats."

"I guess. He's not a bad kid, and he's got guts. I could've run him down the other night, but he never flinched. For a while there, I couldn't get that goddam car under control on the grass. I wondered how I was going to miss him! They must breed 'em tough where he comes from!"

"He was very frightened, which makes him all the braver. Did you catch the driver of Irina's car?"

Sherman frowned. "No. We goofed. The moment the girl got out at the Dorset, everyone came running towards her. I guess they were so excited to get her back, they just ran. There was a car stationed at the end of the street, on the corner of Fifth, but the Buick never got there."

"What happened to it?"

"The driver parked it a few yards up the road and left it standing. He must have stepped out and walked away, cool as a cucumber. That takes nerve!"

"How about the car?"

"Stolen that morning in Scarsdale. The owner was lucky to get it back in one piece. Are you going back for Irina later?" Mark nodded.

"She's a cute girl." Mark said nothing, and Sherman grinned. "OK, I know when to keep my big mouth shut! Listen, I'm sorry about the knock-out pill. I didn't know it was going to hit you that hard."

"Don't worry. It was the cumulative result of the past few days. It's been a busy week!"

"This place has been a madhouse since dawn, what with security and the television crew. They've set up cameras all over the house. It seems they're going to beam the programme by satellite to half of Europe." He grunted. "They even have a special fixed camera, pointing at the presidential box, to catch every reaction. He'll be playing to an audience of millions."

"That was always Viktor's dream."

Sherman grinned. "I was talking about the President!"

They continued to walk, slowly circling the ground floor of the building, then retraced their steps back to the stage door. "I'm surprised Viktor hasn't started to play. I can't hear anything from inside."

Sherman laughed. "You forget, he's got a lot of ghosts to commune with!"

As if in response to their conversation, the sound of the piano became audible. Viktor was playing the opening bars of the Chopin sonata with some of the fierce passion he had displayed at the rehearsal in Lausanne.

Sherman paused by the door, his head bowed so that his ear was next to the panel. He nodded appreciatively. "I don't know the first goddam thing about that kind of music, but he sounds like he plays a mean piano!"

15

"Irina, you're beautiful!"

"Do you like it?" She twirled before him like a fashion model. She was wearing a simple, straight-cut black dress, without sleeves, high at the neck and bare-backed, with a single strand of pearls round her

191

throat like a collar. Her hair was drawn tightly back, emphasizing her high cheekbones and large eyes, and her breasts were sensuously outlined against the soft material. "It was very expensive!"

"It was worth it. The audience will spend more time looking at you than at Viktor."

"Oh Mark, you always say such good things to me! They give me confidence." She locked her arms around his neck. "I am sorry I was so distant yesterday." They kissed. Her arms tightened, and her tongue searched for his.

He released her gently. "We'd better leave."

"So soon? Are we late?"

"No, but if we stay here much longer, we'll miss the concert altogether! Why do you look sad?"

She smiled quickly. "You forget my Slavic blood. In the midst of happiness, we are always able to find a moment of regret! Will we see Viktor first?"

"Yes. He's waiting in the dressing-room. He practised until the last moment. The piano tuner was getting nervous!"

"He is very excited. I was sad for a moment because I wished our mother and father could have been here to see him play."

"Are they still in Russia?" Mark realized that he knew very little about her.

Irina shook her head. "No. They died many years ago. We have only each other."

Viktor was resting in an easy chair in the dressing-room. He had already changed and was sitting in his shirt-sleeves, fiddling with the dial of his transistor radio. He looked up to greet them with a casual wave. If he was tense, he gave little indication. Irina leaned over her brother and kissed him on the forehead.

Mark smiled. "All set?"

"Yes. There is a D-sharp that is a little slow, but the tuner is working on it. Otherwise, the piano is excellent."

They talked for a few minutes until Abe put his head round the door. He was beaming happily. "You're starting out right, Viktor. The box office has closed, and they're turning people away in droves. There was a line half-way down the block, hoping for last-minute returns. I just looked in to say break a leg." Irina was puzzled. "It's OK, honey. It's just an expression of good luck. I guess we'll have to think of something else when you dance! Would you like one of us to stay backstage with you, Viktor?"

"No."

"You're sure?" The pianist nodded. "I'm only asking because the security's fierce out there tonight. Nobody's allowed to come in once the President's seated—not even managers." He grinned. "I guess they're afraid it might wake him! I keep tripping over television people round here. Backstage is littered with them. There must be thirty young broads standing around with clipboards, looking important. They've set up a TV monitor in the dressing-room on the other side, up the little staircase."

Viktor stood and put on his jacket. It was cut in a slightly old-fashioned style, with wide lapels, but it was well tailored, emphasizing his muscular shoulders and narrow waist. Irina tried to straighten an unruly lock of hair, but he smiled and rumpled it again. "More poetic!" A distant bell sounded.

"Time to go!" Abe beckoned. "I have my usual box, at the end of the row. You may not see so well, but you get out first!" He led the way through a rear door close to the dressing-room. It was guarded by an elderly black attendant with frizzled white hair, wearing the house uniform. Mark recognized him from previous visits. The old man had an uncanny memory for names. He gave a quasi-salute.

"You just knock once, Mr. Sincoff, and I'll open up for you." He leaned forward. "Those Washington security men tried to take over from me here, but I wasn't having any. I told them this was my old door and nobody else gets to work it! I'll see you at the intermission."

Myra Sincoff was already in the box, seated in the front row, peering across the elegantly clad audience. She was, as ever, in her black silk "working dress." She stood to shake Irina's hand, then held a cheek up for Mark to kiss. "So how come you haven't called me?" She glanced approvingly at Irina. "You found yourself another girl already?" Most of Myra's comments ended with a question mark, and although she pretended a reproachful manner, Mark knew that her affection was unshakeable. "Abe tells me you were ill. You don't call your friends at a time like that?"

"I'm sorry, Myra. It's been hectic. I'm feeling fine."

"You probably didn't eat regularly. What are you—on a diet?"

A slightly muffled recording of "The Star-Spangled Banner" greeted the presidential party, and the house lights dimmed to an expectant hush. Many heads were turned and necks craned to see the nation's leader and his wife, but they were hidden behind floral decorations and Secret Service aides. Abe winked at Mark. "I told you: he looks just like on television, only much, much smaller!"

There was still an excited murmur of conversation as Viktor walked briskly to the front of the stage. He hesitated momentarily, looking towards the presidential box. Then a broad smile filled his face and he bowed, holding his head low as the applause mounted. The audience was won over by that smile and responded. A man stood, clapping his hands in a wide, exaggerated arc, others quickly joined him, and the entire house rose to its feet, cheering and applauding. Many heads were turned towards the flower-bedecked box and there was a sudden surge of acclaim. The President and his wife had risen also, smiling and clapping, and he waved a friendly hand with that familiar gesture that had won so many votes at the last election.

Abe was delighted. Leaning closer to Mark, he had to raise his voice to be heard over the noise. "Only in New York! Where else in the world do you get a standing ovation before they ever heard you play!"

Perhaps it was the mood of the gala evening or perhaps the occasion inspired Viktor beyond his own expectations, but it seemed to Mark that the pianist played better than he had heard before. The Mozart sonata was beautifully balanced, with a subtle blend of drama and elegance. He seemed to settle into the piece with ease, allowing the music to flow naturally. The piano sang. Following a graceful Adagio, Viktor made the playful finale almost skittish, with dazzling displays of fingerwork. Perhaps it was a little too fast for the purists—he wondered whether Viktor had ever heard Glenn Gould's outrageously iconoclastic performance—but it suited the mood of the evening, and the audience rewarded him with extravagant applause. They were celebrating together.

Mark looked at Abe. "Well?"

Abe was not smiling. For a moment Mark wondered whether he was disappointed. "He's good, Mark, really good! That playing is special. I haven't heard Mozart like that in twenty years." He cast a contemptuous glance at the cheering audience. "Forget about the civilians out there. This is your Uncle Abe talking!" Then his face broke into a mischievous smile. "Why didn't you tell me?"

Viktor had chosen a short, conservative programme, taking out one of the works he had played in Lausanne. Mark wondered whether someone had discreetly warned him that the presidential attention span was likely to be limited. The rest of the first half was to be Schumann's *Carnaval*, with an all-Chopin collection after the interval.

The Schumann was superb, capturing the many and varied moods of the twenty short pieces that made up the work. Viktor played with the same lyrical fantasy that had first impressed Mark. It was intelligent playing, going straight to the heart of the music, and Mark was only aware of the pianist's brilliant keyboard technique as an afterthought. It was never a display of personal virtuosity, and his hands only served the music. The "Davidsbündler March" finale had nobility and strength, and its triumphant melody seemed to capture the imagination of the audience, suggesting that the young Russian *émigré* was sharing with them his first joyful taste of freedom. Long before the final chords had sounded they were on their feet, cheering and applauding, and each time Viktor returned to the stage for call after call he bowed first to the President—always accompanying the gesture with that happy, winning smile—then stepped back, raising his arms to acknowledge the rest of the assembly. They kept calling him back until someone thoughtfully brought the house lights up, to let the interval begin.

Abe led the way backstage, a paternal hand on Mark's shoulder. "He's quite a showman! The audience was eating out of his hand, and I'm not so sure our great leader wasn't too! No wonder Viktor always wanted to play for him! Listen, we'd better plan to meet in my office at seven o'clock tomorrow morning, before the stampede gets under way. If you think today was rough, wait and see what happens when the phones start ringing tomorrow!"

Despite the efforts of the security staff, the green-room was already busy with guests eager to be among the first to offer congratulations. New Yorkers adored success. It attracted them like a magnet. Viktor's door remained firmly shut, and Abe gently sent all the well-wishers back down the broad staircase, the smile never leaving his face. There would be more than enough time after the recital. He turned to Mark. "It's too bad we can't charge admission to the green-room. We could double the take!"

They found Viktor engaged in conversation with the television director, who had run in from his control truck parked outside the stage door. His professional status permitted him entry to the artist's room. "It was all fantastic, Mr. Kaverin—no need for retakes. Have you decided on the order of your encores?"

Viktor smiled. "No changes. I will just play two Rachmaninov preludes, the C Minor and, if they want another, the G Minor."

The director shook his head. "The way things are going, they'll be perfectly happy if you play all twenty-four!" He bobbed his head and departed to prepare the camera crew for the second half of the programme.

Viktor embraced Irina, then hugged Mark and Abe in turn. His excitement was apparent, and he was still riding on the crest of the waves of applause that had followed him from the stage. "What a wonderful audience! I could never have imagined such an evening!" For a moment, he was serious. "I will never recapture such a mood in the second half." Mark smiled inwardly. It seemed that Viktor shared with his sister that Slavic capacity for despair in the midst of joy.

The interval ended all too quickly, and Abe shepherded them towards the auditorium. Irina held back.

"Aren't you coming with us?"

"I think I would prefer to watch from backstage. I would like to see how they are putting it on the television." She looked at Mark. "You go back to the box with Mr. Sincoff. I will be happy here, to watch the monitor. I have heard Viktor play the Chopin many times."

Viktor laughed. "Including all the wrong notes! When I am practising in the apartment, she shouts at me every time I miss one!"

Mark was about to re-enter the box when he saw Sherman walking quickly towards him. There was a strangely fixed expression on the man's face.

"Where's Irina?"

"Backstage with Viktor. She thought she'd watch the second half on television. Why?"

"Something's wrong." Sherman took Mark by the arm, leading him towards the end of the corridor. "Can we talk?"

"Not here." Mark preceded him out of the auditorium to the private door leading directly to the dressing-rooms. He knocked once, and the elderly attendant let them in. The green-room was now deserted. From the open doorway to the dressing-room being used by the television crew, he could hear an American announcer making solemn introductions to the second half of the concert. It was curious that they always adopted such sepulchral tones. Mark kept his voice low. "What's the problem?"

"We don't know yet, but something's going on. Your friend Quentin Sharpe is on his way here." Sherman looked at his watch. "He should have gotten here by now."

"Quentin? What the hell does he want?"

"I wish I knew. Shit! He's been trying to reach me most of the day, but I've been tied up, looking after Viktor. It seems it was serious enough for him to grab the first plane he could find."

"Did he leave a message?"

"No. The only message he left was that it was very important and that he needed to speak to me in person."

"Did he mention anyone?"

"Viktor and Irina."

"Are they in danger?"

"He didn't say, but they may be. The message was only that we should stay close to the Kaverins at all times until he gets here. He should have landed before this, but his damn flight was delayed. There's a helicopter standing by at JFK, waiting to bring him in. Where's the girl?"

Mark pointed. "In that room, watching the television monitor."

"You'd better stick close to her." At that moment, a sudden swell of sound came from the auditorium. Viktor had returned to the stage. "I'm going down to the stage door to wait for Sharpe. I wish to hell he'd told someone what it was about." They were walking down the inside staircase which led to the stage, and Sherman ignored a man in shirt-sleeves whispering hoarsely for him to be quiet.

Mark followed him. "Didn't he give any kind of indication?"

"Only that it was urgent." He paused, remembering. "He did leave a message for you, but my assistant only got part of it. It was something about looking at your hotel bill and phone calls. Look, I can't stay here. Go to Irina. It could be they're going to make another try for her. They could be mad at losing her."

"They could never get her out of here."

197

Sherman's face was grim. "I'm worried about Viktor. Out there alone on that stage, he's a sitting target if some nut decides to take a shot at him. There's nothing we can do to protect him."

"No." For a moment, Mark remembered the PLO demonstration in Geneva. A musician on an empty stage was helpless.

"I'll get back to you as soon as I can. The message has been passed along, and every security man is on the look-out. For Christ's sake, go find Irina!" Sherman hurried away, pushing past a girl holding a clipboard in one hand and a stop-watch in the other.

In the darkened dressing-room, a large colour television monitor was relaying the programme as it was being recorded. Four or five chairs faced it, occupied by silent viewers, including another girl armed with clipboard and stop-watch. Irina was standing behind them, leaning against the wall. She looked surprised to see Mark.

"I thought you went back inside."

"I changed my mind and decided to keep you company."

She gave his hand a squeeze. "You did not have to bother, but I am glad." The girl with the clipboard looked round and glared at them, and Irina stifled a giggle.

Viktor's Chopin programme opened with three of the waltzes. They were gossamer light, almost casually thrown off, in a style reminiscent of Dinu Lipatti. The audience, unable to contain itself, applauded immediately after the first one ended. For a moment Viktor was disconcerted, losing concentration, but the applause continued. He gave a gentle shrug and smiled graciously, waiting for them to settle down again. The gesture had great charm. At the end of the third, he rose from the piano to a thunderous reception and, after several bows, took a brief pause offstage.

Irina's hand clasped Mark's. "It goes very well, I think."

He smiled. "As Abe would say, it goes great!"

The next work was the *Berceuse,* and Viktor made the cradle song into a delicate lullaby, risking pianissimo playing that took the instrument to its dynamic limit. He caressed the melody, adding Chopin's filigree decorations with fragile whispers of sound. There was a moment of total silence when the piece ended, as though nobody present dared to break the spell. Then the audience came to life, and sustained cheers followed. Viktor took several bows before departing.

On the television screen, the title "Chopin: Sonata No. 2 in B-flat

Minor—'Funeral March,' Opus 35" was superimposed over the image, and Mark guessed that the clipboard-and-stop-watch girl downstairs was standing with Viktor in the wings, waiting with him while the announcer introduced the work in suitably funereal terms. He leaned back against the wall, awaiting Viktor's return. This was to be the highlight of his recital.

The pianist returned to the stage, acknowledging the applause for a moment before seating himself at the piano. He did not begin to play immediately but remained motionless, his head lowered, as though mentally preparing himself. The rustle of anticipation in the auditorium subsided to an absolute silence. It was an extraordinary moment of suspended animation.

Viktor began to play. The introductory phrase, low in register, was sombre and ominous. Then the accompanying figure in the bass began, and the right hand played the opening melody, plaintive and yet with underlying drama. There was poetic nobility combined with fire as the performance gathered momentum, and Mark found himself almost hypnotized by it.

He felt Irina's hand on his arm. She put her mouth close to his ear, whispering so that she would not disturb the others. "I am going to the dressing-room for a moment. I will come back shortly." Momentarily distracted, Mark nodded, his eyes still on the television screen. Viktor had begun the development of the poetic theme that formed the basis of the movement, controlling the passionate climax with masterly timing.

It was only when the pianist was embarking on the Scherzo that Mark realized Irina had not returned. Sherman's warning flashed through his mind and he stepped out of the room, pausing for a moment before crossing the green-room to Viktor's dressing-room. What was Quentin's garbled message about the hotel? He felt in his pocket for his wallet. He had hastily stuffed the hotel bill in a back compartment, scarcely bothering to look at it before driving to the Skyliner Hotel. There were various expenses printed in the column, but an item caught his eye. He paused to read it a second time, then hurried to Viktor's dressing-room.

Irina was standing in the centre of the room, carrying Viktor's hold-all. She seemed about to leave.

"Where are you going?"

She did not speak for a moment. "I was just putting Viktor's clothes together in his bag."

"Why?"

She smiled nervously. "Afterwards, there will be so many people here."

"Where are you taking it?"

"I thought I would take the bag downstairs, to the car, so that it would be safely stored. I am used to looking after Viktor when he plays. Sometimes, when I am not dancing, I wait backstage, and . . . Mark, why are you staring at me like that?"

"Sit down for a moment, Irina." She hesitated, looking puzzled. "Please."

She sat, holding the bag on her lap. "What is it? What have I done, Mark? Why do you look so strange?" She laughed uncertainly. "You are staring at me."

The hotel bill was still in his hand. "Irina, the night we left Covent Garden and went to the hotel . . ." He hesitated.

"Yes?"

"When I came into your room, you were using the telephone. Who did you call?" She did not reply. "Do you remember? I was angry when I saw you."

"Yes, Mark. I was calling the operator, to wake me early. You thought . . ."

Mark shook his head. "You weren't talking to the operator, Irina. There's no charge for a wake-up call."

"What do you mean?"

He handed the hotel account to her, his eyes still on hers. "The hotel bill. It lists all phone calls automatically."

"I don't understand."

"There are two calls listed. Look for yourself. I made one of them, trying to reach Murphy at the Skyliner Hotel. It was the only one I made. I didn't want to risk . . ." She looked briefly at the document. Her hands were trembling. "There's a second charge, Irina. Who did you call?"

She did not look up, concentrating her attention on the paper in her hands. "It must be a mistake. I only called the operator. Perhaps you forgot . . ."

"No. The calls are automatically registered. Who was it, Irina?"

When she did not reply, he walked over to the dressing table. There was a loudspeaker in the room, relaying the music from the stage. Viktor was half-way through the Scherzo, replacing drama with a lyrical waltz.

Something on the table had caught Mark's attention. It was Viktor's green card. While he waited for Irina to speak, he glanced at it. On one side of the card, Viktor's photograph stared out, slightly self-conscious, next to the paragraph of government regulations. He turned the card over. There were brief details: his name and a number, his date of entry into the United States, and his date of birth, 6/12/53—December 6, 1953. No, that was wrong. Americans reversed the digits, putting the months first. Viktor had been born on June 12. Mark stood very still, as the information sank in.

Irina was speaking. "Mark, it must be a mistake. I am sure such things must happen from time to time . . ."

"Perhaps."

"It must be." Her voice was barely audible.

"We'll leave that for the moment. I wanted to ask you something else."

"Mark, what is wrong with you?" She laughed uneasily. "Why are you suddenly asking me all these questions?"

He watched her. "That first night we met, in Moscow . . ."

"Yes." Her face softened with the memory. "You kissed me and then apologized! I was very touched by it."

For a moment Mark hesitated. When he spoke again, his voice was gentler. "You said something that stuck in my mind. We were talking about politics and the Russians of your generation, and you said you were born on the day Stalin died. I made a stupid joke, because you said it marked a great change for your country."

"I don't remember. Mark, I . . ."

"I do, Irina. I remember for a strange reason, the sort of unconnected thinking that makes something stick in one's mind." Irina looked bewildered. "You see, I remember the date of Stalin's death because it was also the day that Serge Prokofiev died. Silly, isn't it? I suppose I was about twelve or thirteen at the time, and I'd just discovered his music—not *Peter and the Wolf*, but the Fifth Symphony and the First Violin Concerto. I'd just heard them at a concert, and they'd had a profound effect on me, even at that tender age! So, when Stalin died, it didn't mean a damned thing to me. The date stuck in my mind because my newly discovered musical idol had died on the same day. I was annoyed that the media gave it so little attention."

"Mark, why are you telling me all this? What does Stalin's death mean? What does it matter?"

Mark picked up Viktor's green card and threw it on her lap. His voice was harsh. "Viktor's birthday, Irina! He was born on June 12, 1953. Stalin and Prokofiev died on March 5, 1953. How did your brother get to be born three months after you?"

She stared at the card, but he had the feeling that she was not reading it. "You must have misunderstood me."

"No. Irina. Nobody gets their own birthday wrong! You're the one who made the mistake. Perhaps you didn't realize it at the time, because the plan was so remote."

"What plan? What are you saying?"

"The plan to enlist my services in getting you out of Russia. Either Viktor's lying or you are. Why?" She did not speak. "You're not brother and sister; you can't be. In which case, who are you?"

She kept her head lowered, and the plastic-coated card slipped from her fingers. Mark watched it fall as her hand reached into the top of Viktor's hold-all. When it reappeared, she was holding a small revolver. It was pointed directly at Mark's heart.

"I cannot tell you that, Mark." Her voice was unsteady. There was a noise outside the door, and she stood. Viktor's hold-all fell to the floor, its contents spilling out, but she moved quickly across the room and pushed the door of the dressing-room shut. The gun in her hand remained steady. "Please stand where you are, Mark. I will use this if you force me to."

From the speaker, the last notes of the Scherzo died away and the audience shuffled slightly, preparing for the Funeral March that was to follow. Irina's eyes flicked towards the speaker for a moment, before moving back to Mark. "You are already too late to do anything about it."

16

Irina stood with her back to the door, motioning to Mark to move to the end of the room. He backed slowly, watching her. The gun in her hand was very steady. He needed time. Quentin Sharpe was due any minute and would come in search of him. From the loudspeaker on the wall, the first mournful strains of Chopin's Funeral March began. Mark smiled crookedly and nodded towards it. "It sounds as though Viktor is going to keep us appropriately entertained! Why am I too late?"

"Don't make jokes." Her voice was sad.

"Under the circumstances, why not? What do you expect me to do, Irina—go down on my knees and beg for mercy?" He watched the gun. "You can't expect to get away with firing that. You'll bring half the building running in here."

"No. It does not make very much noise, and they will be too busy . . ." Irina stopped herself. She was breathing unevenly, as though she had been running. Despite the gun in her hand, she looked very vulnerable. She was also very beautiful.

Irina motioned to him to keep his distance. With her eyes fixed on him, she came forward and knelt by Viktor's hold-all, pulling the contents across the floor. She seemed to find what she was looking for. It was the little plastic transistor radio. Holding the radio in her left hand and the gun in her right, she returned to her feet, moving a step backward.

Mark took out a cigarette and lit it. Her eyes followed his movements cautiously, but she said nothing. He had the impression that, for the moment, she was waiting for some prearranged signal. Where the hell were Sherman and Quentin? "Will you at least tell me who you really are, Irina?" She shook her head. "All right. If I'm too late to do anything about what's going to happen, tell me what happened to Murphy in London. Who killed him?"

Irina hesitated, debating whether to reply. Eventually she spoke. "He realized . . . not everything, but enough. Viktor thought at first he was just a thick-headed bureaucrat who drank too much, but when he asked to see . . ." She looked down at her hands momentarily, then shook her head again, as though regretting her words. "It is better that you do not know."

"So Viktor killed him?" She did not reply, but her silence was acknowledgement. "It had to be that. I knew Murphy couldn't have told the operator to hold calls until the morning. I assumed his visitors had, but it didn't make much sense. I should have been thinking more clearly. A few minutes ago, when I saw that extra phone call on the hotel bill, I thought you had tried to call Viktor at the hotel, but were afraid to admit it. Then I thought you must have called someone else, to tell them where to find him. Apparently not." His voice softened. "Who did you call?"

"It's not important."

"I'd still like to know."

"I told my . . . contact where I was. That is all."

"I see." Mark inhaled cigarette smoke. "The whole thing was monitored from the start, wasn't it? You were both programmed to escape—Viktor in Geneva, you in London. That car following us from Covent Garden was simply there to add credibility. I'm impressed! What about Yuri Schedrin? Was he part of the operation too?"

"No. He did not know who you were. It was only when he said you were coming to Moscow . . ." She stopped again. Her eyes met his. "When we were in the hotel in England, and I . . ." She hesitated. "I was not acting, Mark."

"That's very flattering." His voice was cold. "How about the hotel in New York?"

Her face was troubled. "Some of the time . . . I do not know . . . I'm sorry, Mark. By then, it was too late." She glanced at the speaker, listening to the music.

"Well, it's a small tribute to your acting abilities—and Viktor's—but I was convinced. Whoever trained you did a good job. You must have prepared for this for a very long time." He stubbed out the cigarette slowly. "Why the kidnap? It was all arranged, wasn't it? You took me back to the hotel because you knew someone was waiting for me in Viktor's room?" She nodded almost imperceptibly, her head lowered.

204

"Why? Why arrange such an elaborate masquerade if we were going to end up by freeing you?" He smiled wryly, softening his voice. "You owe me some small explanation for that. I'd hate to think I took a beating for nothing!"

Irina seemed to relax slightly. Perhaps the confession eased her conscience, if she had one. "It was necessary, Mark. We needed to make sure we were completely protected, especially Viktor. London was a shock for us. Mr. Murphy was suspicious of Viktor the moment they started to talk. He left nothing to chance. He wanted to examine every . . ." She hesitated again. "We wanted to be sure that no one would ever question our presence." For a moment, her expression clouded. "I was surprised how easy it was. People were very kind. It was not at all the way I expected it to be, but Viktor . . ."

"Viktor reminded you why you were here?" She nodded slowly. "And you convinced everyone by having me knocked cold while you were supposedly kidnapped?"

Her face was stubborn. "It was necessary for Viktor. He had to be sure of protection once he was inside the hall." For a moment, her eyes widened and Mark suspected that she had said more then she intended. He wondered whether she was also frightened of Viktor. But why? The minutes were ticking by. Keep talking!

"Viktor was already protected. They were much more concerned with him than with you. The hall was swarming with FBI and God knows who else! I don't understand, Irina. Whose side are you on?"

"You will understand soon. There will be no need to explain to you." Her eyes met his. "I am sorry it has to be this way, Mark. I believe we could have been . . . close to each other, but there is not enough time."

He thought back. She had offered herself to him in London before she knew he was flying to New York. Did she mean what she had just said? She was still too far across the room. He stepped forward, and she immediately raised the revolver level with his heart. Mark backed away. "Why?"

"I will be leaving shortly."

"You can't hope to walk out of here after this. What about Viktor? Are you leaving him behind?"

"No one will notice Viktor leaving. There is a car waiting for us at the stage door." She glanced towards the speaker again. Viktor was still playing the opening theme. The tempo seemed majestically slow. As it developed, he was gradually increasing the volume. The long, poetic centre section was still to come.

"You seem to be talking in riddles, Irina. You knew that we would save Viktor the other night in Washington Green?" She nodded, offering no explanation. He laughed. "That's a let-down! Sherman and I thought we'd done such a good job outsmarting them! Weren't you playing it rather close? We only just saved him."

"My car was supposed to arrive sooner at the hotel, but it was held up by the traffic on Seventh Avenue. I was to be at the front door of the hotel when Viktor was only a few steps from your car." She almost smiled. "He was very angry."

"I'm not surprised. We nearly ran him down." He kept his voice conversational. "Viktor gave a marvellously convincing performance. If he weren't such a fine pianist, he should put in for a transfer to the Moscow Art Theatre! Was there an alternative plan?" It was essential to keep her talking. She seemed to be relaxing, or was she still waiting for the pre-arranged moment? Where the hell was Quentin? "What would have happened if Viktor had crossed the Green to the other car before you reached the Dorset?"

She shrugged. "We would have arranged for him to escape again. He did not want to risk that a second time, after London." She looked up. "Mark, I have to go soon . . ."

On the loudspeaker, Viktor was building to one of the great climaxes of the Funeral March, his right hand playing the theme in powerful octaves. Irina listened for a moment. It now seemed clear that her signal came from the music. Perhaps because the volume of sound had increased or because of some inner struggle, Irina had not noticed that the door behind her was slowly opening. Mark fixed his eyes on her face, willing himself not to look past her shoulder.

"Where are you going—to give Viktor his radio?"

She seemed distracted, torn between conflicting emotions. "No. This one is mine. I . . ."

Mark watched. The door behind her had stopped. She remained in the same position, too far away to be reached.

"Viktor's playing better than I've ever heard. He's a great artist."

"It is not important." Her voice was lifeless.

"Not important?" Mark took a step forward but she raised the gun slightly, motioning him back. "You're not serious, Irina? Pianists like Viktor come along once in a decade. Don't you realize what you're hearing?" The door had opened wider, but he could not see who was there. Irina's body masked the entrance. "He's not just another pianist. He's a great artist. He has a lifetime of music ahead of him, anywhere in the world. Listen to him! Is it worth killing me for some crazy plan that will be forgotten a month from now?"

The gun in her hand wavered. "It does not matter. There are other things . . ."

"What other things? Listen, Irina! God gave Viktor a talent that few musicians ever possess!" The door was four, then five inches open, and widening more quickly. Mark's eyes flicked towards it for a moment, and Irina saw the movement. She gasped and swung round, preparing to fire.

Sherman shot her through the heart. The sound of his silenced revolver was drowned by the music from the loudspeaker. The force of the bullet threw her slim body several feet back, so that she toppled like a rag doll over the easy chair. Mark ran forward, conscious that her blood had spattered his chest and face. The bullet had flattened on impact, emerging from her back in a shower of flesh and gore. As Mark ran to Irina, her eyes met his for a moment. He thought there was recognition in them, and she started to speak. Then blood poured from the corner of her mouth, flowing in a thick stream across her chin, and her eyes glazed over in death.

Sherman elbowed past Mark to stand over her body. He turned round. "I guess we had no choice. I'd like to have taken her alive."

Mark looked at them. "How did you know?"

Quentin was standing in the doorway. His face was pale. "I opened the door fractionally, to hear what she was saying, but you were doing more of the talking than she was."

"Then you heard enough. Why didn't you come in sooner?"

"I needed to be convinced that you weren't working with them."

"What?" He felt a sudden, blind rage.

Quentin leaned against the door-jamb. "Look at the facts, Mark. You went to Moscow. You put yourself right in the middle of this. You were the one who brought them out. How the hell could we be sure that you hadn't changed sides somewhere along the way? Did Kaverin kill Murphy?"

207

"Yes. Didn't you hear? He spotted something we missed."

He shook his head. He was regaining some of his poise. "We came in after the big picture had started. We didn't believe that cock-and-bull story about running away from the hotel." His eyes narrowed. "We thought it could have been you."

"What changed your mind?"

"I couldn't get hold of the Skyliner's night porter until the early hours of this morning. He went off duty at seven on the morning in question, for a week's holiday, and it took us the last four days to find him. The moment he told us there'd been nobody in or out of the hotel after midnight that evening, we knew where to look. Airport hotels are pretty quiet places at night, once the last flights have come in. The man confirmed that the place was shut tight by twelve."

The contents of Viktor's bag were on the floor, where Irina had scattered them. Sherman took a towel and draped it over her head and the upper half of her body. It only reached to her waist, and her legs dangled grotesquely over the side of the chair. He turned to Mark and silently handed him a second towel.

Mark held the towel to his face for a moment. "Who is she?"

Quentin moved into the room. "We don't know, but we think we know something about Viktor."

"How?"

"It isn't definite, but it seems conclusive enough now. There's a violinist called Avram Gutman. He's a Russian, but last year he—"

"I know who he is. I met him in Geneva last November."

"Really? Well, Gutman was in London this week, playing at the Festival Hall. I sent one of our people to talk to him last night, after the concert. He showed him a picture of Viktor Kaverin, the one that's been in all the newspapers. It must have been taken several years ago, and it's pretty blurred. We thought Gutman might have come across Viktor before he jumped ship. It was something of a long shot, but it seems to have paid off."

"How?"

"Gutman was shocked. It seems he played a concert somewhere near Ryazan a few years ago, and the local people asked him to listen to some promising students at their academy. Gutman thought he recognized Viktor's face from that evening, but he couldn't be sure. He was very upset."

208

"Why?"

"It wasn't a music school that he visited. The students were part of a specialized academy that the Russians had set aside for élite young men and women, chosen from all over the country. His hosts claimed it was some kind of special training course for students with a very high IQ. Naturally, there were several musicians among them, which was why they asked him to audition them. But Gutman insists that the place is run by the KGB as a training school. He's convinced that if Viktor is the young man he heard, you've just offered asylum to a highly trained agent."

Sherman was angry. "Why the hell didn't you call us immediately?"

"I tried to. We only heard this last night and I started calling you today, but I couldn't reach you. Gutman only said he *thought* Viktor looked like that student. It wasn't a positive identification, and I didn't want to start a panic. But that information, combined with what the night porter had to say, convinced me to come over here in person."

Mark was thoughtful. "It explains why Viktor refused to appear with Gutman when it was proposed."

Sherman said, "I thought he changed his mind."

"That's right! He did."

"When?"

"After he learned about this recital." In the hall, Viktor was playing the lyrical centre section of the Funeral March. His right hand gently expressed the melody. Mark spoke to himself. "Both he and Irina kept saying that everything would be different after the recital. Of course he was prepared to accept the foundation offer. He didn't intend to be here!" Quentin and Sherman were watching him, and he turned to them, his voice urgent. "We haven't time to talk about that now. Something's about to happen here."

"What do you mean?"

"I'm not sure. Irina was preparing to leave. She said I was already too late to do anything about it."

"Where was she going?"

"I don't know. She was trying not to tell me and only hinted at it. I had the feeling that she half wanted to tell me, but couldn't. All she said was that she and Viktor were leaving shortly and that there was a car waiting for them by the stage door."

Sherman looked puzzled. "What do they have in mind—some sort of disappearing act? Why?"

"I don't know. She said something very strange. When I suggested that she and Viktor could never get away, she said that everyone would be too busy to notice them." He remembered the demonstration by the PLO in Geneva again. "Do you think they're about to bring someone in to . . ."

Sherman shook his head. "They'd never get away with anything like that. The place is filled with security men."

"What's that?" Quentin was pointing at the small plastic container that had fallen from Irina's hand.

Sherman glanced down. "Viktor's radio. It must have fallen out . . ."

"No!" Mark's voice silenced them. "I thought it was Viktor's, but she said it was hers. It happened just before you came in. She took that radio out of the bag when she was holding a gun on me. Let me try to get the sequence right." He closed his eyes for a moment, remembering. "I came in here, looking for Irina. She'd been watching the television monitor next door with me and said she was going to the dressing-room. It was when I was on my way here that I remembered I had the London hotel bill in my wallet. That was when I found the extra phone call."

Quentin looked up. "Did you get my message? You said you'd only made one call that night, and—"

"Yes. You were right. Thanks! For someone who'd said he wasn't involved in what was going on, you were remarkably well informed!"

Quentin smiled. "I was checking up on you at the time!"

Sherman interrupted. "What are you talking about?"

Mark waved him to silence. "I'll explain later. I came in here and found Irina preparing to leave. Just after that, I saw Viktor's green card and realized that she couldn't be his sister." Quentin and Sherman looked at each other. "It was something she said in Moscow last year. It's too complicated to go into now. That's when she pulled the gun on me. I thought she'd taken Viktor's radio because there wasn't time to take all his things out of here. Ever since he reached London, Viktor's been concerned with that damned bag and his bloody radio!" Mark closed his eyes again. "I'd just seen the door starting to open behind her, and to keep her occupied I made some stupid remark about taking

Viktor his radio, but she said 'No, this one is mine.' It looks the same as Viktor's, but there must be two."

Quentin frowned. "Let me have a look at it. I think I've seen one of those before." Sherman picked it up and passed it to him. Quentin turned the radio over, then inserted his fingernail in the narrow slit running down the side of the box where the two pieces of grey plastic met. They broke apart, and he examined the complicated network of tiny transistors and capacitors. When he looked up, his face was grim. "It's the same as one I saw in Belfast."

"What about it?" Sherman was peering over his shoulder.

"It's a radio, all right, and you can listen to it, but it's also a short-range transmitter, effective up to about fifty yards, as long as there's not much in the way." He looked from Sherman to Mark. "The IRA use them to detonate bombs."

In the silence that followed, Mark could hear Viktor playing the repeat of the central section. The piano was barely audible.

Sherman looked at Quentin. "Christ! Are you trying to tell me there's a bomb in the hall?"

"I don't know. All I can tell you is that if there is one and you have the right detonator, you can set it off with this radio." He held it up to the light. "Look. There's a small button set into that moulded hollow on the surface, just next to the tuning dial." He pulled the battery out of the inner shell to make sure the radio had no power. "You can just fit your finger into the space provided."

"What sort of explosives would you need?"

Quentin shrugged. "Plastics usually, but I suppose it would work with anything." He turned to Mark. "Could Viktor or his sister have got their hands on something like that?"

Sherman nodded slowly. "Sure they could. Irina was supposed to have been kidnapped for six hours."

Quentin looked surprised. "When was that?"

Mark ignored the question. Instead, he picked up Viktor's hold-all, turning it upside-down until the rest of the contents had fallen to the floor. Then, pulling the two sides of the bag apart, he held it so that the two men could look inside. The cheap cotton lining had been ripped away for the length of the seam. "I think it was in there, ever since he left Russia. That was why he was so concerned about his luggage and kept going on about his only worldly possessions. All he had to do was

211

get the bag in and out of Switzerland. If the plastic explosive was well sealed, it would have passed through undetected. After that," his eyes met Quentin's, "we were carrying it through for him."

Quentin said, "We're still guessing. Suppose we're right." He looked at the bag. "He could carry enough plastic down the side of that to blow a wall off this building, but he's still got to get in and place it. I thought you said this hall was absolutely secure."

Sherman nodded. "It is. With the President on his way here, they spent the morning with metal detectors, sniffer dogs, and God knows what-all. There was no way Viktor could have placed anything . . ." He stopped, looking at Mark. "Jesus Christ!"

"What are you saying?"

Mark spoke quietly. "Before Viktor rehearsed this afternoon, he asked us to clear the hall for him and keep it empty. We moved everyone out for half an hour—cleaners, television crew, stagehands . . . and security men."

"What?"

"He asked for some time in an empty hall to prepare himself." Mark's voice was bitter. "He wanted to commune with the ghosts of all the great artists of the past! We persuaded all the extra guards and security men to stand outside the auditorium, making sure that nobody could enter. Viktor was alone in there for half an hour. He kept this bag with him the whole time!"

Sherman added, "And you noticed that he took a long time before he started to play. Oh God! Could he have climbed up to the President's box from downstairs?"

Mark took a deep breath. "As a teenager, he trained as an Olympic gymnast. A rope with a small grapple would be enough. I think I saw a ladder being used by the television crew. Now I understand why Irina said they staged the kidnap to be absolutely sure of being protected."

Sherman turned. "I've got to reach the President—"

"No!" The American halted, staring at Mark. "It's more complicated than you think."

"Why?"

"Irina." He indicated the radio. "This one's hers. She was distracted when we spoke, otherwise I don't think she would have admitted it."

"What of it?" Sherman was anxious to leave.

"I think Viktor's radio is in his pocket on-stage. Irina was going downstairs. She was probably there to stand by, in case anything went wrong. That's why she said nobody would notice them leaving! Viktor's going to detonate the bomb from the stage!"

"Then I have to get the President out fast!"

"You can't risk it. If Viktor sees any kind of disturbance, all he has to do is reach into his pocket and press the button. They'll never get the President and his wife out before he does!" He listened to the music for a moment. "The only time we know we're safe is when he's actually playing. When he stops . . ."

"He won't stop." Sherman was unscrewing the silencer from his revolver. "Unless it's a suicide mission."

"I think he has something simpler in mind. At the end of a long movement, it's normal for a pianist to pause for a moment, then reach into his pocket for a handkerchief to wipe his face or hands. Playing an instrument is a sweaty business. If he uses that moment, nobody will even suspect he's done it."

"How long has he got to go?"

Mark listened. "About two minutes."

"Jesus!"

"After that, he still has the last movement. In the Chopin, they're very often joined together, but not always."

"Giving us how long?"

"Very little. The finale's very short—about another minute and a half."

Sherman had unscrewed the silencer and put it in his pocket. His face was set. "If I'm standing at the side of the stage, I could put one shot—"

"No."

"Why not?"

"Because we don't know for sure that he's going to do it. You have no proof! Are you going to risk killing a man in cold blood in front of that audience—let alone worldwide television—because you think he might set off a bomb?" Sherman hesitated.

The movement was drawing to a close. Quentin asked, "What else can you do? He's about to stop, isn't he?"

"Yes, but I think we've got that extra minute and a half. I know Viktor. This sonata means everything to him. It's more important than

213

any other piece he plays. His pride and his musicianship won't let him do anything until it's finished."

"Are you sure of that?"

"I'd bet my life on it. The last movement is fiendishly difficult. It will take all his concentration." He turned to Sherman. "Do you know the guard on the rear door downstairs? Will he let you in?"

"Yes."

"You've got just under two minutes. Here's what you do."

Mark was on the side of the stage, standing next to a television cameraman and his assistant. Fifteen or twenty feet away, his back to them, Viktor was playing the final bars of the Funeral March. The pianist bent low over the keyboard, playing the left-hand trills slowly and with great strength. The music returned to a final reprise of the march theme, and he allowed the sound slowly to die away. Then he lifted his hands from the keyboard, his head still bowed. There was absolute silence in the hall. Mark waited, feeling a pulse beating in his temple. At any moment, in the brief pause, Viktor's hand could reach into his pocket.

Mark looked into the hall. At the back of the auditorium, there was a slight movement. Sherman and Quentin had entered silently and were standing together at the end of the aisle, just behind the last row of seats. Both men had taken off their jackets and ties and had put white towels over their hair, held in place by belts. From a distance, these vaguely resembled Arab head-dresses.

Mark's attention returned to Viktor. The pause had lasted only a few seconds. The pianist raised his head. His hands were still below the keyboard, resting lightly on his knees. He sat very straight, staring across the stage, his body immobile. Then he slowly brought both hands up until his fingers were resting on the piano keys. He looked down and began to play. His fingers moved like lightning as they began the final movement of the sonata.

For a moment Mark watched the two men at the end of the aisle. They had started to walk forward. Then Quentin began to shout, waving his arms. Viktor was still bent forward over the keyboard, totally engrossed. The sound from the piano swelled. He might not even have heard the intruders.

Mark launched himself across the stage, running with all his strength. The light was dazzling, blinding him momentarily, and he was no longer conscious of the sounds around him. Five feet away, Viktor suddenly straightened and looked up. He had heard the noise in the auditorium but his fingers were still on the keyboard, continuing to play.

He stopped as Mark crashed into him, knocking him from the piano stool to the floor and covering him with his body. Quentin was still shouting, and new sounds were coming from every direction—shouts and cries, a woman screaming. Viktor turned his head, looking straight into Mark's eyes. He said nothing but realization dawned, and his right hand moved down towards his pocket. Mark sensed as much as saw the movement and reached to hold Viktor's wrist.

He was immensely strong. The bare skin, slightly damp, slipped under Mark's fingers, inching towards the pocket. Mark held on to the wrist, trying to wrench it sideways. For a moment he halted the movement, but Viktor gritted his teeth and exerted new pressure. Mark looked down. The pianist's fingertips had already disappeared into the pocket. From the auditorium he was aware of voices shouting and calling, and he looked again into Viktor's eyes. His voice was a hoarse whisper. "Irina is dead!"

For an instant the pressure continued. Then Viktor's eyes widened with horror and his body went slack, offering no further resistance. Mark pulled the pianist's hand clear and reached into his pocket. His fingers touched the plastic surface of the little radio and he gently lifted it out. Viktor lay still.

In the auditorium, the noise had abated. Mark looked towards the presidential box. It was empty. Downstairs, there was no sign of Sherman and Quentin, who had run out of the hall by a side door near the front. He dropped the radio into his own pocket and rose to his feet. Reaching down, he grasped Viktor's arm and pulled him up. The pianist stood slowly, a dazed expression on his face, and Mark led him away. From somewhere in the audience, a man started clapping his hands and calling out. Others joined him, and before they reached the side of the stage, there was a great roar of acclaim. The audience thought he had saved Viktor's life.

In the wings, a burly policeman, revolver in hand, was waiting. Behind him, Quentin and Sherman, having shed their Arab costumes, had entered by a door from the outside corridor. They were both panting and breathless, but Sherman was grinning broadly. Mark handed Viktor to the policeman, who grasped the pianist's arms, locking them behind

215

his body. Viktor's head was lowered, his face expressionless. From the direction of the stage, Mark could hear the audience shouting and applauding. The noise was awesome.

Sherman stepped forward, still smiling. "Why don't you go out there and take a bow? You earned it!"

They were standing in the green-room, which had been cleared. The television team had complained, but the stony-faced security men had stolidly removed them. Viktor's dressing-room had been locked and one of the guards stood silently in front of it, his shoulders touching the door. Only Abe and Myra, admitted through the private entrance, were allowed to remain.

Mark suddenly felt very tired and sat on the stairs leading up to the second dressing-room. Sherman handed him a cigarette. Nearby, Quentin was putting on his jacket. He removed a wayward piece of fluff from the lapel with an irritated frown.

Abe stood in front of Mark. "How're you doing, kid?" Mark nodded wearily. "I guess you can tell me about it when you get your breath back."

"I will. We can cancel our seven o'clock meeting tomorrow morning."

"Oh?"

"Viktor just retired, Abe. It wasn't quite what you thought." Abe was silent.

There was a sudden hammering on the private door, and the old attendant opened it. He tried to stop the two intruders who entered, but they brushed him aside and walked over to where Mark was sitting. Greg Laufer was closely shadowed by Larry Austerklein. They were both dressed in dinner jackets, and Laufer sported an outsize maroon bow tie.

"Jesus, Mark, that was fantastic!" He reached down to shake hands, but Mark ignored the gesture. "I never saw anything like that in my life!" Abe tried to intervene, but the vice-president of Magnum Records was determined. "Listen, I'd as soon release the tape just as it happened, demonstration and all. That's a piece of musical history! But the public would never buy it." Austerklein nodded in silent agreement. "They'll want the whole sonata. We'll have to do a retake to finish it."

Mark smiled, closing his eyes. His body shook. He fought against the sensation but he was too tired, and he began laughing uncontrollably.

216

Laufer was furious. "Listen, I'm not kidding! We can't put out a tape like that. You signed a deal!"

Mark continued to laugh. He felt himself growing slightly hysterical, and tears were forming in his eyes. It was infectious. Abe started to smile, and quite unexpectedly let out a high-pitched giggle.

Laufer glowered at them. "It's no damned laughing matter, for Christ's sake! A deal's a deal! Either he finishes the sonata or the whole contract's void! There's only a couple of minutes left, damn it! If necessary, I'll pay him extra. We've got a contract!"

Hearing the word "contract," Larry Austerklein spoke almost involuntarily. Looking smug, he sidled forward, adding, "Our usual terms." His voice was drowned by their laughter.

ABOUT THE AUTHOR

Paul Myers has had an illustrious career as a classical record producer. A Londoner by birth, he spent eighteen years producing classical records for CBS Records, commuting between New York and London. His extensive travels have taken him to virtually every capital city in the world. Since 1980, he has been Manager of Classical Production for Decca International in London. He has made some five hundred classical recordings, many of which have won major international prizes. He has worked with world-famous musicians, conductors, and singers. In addition to his prolific record-producing career, Paul Myers presented a series of classical music programs for New York's WQXR radio station which were syndicated to thirty American cities. London Films and Tele-Hachette have bought the Mark Holland character for a television series.